Andrew Mason

86 Hours

in

England

Rainwolf Press

A Division of Wallace Mason Media

86 Hours

in

England

First Edition 2011

Rainwolf Press ISBN: 978-0-578-09453-3

www.86HoursInEngland.com

"The view from the top of the Eiffel Tower at night was not that different than that from the top of the Old National building in Evansville. Through squinted eyes the Lloyd Expressway looked just like the Champs-Élysées."

Romance, Betrayal, Sex, Drugs, and Shakespeare...

Sam Thompson is an American exchange student at a small liberal arts college in England in 1995. He lives in a hundred year old mansion, gets to travel throughout Europe almost every weekend, and he has been romancing the most interesting girl at the school. It should be the greatest time of his life, but for some reason he decides to quit sleeping. Through parties, bar fights, and a school production of The Taming of the Shrew, the hours add up as he continues to make decisions that he may regret for the rest of his life.

"I read the first page...and love it already."

> **- Chad Williamson, author of *What Comes Around***

"A clever, nostalgic, hilarious tragedy about those final hours before adulthood."

> **– A. Thomas Mitchell, editor, *The Oak Tree***

"Written with raw honesty…a coming of age tale for our generation: travel abroad to find oneself, tales of alcohol and drug indiscretions, youthful philosophy, the sex we regret having, and the sex we didn't have that we regret more."

- Ericka Thessen

"Of all the books that I've read recently, this is definitely one I would recommend that everyone picks up! In fact, it is the first book I have read twice in quite some time!"

– Scott W. Ramsey, Publisher, *The Claremont Courier.*

"Brilliant. A funny, heartbreaking, mind-bending slog through those first excruciating moments which mark the very emergence of that ill-documented condition known among survivors as post-Harlaxton psychosis."

– Audra Douglas, *Harlaxton College 1995*

"Writing a book is a lot like dropping your pants in front of people. Mason's book proves that he's got a big one, and it's probably going to keep getting bigger."

– Andrew Odom, author of *Minus 55*

For Kat…and Katherina

"Those who are faithful know only the trivial side of love: it is the faithless who know love's tragedies."

- Oscar Wilde

Tuesday

In all honesty I have no idea from where my decision to stay awake indefinitely had come. Months of rock-star living as a foreigner on credit cards, student loans, and delusions of grandeur I suppose. A mad rebellion against everything in which I had grown up believing, true love, the opposite of chaos, truth, justice, and the American way. All of that shit made sense to the captain of the football team, the B+ student, the Eagle Scout all those years ago in Paradise, Indiana. Good Lord what had gone wrong? What devious forces could have brought this all-American kid across the Big Pond to his ethnic homeland only to have him kneeling before a filthy fucking toilet with his pants around his ankles, bare ass in the air, praying to whatever gods might be listening to rid his system of some horrible drug that those assholes from Liverpool had promised him would be better than any pot he had ever smoked back in the States?

I wonder sometimes if there actually is anything important to say about the whole trip, half way around the world for no good reason whatsoever, taking twelve semester hours, all history and English. There were thousands of places in America where I could have done that. Of course I could justify it as an exercise in broadening my horizons, the sort of cultural experience that an average Midwestern education might not have provided. Back then it was quite common for college students in Europe to spend time abroad as part of their education. Why shouldn't I?

And it was great living in England, a pilgrimage of sorts. I was able to travel to places that I'd probably never see again, and even at the foolish age of twenty I truly tried my best to appreciate the opportunity that was before me, tried to force myself to focus on the details that I thought would be important to me later.

But even great memories fade, and, believe it or not, sometimes it's hard to remember just what was so great about them at all. The view from the top of the Eiffel Tower at night was not that different than that from the top of the Old National building in Evansville. Through squinted eyes the Lloyd Expressway looked just like the Champs-Élysées.

I suppose that what you learn at a time like that is not as important as what you learn about yourself...

The first twenty hours or so had gone off without a hitch. Actually, I hadn't been paying much attention. I had no idea when I rolled out of bed around noon on that wintery Tuesday that I was beginning that silly marathon of consciousness. It had seemed like an average, unimportant, lazy one-class college weekday. Little did I know what horrors lay ahead.

1:05PM Tuesday (Hour 1:09)

The first thing I really remember was Lopez walking in the room a little after 1:00. I had been awake for an hour or so, and I was quickly approaching the deadline of preparation for my 2 O'clock Shakespeare class. I had done the intellectual work, but I had not yet begun to look for my pants. I was sitting in the Big Chair, a lavishly upholstered example of lounging finery that was a perk of having the only three-bed room in the dorm, smoking a cigarette and watching the pigeons shit on the ornate roof of the opposite wing of the castle.

"Hey Sammy!" she said. Lopez was one of those people that were always happy in the morning. It was as if to her the beginning of each day signified a chance that life might get better, and, it was for that reason that her little brand of depression never seemed to set in until after dinner. Mine was in full swing already...or maybe it wasn't depression at all...perhaps I was just numb...

And I hated that fucking name!

"Jeez, what's the matter with you?" she asked after I snarled at her greeting. "It's Halloween, man. Smile!"

I didn't know what to make of it. I just looked at her for a moment, a tiny half-breed squaw from some Texas hell hole full of charisma and hope and vehement contradictions. Damn, if she were twenty pounds lighter she'd be the sexiest girl I'd ever met.

"Yeah," I finally managed to say, "Halloween…" The word trailed off as if I had been in deep thought, but I don't remember what I had been thinking. Perhaps I had only been pretending to think, feigning a level of brooding that would surely communicate the melancholy of this nameless morning. It had no effect.

"So, what are you going as?" she bubbled.

"Santa Claus," I said.

"Seriously?" she asked, as if she knew that I just might do it.

"I don't have a costume yet," I answered, "but Taylor and I were tossing around the idea of a Christmas theme."

"For Halloween?" she rolled her eyes.

"Yeah, why not?" I said. "It's not like they care around here anyway. They've already started building the bon fire for Guy Fawkes." I lifted my cigarette hand in the direction of the window, motioning towards the huge pile of brush that had recently appeared in the field in front of the manor gates.

"Yeah, what's that all about anyway?" she said.

"I'm not really sure," I said. "I think it's like their 4th of July or something like that." I needed to move, get up out of this huge chair, tear myself away from the gravity of it, but I just couldn't find the ambition.

"Are you ready for the play?" she asked. As one-sided

as it was, this conversation was moving way too fast. I hadn't had time to get my bearings. There was probably still whiskey and evil scotch in my belly from the night before. I felt queasy and submerged, and now I had to deal with all these questions, this fucking conversation! Get a grip man. What the hell was she talking about? Play? Oh yeah, the play.

"Oh yeah," I said thinking with the speed of thought, "Yeah, I'm ready for the play."

It had been her brainchild all throughout the semester, some dramatic presentation exhibiting an alternate interpretation of *The Taming of the Shrew*, the capstone of *English Literature 350-Shakespeare: Studies in Drama*, the October 31st, 1995 meeting of which was looming ominously in my very near future.

"Good," she said as I somewhat apprehensively took a drag off of my dwindling cigarette. She seemed as if she was worried about my upcoming performance. She was, after all, half Apache. Perhaps she had had a vision of the coming tempest, maybe her spiritual ancestors had warned her of the chaos and depravity, or maybe she was just upset about me missing rehearsal on Monday. Lopez had put a lot of time into this production. It was a living, growing thing to her, and she cared for it deeply, as a god might care for the glorious race she had created.

But I wasn't worried about it. Opening night wasn't until Friday, and I made it a habit never to worry about things that were more than twelve hours into the future. Hell, the whole wide world may have changed in twelve hours. The planet used to be flat for Christ's sake.

And besides, I had tore the roof off of the Castle High School auditorium in my acting debut as John Bender in a rousing, if technically wanting, production of *The Breakfast Club* some three years ago; surely I was ready for Shakespeare.

"*Now go thy ways, thou hast tamed a cursed shrew,*" I quoted in my best Richard Harris accent. I hoped that my big line from Act V would appease the wench.

"It's supposed to be sarcastic," she whined. "Hortensio sees that her spirit has been broken!"

"Maybe..." I mused, "...or maybe he's just giving Petruchio a big pat on the back."

"It's not that simple," she said. I'd done it now. I was in for the whole interpretation thesis. Damn! What had I done to deserve this early morning grilling? Just sitting here in my undershorts, in my Big Chair, meditating in my own way, and trying to will away this fucking hangover as she droned on and on about that damn play. Maybe we should have shut the door to our room as a matter of regular practice.

"Where's Taylor?" she finally asked, and perhaps revealed the genesis of this visit. Her eyes always seemed to widen with anticipation when she mentioned his name.

"I don't know," I said, "I don't think he spent the night here last night."

And then those bright eyes would dim. I almost enjoyed it every time; maybe it soothed my jealousy. For an instance, I fantasized that I had lied just to watch the hope fueling those big hazel half-breed eyes fade, but I hadn't. I really didn't know where he was...or who he was with.

This had been going on for months. Harlaxton College was the name of the place, a small liberal arts school outside of Grantham, Lincolnshire. The school was actually an overseas annex of the University of Evansville, a small liberal arts school back in Indiana. It was a strange place, mystical and enchanting yet artificial on every level. The building itself was a lie. An elaborate and ornate homage to the great English manor houses of the eighteenth century, the castle had actually been built in the late 1800s by a wealthy nobleman named Gregory Gregory who, himself, must have longed for that great and bygone age. In fact, the old boy had gone all but broke funding the construction, and the grand giant, bewitching and omnipresent yet ironically purposeless, never really functioned as the great manor house he must have envisioned. Still, it did look impressive. A year or so after I was there they used the place as a haunted house in a rather forgettable Liam Neeson film.

Sometime in the early 1900s, after Gregory Gregory's death, one of his descendants turned the place over to the Jesuits, and it became a monastery. Then, somehow Stanford University got the deed in the 1970s, but their plans to turn the old castle into an overseas campus fell through when the house was *gifted* to the University of Evansville under questionable circumstances a few years later.

And so the old mansion became Harlaxton College, a place for American students from colleges all around the country to come and pretend like they were studying overseas for a semester. The odd thing was that most of the students who attended Harlaxton College in Lincolnshire, England were, like my spunky Texan friend, Americans.

Though proud of the fact that she had studied theatre at Yale, Lopez still held a grudge against those damn uppity snobs who had rejected her at Julliard. She had taken it personally and that insecurity was never far from the surface. Of course there was no reason for it; her talent was quite obvious to everyone except her. Besides, I always suspected that those uppity Julliardians would have had no idea what to do with her anyway. I often wondered where she thought a short, chubby, half Mexican half Apache hydrogen explosion of a woman would have fit into the uppity contemporary world of performing arts, but then, I have, myself, been accused of pessimism quite often.

But I respected Lopez. She possessed a certain uniqueness that was beyond facsimile. Under different circumstances I might have been able to fall in love with her, but she was in love with my roommate, Taylor. Of course, she would never have admitted as much.

Taylor Beckett was, at very least, an agent of Satan, tall, dark, and evil as Hell in that charming sort of way that makes it impossible for you not to like the guy. I figured him for what he was the moment I met him, one of those liberal, touchy-feely, manipulative city fellas that frequent coffee shops and used books stores, but damn if that angle didn't work for him. He was not particularly dashing, nor was he overly ugly, as Jesus is described in the Bible, but there was something intriguing about his aura to which no one in his presence was immune.

The evil bastard had sunk his claws into Lopez right away. They had spent nine hours next to each other on a 747 heading from Chicago to London. No doubt thinking about passing the awful minutes of a layover wait with a time-killing rendezvous, my future roommate immediately began to work on the unsuspecting lass.

And work it did. He told her enough to keep her guessing and asked her enough to let her know he was interested. It wasn't until a few minutes into the conversation that they discovered their mutual destination. Shrewdly, Taylor began a full-scale retreat, but it was too late. The damage was done, and she might very well love him forever.

I realized this the first time that I met them. I had just completed the long haul up three flights of stairs to the third floor of Harlaxton Manor where I hoped to find my new home. Down the hall, around the corner, down the steps, damn this was some archaic architecture, up the steps, watch your head, and, eureka, there it was, the Vortex, room 333. The door was open, as it would remain for the next three months, and I could make out one of those liberal, touchy-feely, manipulative city fellas smoking a hand-rolled cigarette and talking to a short, chubby, half Mexican half Apache hydrogen explosion of a woman who was looking at him as if he had just finished hanging the moon. They turned toward me as I walked into the room.

"You must be Samuel Thompson?" the fella said. He smiled warmly, and, right away, I didn't trust him.

"Yeah," I said. "How'd you know that?"

"Well, Daniel Beam got here this morning, stowed his stuff, and headed to the pub," he answered, "And *Samuel Thompson* is the other name on the door." He gestured with his hand-rolled cigarette holding hand in the direction of the ink on paper sign that I had failed to notice.

"Oh," I said as I stood there looking stupid.

"I'm Taylor," he said, again with that fucking smile. "This is Lydia." He gestured toward the girl. "She's from Texas. You want a hit of this?"

As it turned out, the hand-rolled cigarette was no cigarette at all, but, rather a tightly rolled joint of Kentucky Homegrown that Taylor had smuggled out of Louisville as a house warming gift for whoever his new roommates would be. I took the damn thing from him and inhaled deeply and coughed as I said, "Do you think we should close the door?"

"Why?" was his response. I had no idea how tired I would get of hearing him ask that.

And so it began, this weird pattern of backstage living that had ensued up until this morning. Room 333, the one I shared with Taylor and Dan became known as the Vortex. All the other rooms on our floor were typical dorm rooms, two beds, two desks, two closets, standard Benedictine cells. But 333 was different in every way. Set in a corner of the manor that was completely separate from the rest of the floor, our room consisted of three small sleeping chambers divided by a cozy common area and, as a result of the unorthodox layout, was adorned with a bevy of amenities unknown by the other students. We had a large window that overlooked the courtyard of the faculty quarters, a large table and bookshelf for studying, a mirror and sink with hot and cold running water, and the Big Chair, the throne of room 333.

On that first evening and during every conversation that followed I took notice of who sat atop the throne. It was always interesting to me to watch the power struggle play back and forth during a conversation amongst any group of people more than three. At any given moment there is a leader, the person who is in command of the room, and it isn't always the person who's talking. Most conversationalists are followers and, though they may contribute a great deal to the discussion, really never even understand the game. A few special people, maybe one in a group, are like Taylor, natural leaders who command attention simply by projecting a level of charisma that cannot be resisted. Others, however, will wait and listen and manipulate, and they prefer to guide the conversation with tiny, covert nudges. In any event, I noticed earlier than most that possession of the Big Chair was a huge subconscious advantage.

And then there was the sink.

Never one to keep a thought to himself, Dan brought the question up on the first day that we were there. "Welp," he said in his thick Chicago accent, "we..ah..gonna pee in da sink or not?" An interesting query indeed. Of course we were all civilized young men, well on our way to becoming educated, respectful members of society. Should we not be above resisting the medieval temptation of the glistening white porcelain basin when faced with the early morning dilemma of trekking outside the room, down the hall to the semi-public facilities we shared with the rest of the men on the floor? Would that be too much to expect?

"I'm not pissing in the sink!" Taylor said with the kind of authority that should have rendered the entire issue

16

moot. However, the emphatic strength of his declarative statement was weakened when he looked in my direction for backup. For I knew that we might not always be able to resist that evil temptation, and the air of defeat hung upon his brow as I shrugged my shoulders and registered my *undecided* vote.

"Look guys," he tried one more time, "I'm not brushing my teeth in a fucking toilet!"

"Yeah, okay," Dan, who would eventually become known as *Elwood*, finally said. "You're right, pal. No peein' in da sink."

Within a month we were all three doing it anyway, and that became the only real secret of the Vortex, the only piece of questionable knowledge that was actually kept between the three of us. For, besides that, The Vortex became as public a place as any of the pubs in town.

Our sleeping chambers each had curtains that served as doors and provided us with a level of personal privacy that allowed us to keep the actual door to the room open at all times, and that open door proved to be as inviting to anybody who walked by as the neon sign outside a Bourbon Street strip joint. People would just walk in and introduce themselves. And they'd get stuck there too, like flies in a web, drinking up the atmosphere of rambling conversations about every possible existential interpretation of whatever was being discussed. We had even had people stay in there for days, sleeping on the floor, missing classes. In retrospect, I guess it really was an interesting phenomenon, and I've never lived anywhere like it since. The pull of the great magnet was like the song of the sirens, and that was from where the name came. I think Lopez, who was fairly well-versed in the *classics*, coined the term.

And so it was not surprising that the first minutes, the first ones I really remember anyway, of that first day of my waking marathon were spent with that cute little half-breed raving on about something or other as I sat in a daze deep within the bowels of room 333.

1:49PM Tuesday (Hour 1:53)

Eleven minutes to make class on time. Considering the fact that I still had not located my pants, it was going to be close.

Lopez had given up on Taylor and headed down the stairs a few minutes ago, but, giving into the desire to selfishly savor it in the silence she had left behind, I had lit another cigarette upon her departure. A dedicated student-athlete all through high school, I didn't start smoking until I was 19. I had always idolized hyper masculine characters like Clint Eastwood's *Man with No Name* and the *Wolverine*, and they made it look so fucking cool. The bad guy would threaten them. There would be a pregnant pause, then a drag of the cigarette, and then a violent and righteous ass-kicking. The reality of my smoking habit, the daily morning phlegm, and the shortness of breath in my formerly well-conditioned lungs was not nearly as romantic, but when I raised my hand to my lips, narrowed my eyes, and inhaled that sweet Turkish and domestic blend I felt petty Goddamn cool.

When I had sucked in the last bit of cancerous euphoria I tapped the little devil out and sprang into action. A quick survey of the room told me most of what I needed to know. My books and papers were on the desk where I had left them, my Converse One-Stars were on the floor by the door, and...if memory served me... yep, there were my pants wadded up under the covers at the foot of my bed. Dressed and equipped with the day's lessons, I was out the door, around the corner, down the steps and on the way to my Tuesday afternoon class with Dr. Helen White.

Dr. White was a kind-hearted sort of English professor who spoke with an upper-class accent and exhibited an alarming expertise in regards to the works of old Bill Shakespeare. She appeared to be in her mid-thirties and was quite pregnant during my time at Harlaxton. She was the kind of woman who probably would have looked frumpy and nerdish under normal circumstances, but the pregnancy had given her that alluring glow that pregnant women sometimes get. The sparkle from her eyes reflecting off the rim of her glasses or the occasional engorged nipple visible beneath her silk blouse had played havoc with my hormones over the course of the semester, but any distraction that she had caused had been due to simple, primal lust. That was something that I understood and with which I had found no trouble squelching.

The origin of all action is motivation. The evil deeds of men, especially young men, are inconceivable without proper consideration of the motivation behind those actions. The same, of course, is true in regards to good deeds. However, the system is flawed. One of the true tragedies of life occurs sometimes, when good intentions lead some poor soul down the wrong path. Oddly enough, the opposite occurs as well.

I'm not sure what motivation had been responsible for my lustful thoughts about pregnant Dr. White over the last few weeks, but that was not what had gotten me out of bed and to class on time that day. No, sir. My motivation for never missing Shakespeare and, ironically, the real obstacle to my educational experience while I was in England had been Miss Katherine Graham. Under normal circumstances I would probably have wasted away the afternoon smoking Camels and preaching my perpetual pessimism from the pulpit of the Big Chair, but Kat was in my Tuesday

Shakespeare class and I was not going to miss an opportunity to see her.

I met Kat the first night I was in England. My plane had landed at Heathrow several hours earlier, and I had boarded a bus chartered by the school to ferry us up from London. The ride was excruciating. Being a larger-than-average fellow, I had never been comfortable in any of my experiences using public transit, but the long plane ride had conditioned my body for the physical challenge of sitting on that bus for three hours. The difficult part was the anticipation. I had never lived anywhere other than southern Indiana, safe suburbs of Evansville, Newburgh, Paradise. That semester was to be quite an adventure for me, and I couldn't wait to see my new home. Of course, I had seen pictures in the brochure, but photographs only take me there when they are used in association with the memories of my own experience. Otherwise, it's just a glimpse into a world of which I know nothing. I'd seen pictures of the Taj Mahal and it might as well have been on Mars.

So far, this trip had, unfortunately but necessarily, utilized the most efficient and very worst ways to travel, and I was weary. Riding in a bus is too passive an activity for the human spirit, and the plane was even worse. Our primal tendency has always been to take action, challenging ourselves and forcing change, making our environment adapt to our needs. However, as I sat there with my legs going numb and my eyelids getting heavy, I vowed to make up this lost time watching the sheep and crawling through the roundabouts, and as we approached Harlaxton Manor for the first time, I was not as interested in the old castle on the hill as I was in the quaint English pub that sat across the street from its gates.

The Gregory Arms led a duel life, neighborhood pub to the small village of Harlaxton during the offseason and nightly hot spot for the American students during the school year. Andy, the owner, was okay with this and used his English countryside charm to bring both of these worlds together surprisingly well. For a few quid, one could relax with a pint of the black stuff or raise hell on shots of tequila, and, either way, the mood always stayed cool. In almost three months, I had never seen anyone be asked to leave the Gregory Arms before the lights came up at 11:30.

Katherine Graham had a very short pixie-bob haircut, and the stubble on the back of her cream colored neck was the first detail about her that I could remember noticing. She was sitting at a table with some other Americans, facing away from me as I walked up to the bar to order a drink. Being only twenty, I couldn't have legally entered a pub like the Gregory Arms in my own country, and I had only successfully sneaked into a couple. In preparation for my debut in this new world of socially acceptable alcohol consumption, I had made sure during my long walk down from the manor to have my order ready, but when the bartender asked me what I wanted I was distracted by the downy stubble at the base of that delicate scalp.

As I remembered it, Kat had been rather sophisticatedly dressed for a woman of her age in 1995. She was wearing a dark colored woolen sweater, a perfectly fitting pair of dress slacks, and black patent leather high-heeled boots that looked like might have gone up all the way to her knee under the trousers. It had been cold out on the moor, and I had exercised utilitarian reason when choosing to throw a tee shirt over my long-underwear top. I was rocking my well-travel hiking boots and a trusty pair of American jeans, and I had the whole ensemble wrapped in my Gortex rain jacket. To keep the cold off of my ears, I had taken my ponytail down, but the wind had blown rats in my hair and it was beginning to take on an agenda of its own. The pub was

21

classy and quaint, and she looked like she belonged there. I looked like a professional wrestler from one of the low-dollar regional circuits who had missed his bus to Provo and wandered around in the desert for a few days. However, in spite of my awkward self-awareness, it had only taken a couple of hours and a few rounds of drinks for me to find myself in a dark back room of the crowded Greg in deep conversation with the sophisticatedly dressed, pixie-haired girl that I had noticed when I first walked in the pub.

An annoyingly perky friend of hers, Sara, had been responsible for our meeting. I remember her running her fingers through my hair and saying, "Oh my God, there is someone I have to introduce you to!" She had then taken me by the hand and pulled me away from the bar towards the rear of the building so impulsively that I had barely had time to pick up my drink. "My friend, Kat, is so crazy about guys with long hair," she bubbled as she led me past the burning fireplace and into the back room.

I never found out if what Sara had said about the hair was true, but Kat seemed to take a liking to me right away. It made no sense, I could not reconcile it logically, but all of the signs were there. She was laughing at my jokes and thinking about the thoughts that I shared. Sara had floated back to the crowd, and Kat and I shared another round of drinks and then another. I had been in an adventurous mood that night, and I had purposely steered the conversation away from the *where-you-from* and *what-are-you-studying* that had been going on all around us. I got deep fast with Kat, and, while most people were fearful and untrusting when I did that, she seemed to thrive. I don't think either of us was ready to leave that delicious little temporary world when the lights came up and Andy began his rounds.

Flickering and emitting their fluorescent hum, the lights in Dr. White's classroom were up as well. It had been

22

months since that first night with Kat at the Greg, but I felt the same rush when I saw her there in class. Over the weeks, the cosmopolitan look had given way to comfort and practicality, but the fuzzy slippers and pajama pants were just as endearing to me. She was a wood nymph, a scarred and sacred sculpture from a glorious and forgotten age. She had done nothing to her short black hair that day and it framed her tiny head perfectly. Her ears were too big and I liked to pretend sometimes that she was part elf. At least that would have explained the spell I felt cast on me. She looked up through her glasses and smiled at me as I walked in the room. There was a little part of her that loved me too.

Because most of class was spent that day in final preparations for Lopez's play, I didn't get much of a chance to talk to Kat. She was, of course, playing the lead, and the pressure of our upcoming performance had motivated her to take the role quite seriously. As Hortensio, I had little to do except run my lines. I did go through my scene with Lopez, who was playing the widow as well as directing, but afterward I just sat there and enjoyed Kat's charisma as she breezed through the difficult dialogue. As she finished the Act V monologue, sarcastically and sadly, a tiny round of applause foreshadowed the response our patrons would have on Friday.

At the end of class, Kat gave me that same smile as she threw her bag over her shoulder and headed back towards her room, and that was it, the highlight of my day.

4:36PM Tuesday (Hour 4:40)

I was back in the Big Chair, well in command of the conversation I was allowing Lopez to have with me, when Elwood stumbled out of his chamber. He had been drinking all day the day before, as was his custom, and he headed towards the sink to relieve his morning need. He shot me a quick glance as he noticed Lopez in the room and, in accordance with our unspoken pledge of secrecy, adjusted his flight path away from the alluring basin on the wall and towards the bathroom down the hall.

"Mornin'," he managed as he passed the two of us, and I took a moment to admire his carnival uniqueness.

James Daniel Beam, only son of Jeremiah Beam Jr., had lived a life of which many of us dream and none of us would want. In the lush countryside of Kentucky, somewhere between Lexington and Louisville, Elwood's vaunted ancestors had perfected a distinctive recipe for sour mash bourbon. As is often the case in these stories, the recipe had been kept in the family for generations before Elwood's great grandfather started selling it to friends and neighbors. The bourbon was good, people bought it, and it was Elwood's grandfather who built the distillery and founded the company that had made his life what it was.

Therefore, at least in function if not in theory, there had never been any reason for Elwood to take anything seriously. His lifestyle consisted of sleeping until three or four in the afternoon, at which time he would pull himself out of bed, wash himself clean of whatever evidence of the previous night's follies had crusted up overnight, get dressed, and head to the pub. About seven or so that evening he would stumble back up to the Vortex and fall into bed, usually fully clothed, to sleep off his afternoon drunk. Then, later that same night, usually about eleven or twelve he would repeat the process. Elwood held firm to this regimen. In fact, in the time that I had known him I had never seen him eat.

It was no surprise then, a few minutes later, when Elwood trudged back into the room and said, "Hey, I'm headin' down to da Greg. You guys wanna tag along?"

I had maybe smoked five cigarettes by this time and they were definitely not helping my foul mood. The intoxicative effect of my earlier proximity to Kat was wearing off, and I had been thinking about something stronger. Whiskey sounded like a good idea. Perhaps, I thought, the change of scenery would be healthy as well. I looked towards Lopez to see if I could garner her opinion of Elwood's proposition, but she seemed preoccupied, horrified and fascinated by the site of my skinny roommate in his tight white skivvies. Whatever her quiet thoughts might have been, she was with us a few moments later when we sauntered down the steps and out the front door of the manor after Elwood had returned from the WC and graciously sheathed his glorious ivory gams.

The driveway to Harlaxton Manor was perfectly straight, narrow blacktop, and legend had it that it was exactly a mile long. During my time there it was not unusual to hear the thunder cracking boom of an RAF fighter pilot swooping down to use the long narrow drive as a point of reference during a practice bombing run. Also, there was supposedly a tradition at the college of students stripping naked, probably while inebriated, and jogging the entire length of the drive, but I had never actually known this to occur. In my assessment, the damp English air would have made the inebriation a prerequisite, and I found the jets to be more exciting anyway. However, to the majority of students at Harlaxton College the main purpose of the mile long drive was walking to and from the Gregory Arms.

Of course, the walk to the Greg was always easier than the walk back. The ingestion of adult oriented alcoholic beverages was the main factor in this difference. However, there was a slight but consistent uphill grade on the way back as well. For the observant traveler, the key to a successful trip was measuring one's progress using the two major landmarks that existed on the path back to the manor.

The first, about a quarter of a mile up the drive, was an old stone bridge, flat and wide but fairy tale ornate, like a miniature version of London Bridge. In accordance with the Harlaxton theme of illusion, the bridge crossed a pond that had been cut into the countryside in such a way as to resemble a naturally occurring river that had never been there. Standing by the short stone rail of the bridge, it was impossible to see either end of the lake, and I had been living there for weeks before I realized the illusion.

The other landmark on the trek was about three quarters of the way up the drive. A large gate house built in the same style as the manor, it consisted of two towers on each side of the drive connected by a high stone arch and it was all under one roof. The structure was small in comparison to the main house but almost as large as some of the private residences that I had seen down in the village.

"I can't believe we rode through this thing on one of those giant buses!" Lopez said while looking up at the bottom of the gatehouse arch as we walked through it. Inversely, the gatehouse was the *first* checkpoint on the way *to* the Greg.

"I wonder what they use it for," she said.

"I think the maintenance guys use it for storage," Elwood said as we continued on.

It was chilly and damp that day, and the invisible rain hung motionless in the dishwater sky. The weather had been getting worse over the last couple of weeks, but I noticed that my comrades were cheerful as we made our way to our favorite watering hole. As usual of late, I was silently somewhere else, thinking about the first time that I walked back from the Greg that first night all those months ago.

I couldn't remember about what Kat and I had been talking that night, but I remember the mild shock of noticing that the pub was empty except for us when the lights came up. Kat started and then smiled and her eyes narrowed and her nose wrinkled as she did. I probably said something like, "Well, I guess we should get going," but I don't remember whether or not I did. I remember that her gloves matched her scarf, and she had a black wool jacket that she put on over her wool sweater before we walked out the door. I'm sure that I was drunk that night, and she probably was too, but in my memory it didn't feel like we were.

In retrospect, I suppose the atmosphere alone could have induced the moment. Two American kids, our first night in England, enchanted by the mystical magic of travel, our discovery of this new and ancient countryside. As we walked side by side onto the fairy tale bridge her gloved fingers became woven into mine. Our pace slowed as we simultaneously noticed the reflection of the moon melting into the surface of the pond. We might have looked at each other, but neither of us said anything. It felt good to have her hand in mine as we continued up the drive, and she leaned into my body in reaction to the cold. The night was quiet and bright, and we saw a couple of hares scramble as we came upon them. There seemed to be an inexplicable familiarity between us, and I felt sure that we were on the first of many romantic walks to come.

We stopped in the darkness beneath the roof of the old gatehouse, and I asked permission to kiss her. I saw that somewhere, in a movie or a silly daydream, and I had always wanted to try it. The chivalrous ritual of honorable courtship had been a fantasy of my youth. Maybe it was the moment, but she granted my wish, and I think I remember her smiling, wrinkling that tiny pointed nose a bit as if she had never before been asked such a question.

Facing each other, we stood holding hands at our sides, and the silhouette of my larger head cast her glowing face in a shadow as I leaned down upon it. As our lips touched, her hands fell from mine and found each other at the small of my back. I cupped her delicate head and my fingertips grazed the short hair above her neckline that I had first noticed in the pub. She pushed her weight against me, and I responded by holding her a little tighter. Her lips were very narrow and her tiny tongue playfully tapped against mine. Her head felt very light in my hands. Her breath was warm against the cold skin of my face, and a small cloud of steam danced in the air above us.

A charming old English gentleman named Harold was the head groundskeeper for the college, and he was the one who finally happened upon us there in the dark. Awkwardly, we broke our kiss as the beam of his big chrome flashlight founds our faces.

"Sorry," he said in his charming old English gentleman's accent as he turned the light away from us. "I was afraid someone was messing about over here."

Kat's cream colored face turned red, and I smiled sheepishly at Old Harold.

"Carry on," he said nervously as he walked away with his eyes fixed on the pavement in front of his feet.

I looked at Kat, and she giggled a bit as the crimson began to fade. I put my arm around her and we resumed our walk back the manor. We stopped as we came to the front door of the mansion. Her room was in a different wing of the great old house than mine, and this was to be where we would part ways. We kissed again, just a peck this time. She smiled as she backed away, but I don't remember her saying anything. She turned around and I watched her fade into the darkness of the entrance hall on her way to the old cedar staircase. For a moment, I stood there, stupid grin on my face, thinking about what the future might hold.

I didn't think about what the future might hold anymore, but, as Lopez and Elwood and I made our way to the Gregory Arms that day, I resolved to no longer think about the past. The decision came to my mind quickly, and I embraced it with rash abandon. All thoughts of Katherine Graham were driven completely out of my head by the time we crossed the old stone bridge, and I felt confident that my conviction would hold true for at least a few hours.

6:52PM Tuesday (Hour 6:56)

As I rested against the door frame of the men's room at the Gregory Arms, I spied my empty stool across the crowded room, and I remember thinking that my mission was simple. Operation: Upright. All I had to do was focus. Lead with the head and the body will follow. I was not deterred by the fact that I had needed a break to regain my balance after my harrowing but successful trip from the urinal, through the swinging doors of the john, back into the fray. I had made it this far, and I was not the type of fellow to just give up.

It had all started quite innocently a few hours earlier with a pint of McEwen's ale, but it hadn't been long before we were working our way down the colorful row of bottles in front of the mirror behind the bar. The itinerary had been reckless and foolish, no thought at all put into the chemistry experiments gurgling in our bellies, Beefeater and tonics followed by shots of Cuervo, Glenfiddich on the rocks, then some devil shite called Connemara. Amazingly, I had felt fine until I got up to use the facilities, but, as I started walking towards the restroom, I was surprised to discover that my left leg was no longer the same length as my right. This, of course, made bipedal locomotion, something with which I normally had no trouble at all, a bit of a challenge. Trying to concentrate, I suddenly noticed how loud it was, and I thought for a moment that we might be seaborne until I remembered that we were nowhere near the ocean.

I had made it to the head and evacuated my burdened bladder but was now caught in *no-man's land*, treed, unable to move from my perch on the wall by the bathroom door. I might have been there the rest of the night, gradually melting into an unconscious heap, had Paul not strolled in through the side door.

"Cheers, Sammy!" he said. I didn't hate the name when he said it. "What you doing pissin' round the loo, mate?"

"Paul," I said in a guttural slur, "What's up?"

"It's me slumming night," he cracked, "You got a fag?"

I quit concentrating on my balance as I reached into my shirt for a cigarette, and my knees buckled momentarily as I shifted my weight against the wall. Paul, who couldn't have caught me had I fallen, steadied me by grabbing my arm and said, "Easy, big fella, let's get you a stool."

"Right on," I nodded as we double-teamed the trip back to my party.

"Paul!" Lopez howled as she saw us approaching. A glass ash tray lost its life in her rush to get up and hug him.

"Cheers!" Paul said as he guided me to my seat.

Elwood, who rarely exhibited the effects of alcohol consumption, lifted his glass and said, "Cheers, buddy."

One difference that I had noticed over the last few months between Americans and Britons was in the very nature of how they defined themselves. The key factor seemed to be occupation back in the States. A doctor had achieved a certain level of success in life simply because he or she was a doctor, while a ditch digger was merely a ditch digger. Paul Patmore, 22 years old, native of Gratham, worked at a chicken processing plant. Despite the fact that this was, in his part of the world, a fairly decent job, Paul's character was not defined by the way in which he earned his money. A legend among the townies of Gratham, Paul was a dilettante of social diplomacy between the locals and the Americans. Unflappable, he seemed to be ever present, smile on his face, pint in his hand.

"What's got into to him?" he asked the others as he nodded towards me. I was settling onto my stool with the painstaking precision of a Harrier jet landing.

"One too many trips to the well, my friend," Elwood answered. I was beginning to realize that they were talking about me.

"Right, a nice cuppa then," Paul said loud enough that Andy nodded and reached for the kettle simmering behind the bar. "I'll not be the one to carry the big bastard up the hill," Paul cracked as he got up to collect my tea.

I felt the aromatic steam on my nose and lips as he set the cup and saucer under my randomly undulating face. For three hundred years the English had been drinking tea, and, like coffee back home, one of its rumored benefits was that of a head-clearing agent for fellows in a condition such as mine. Like coffee, it didn't really work.

"Pull yourself together Sammy," Lopez slurred a bit as she put her arm around my head to pull my ear closer to her lips. "We still have to make it to the Halloween party in the Bistro!"

I remember being surprised by Elwood's pace as he had steadily pulled away from me and Lopez on our way up the drive. It was as if the hours of mid-afternoon drinking had had no effect on him, and he mercilessly left the two of us in his dust. Lopez and I parted ways as we entered the manor.

"I gotta go get dressed," she slurred. "You better be there, Sammy. You gotta see my costume!"

I don't remember saying anything. I just watched her stumble down the hall with my own blurry vision. With a bit more effort than should have been necessary, I made it back to my room. I felt confident that I was not going to be sick, but the awful industrial carpet in the hallway of my floor kept catching my feet as I tried to pick them up. I felt, at times, as though the walls were falling inward so I decided to lean hard against the one on my left and drag myself down it to ensure that it did not cave in. That system seemed to work pretty well. Before long I made it back to Room 333, stepped off the merry-go-round, and slumped into the Big Chair to await my fate.

"What d'ya think?" Elwood said as he emerged from behind the curtain of his sleeping chamber, black suit, white socks, skinny tie, and fedora. I was now thinking more slowly than the speed of thought because I didn't realize until he put on his shades that he was dressed as Elwood Blues.

"Nice" I chuckled, "clever."

"I'm on a mission from God," he quoted. He didn't even have to change his accent.

"You need sideburns," I said as I began to look around the desk for the black felt tipped pen that I had seen a few days ago.

Suddenly but with little fanfare, Taylor strode through the open door of the Vortex as I was sketching a soulful set of sideburns on the sides of Elwood's head.

"Hey guy," Elwood said without calling attention to the fact that Taylor had been MIA for over 24 hours.

"Nice," said Taylor, no doubt in reference to Elwood's costume choice as well as my artwork. He had a black garbage bag with him that he set on his bed on his way to the sink where he relieved himself and then took out his toothbrush.

"Two sideburns," I said as I finished up the artificial facial hair, "No charge."

Elwood moved like a boxer, bobbing and weaving as he checked himself in the same mirror that Taylor was using to brush his teeth. Satisfied, he turned to me, said, "Thanks buddy, I'll see you guys down there," and walked out the door. As he left I noticed a slight change in his gait, as if he had actuality become Dan Aykroyd.

"Got something for you," Taylor said as he set his toothbrush down and headed back toward the garbage bag. He rummaged through what looked like two days worth of laundry and produced a large blue bed sheet and silly foam reindeer mask. He smiled his *you-didn't-think-I-was-really-going-to-do-this-did-you?-smile* and said, "Do you want to be *Jesus* or *Rudolph?*"

As I remember it, the British didn't care much for Halloween, which I found ironic seeing as how the holiday had its origins in the pagan harvest celebrations of the ancient people of those very isles. In fact, the festival of Samhain had been such an integral part of Gaelic culture that the Romans thought it less trouble to Christianize the holiday rather than try to eradicate it. In northern England, the festival evolved into Mischief Night, an excuse for angst ridden young people to steal garden gates and set street fires, but that had all but ended by the time I was there. Gone were the punkies and soul cakes, and the few trick-or-treaters that did come out seemed to be regarded more as a nuisance than anything else. Yet, as a service to the primarily American student body, the Evil Student Activities Committee of Harlaxton College had planned a costume party in the Bistro. Clever bastards.

The Bistro was something that would not be found on an American campus. Nestled into the arched stone foundation of the old manor house was a private lounge, open only to students and faculty, although I *had* seen Paul there on more than a few occasions. Far from palatial, the room was cold and damp with an uneven concrete floor and looked to be furnished with old church pews and tables out of a Viking long house. The flaking cement walls were covered in student-painted murals, most of which depicted common British tourism locations, the London Underground, Stonehenge, Tower Bridge, and the like. The saving grace was a portable bar set alongside the east wall, usually manned by charming old Harold the groundskeeper, with two taps, one ale and one cider, and a very limited variety of wine and bottled brews. As far as bars go, it really wasn't impressive; however, it *was* in the basement of the school.

For all of its shortcomings, the Bistro was a safer alternative to the pubs in town. There were no unruly townies to worry about, no liquor, and no matter how drunk you did get you were only a few flights of stairs away from your bed. However, despite these built-in safeguards, I was still weary of a trip to the cellar. The night's leisure had started too early and at too brisk of a pace, and, though I had fought through the drunkenness, the sedative quality of the alcohol was beginning to take effect. Months before, someone had put a poster of the Queen up on our wall, and Taylor had covered her Majesty's face with an Elvis postcard from one of the kiosks outside King's Cross Station in London. As I sat there nodding off, the irony of his interior design suddenly struck me as very funny, and it was my own laughter that jolted me back awake.

If it hadn't been for that postcard, I could have just passed out in that comfortable behemoth of a chair like I had so many times before, and that would have been the end of it.

"What the hell's so funny?" Taylor said from inside his bed chamber.

"Your artwork," I said.

"What's that?" he said inquisitively as he stepped half way through the curtain hanging in the doorway.

"Your collage piece," I said as I motioned towards the wall. "*King on Queen*," I named it.

"That was commissioned, you know," said Taylor, playing along.

"Sweet, how much?" I feigned.

"Doesn't matter," Taylor said, "the rat never paid."

"Fuckin' Elwood, "I added. Then I chuckled again remembering the sight of him *Aykroyding* down the hall. "Did you see that fucker's costume?"

"Yeah, fits him, doesn't it?" Taylor laughed. "Are you going down?"

"I don't know," I groaned. "It's been a rough night already…"

"Why come?" asked Taylor, mocking the parlance of our times.

"Well, let's just say we had old Andy slinging the bottles down at the Greg all afternoon."

"Hey man, Elwood looked fine."

"That's because he's always that drunk," I said.

Taylor chuckled and then reached back into the garbage bag he had carried in with him and produced a small brown glass bottle with a plastic lid and a colorful paper label that said: *Liquid Karma Room Odorant*. He tossed it into the air towards me and then said, "Here, take a whiff of this."

"What is it?" I asked after I missed the catch and picked it up off of the floor.

"Popper," he said. Then he realized that had not answered my question. "Rush, amyl nitrite, it's kind of like a whippet."

I had heard of whippets but I had never done one. "Where'd you get this shit?" I asked.

"Head shop in Grantham, got a new one-hitter too. Check it out," he held up what looked like a cigarette but in all probability was not at all.

Meanwhile, I examined the bottle he had given me. *Active Ingredient: Isoayml Nitrite (CH₃)₂CHCH₂CH₂ONO*. I had no idea what any of that meant. *Warnings:* That was what I needed! *For aromatic purposes only, do NOT inhale directly from the bottle.*

"So what do I do with it?" I asked.

"Put it under your nose and take a big whiff."

9:45PM Tuesday (Hour 9:49)

My first hit of amyl. That sweet-and-sour chemical smell was the first thing I remember, but the entire rush was almost immediate, heart pounding, blood rushing, warm and fuzzy behind the bridge of my nose. My eyes seemed wider, my nerves seemed sharper, and I felt the color red. Then, over the course of the next couple of minutes, the rush gradually drifted away like the last few sparks of a fourteen dollar firecracker.

"So," Taylor said, "do you want to be Jesus or Rudolph?"

9:52PM Tuesday (Hour 9:56)

Taylor's little brown bottle seemed to be just what the doctor ordered. The high was subtle and didn't last very long, but with repetition I was able to emerge from my drunken stupor. Blown by this second wind, I was finally able to seriously contemplate attending the costume party downstairs, and we began to make preparations.

Taylor had shown generosity in his offer, but, seeing as how I was the one with long hair and a beard, it seemed obvious to me who would be *Jesus* and who would be *Rudolph*. Our costumes were rather simple really. Taylor just added the mask to the clothes he was already wearing, and I didn't do much. I had a red Henley that I knew would work perfectly. I located it, pulled it on, threw on some shorts, and wrapped the blue sheet around my body and over one shoulder toga style.

"You look like Jesus on steroids," Taylor said. His Rudolph mask looked ridiculous.

"Yeah," I said, "Why is Jesus always so skinny?"

"We like to think our Lord and Savior was in shape," Taylor said. "Who wants to think of their god as a slob?"

"Buddhists," I answered.

"Here," he said as he produced a couple of fat and sweet smelling cigars, "duty free."

He cut and lit his own as I asked, "Should Jesus show up smoking a cigar?"

"Why not?" he asked and I didn't have a good answer.

After a jovial descent down four flights we walked into the crowded Bistro arm-in-arm as if we were each other's dates. In retrospect, I guess we were.

In the States there are two Halloweens. The first one takes place early in the afternoon. Thirty-something parents dress their children as cute as possible and escort them around the neighborhood on their treat-gathering rounds, fairy princesses and tiny Jedi filling their plastic Jack-o-Lanterns with sweet, sugary goodness. The second celebration of the holiday takes place later, after dark, and is more true to the pagan origins of the day. The participants in this version are older teens and singles in their early twenties, and the focus is almost entirely on the practice of dressing up. It's an excuse, a license for the night to be someone else, a little sexier, a little sillier, or a little darker. This second version of the holiday is what was being celebrated in the Bistro that night.

Being on what was in essence an extended vacation, living out of the suitcases they had lugged onto the plane with them, the students at Halaxton should have been limited in their wardrobe options. With this in mind as we merged with the partiers, I was surprised at how elaborate and pre-meditated some of the costumes seemed. A frat boy from my floor named Adam had put together an impressive caveman costume which I thought amplified his personality perfectly. A pothead buddy of mine named Ben had woven his unkempt hair into giant *Pippi Longstocking* braids, and he had somehow located a dress that completed the look. It is incredibly liberating to expose certain aspects of one's true persona in the ruse of taking on another, and opportunities to do so are rare. It was obvious as I looked around the room that my fellow students had put a great deal of effort into making sure the opportunity was not wasted. In fact, our little Christmas gag seemed a bit overshadowed.

Not surprisingly, Kat had outdone everyone. She had somehow obtained an appropriate blonde wig and gold-rimmed glasses that perfectly complimented her borrowed maternity pants and the pillow under her button-down shirt. At first, I actually thought she was Dr. White.

As we walked up Kat, in the voice of an overly excited kindergarten teacher, said, "Someone's going to hell!"

"I'm driving the bus, baby," Taylor said as he walked on past her towards the bar.

"What?" I said as her magnetism pulled me to a halt. "You don't get it?" I said and unfortunately realized that I was still too drunk to be clever or endearing.

"Oh, I get it *Hey-Zeus*," she said. "What do you think of mine?"

"That's fucking sexy," I said. I was serious, but when she laughed I realized that she had mistaken my enthusiasm as a well executed joke.

"I didn't know the Christ was a smoker," she smiled as she pointed at my cigar.

"I didn't know Dr. White was a drinker," I failed again at being clever. "I mean, you know, while she's pregnant.." God, I had turned into an idiot. I even slurred the word *pregnant*, inadvertently emphasizing my boobery.

"A pregnant drinker?" she finished for me.

"Right," I sighed. I was losing her fast. The entrance had been good. She thought the costumes were funny, but the second I opened my drunken, oafish mouth her eyes had started to move around the room. My mind reeled, spinning aimlessly out of control, so much activity in such a short period of time and absolutely nothing to show for it. Talk about her, I thought, and I was just getting ready to tell her how clever I thought her costume was when time expired...

"Well," she said, "I'm going to go find Liz and Sara."

"What?" I said.

39

"Liz and Sara, they never came back from the bathroom."

"Oh, right on." I said. "Maybe I'll catch you later..." but she was already walking away.

While it is undoubtedly true that excess consumption of alcohol reduces brain function greatly and on many different levels, it is strange how being shitfaced can make you focus on a memory or a detail that you would have otherwise missed. There was no music playing in the Bistro that night, but I heard Cyndi Lauper singing *Time After Time* as Kat disappeared into the costumed crowd. It took me a moment to realize why. The first night I was in England, I had been sitting with Kat in the semi-private back room of the Gregory Arms when someone played that song on the juke box.

"Oh my God, I love this song!" she had scream-whispered as she grabbed my forearm from across the table. That was the first time that we actually touched.

"Cyndi Lauper?" I cringed.

"Yeah!" she said. "Come on, you can't tell me you don't love Cyndi Lauper."

"She was great on wrestling," I laughed.

"Listen to the words," she said, "It's really a beautiful song."

I had heard the song before, but I had never really listened to it. That night I did, and she was right. It was beautiful, haunting and ethereal, and for some reason, as she walked off in the Bistro that night, I remembered that song and the conversation that we'd had at the Gregory Arms that night while it played in the background.

"Paradise, Indiana," I had told her when she asked me where I was from. I had always thought the name of my home town was cool, and I was secretly proud anytime I had a chance to announce it.

"Been there," I was surprised to hear her say.

"You've been to Paradise, Indiana?" I had asked in disbelief.

"I'm from New Albany, "she said, "We squashed Castle in football my senior year."

"You played football?" I asked feigning disbelief this time.

"Yeah," she said, "I know I'm a little under-sized, but I'm fast!"

"Wide receiver?" I played along.

"No," she laughed, "I played clarinet. The band gets to travel for play-off games!"

"So what did you think?"

"Of the game or of Paradise?" she teased.

"Paradise," I said.

She shrugged her shoulders. "It seemed pretty much like New Albany, just smaller."

"Okay the game then."

"Ugly," she said, "We beat you guys like 50 to 20."

"49 to 28," I said. "I played in that game."

"Ouch, sorry," she said as she took a drink of her Stoli and cranberry.

"I'm over it," I said.

"No you're not." Her eyes narrowed as she smiled mischievously.

"You know, I'm really not," I laughed after my confession and wondered if that had just been a lucky guess on her part.

"What's your sign?" she asked as she leaned closer to me, conveying interest in my forthcoming answer.

"Like zodiac sign?" I said, "Pisces."

"Wow," she said as she leaned back in her chair, "So cool for you!"

"Really," I said. "What's so cool about being a Pisces?"

"Well," she said. Her face was electric with energy. "Pisces is the last sign in the zodiac, some people believe when your soul is born under Pisces that you've already been born under all the other signs."

"You talking about past lives?" I asked.

"Yeah," she said. "You're supposed to be an *old soul*. You've gained all this wisdom by living through all the lessons of the other eleven signs and now you're really close. As a Pisces you have the most potential to reach Nirvana this time around."

"Potential?"

"Well a Pisces may start out closer to Nirvana than the rest of us, but you still have to make it. You know, you still have to live a good life. They call it the *last chance lifetime*."

"What if I don't make it?" I said.

"I guess you start all over," she smiled wickedly, "...as a worm!"

She was a Sagittarius, but at the time I was ignorant of how that should have been a warning to me. She had been an actor and a singer in high school, but she told me she was discovering that writing was her true passion. She said that she thought it was more exciting because it was a challenge, and that acting had always been easy for her. I guess I started to fall in love with her right then, listening to her, watching her listen to me. We seemed to have so much in common that night.

That feeling, that strange familiarity that I had sensed so many weeks ago, seemed very far away as she waddled her mock-pregnant self away from me in the Bistro that night. The last bits of my earlier drunkenness were draining away, and I feared my impending sobriety. I needed to go to the bar, but I ended up just standing there. Luckily, Taylor arrived with a lukewarm McEwen's just as I was about to lose all hope.

"Dude," he said upon his arrival, "You need to come with me now. Alyssa and Audrey are dressed as Batman and Robin…and they're making out with each other."

"The Caped Crusaders…" I said as I slowly accepted defeat, "…I knew it!"

11:40PM Tuesday (Hour 11:44)

I had ordered four more ales at last call. Bistro rules clearly stated that a person was only allowed to order two drinks at last call, but I had cleverly circumvented this rule by being first in line at the bar, buying my two beers, and then drinking them as I moved to the end of the line. Although I had never previously tried this tactic, it worked quite smoothly and I was allowed to purchase an additional couple of beverages. The only flaw in my plan was that the place got empty too fast, and Old Harold had to ask me to leave before I could finish my fourth.

That should have been the perfect opportunity to stumble up to bed and pass out peacefully, but it occurred to me as I sloshed up the stairs that I had not seen Lopez at the Bistro all night. This surprised me because she had been quite intent upon us attending the costume party earlier in the day. I remembered her saying something about how I needed to see her costume, and I thought she would be disappointed if I missed it so I decided to find her. The fact that I was still dressed as Jesus did not, at the time, seem relevant to my decision.

My search led me to the fourth floor of the manor, residence hall of dozens of young female students, and strictly off limits to any persons of the male persuasion at this time of night. Even in my drunken state, I was quite surprised at how easy it was to move in restricted areas of the house at this hour. Perhaps it was the costume. It was also surprising to me that I was able to remember Lopez's room number. Finding her door was easy, but I don't think she was there. Also, I must have underestimated the volume and vigor with which I had been hailing my small Texan friend. Even though she never answered her door, I was greeted by a few of her floor mates, none of which seemed happy to see me.

"What the hell are you doing up here?" Kat's friend Sara said as she pulled her robe closed over her flat stomach and walked aggressively towards me. "People are trying to sleep!"

"I was just looking for Lydia," I said, but she and the others did not seem sympathetic.

"It's like midnight, Sam!" Sara continued. She made a sour face as she got close to me. "Good Lord," she said, "have you been drinking beer tonight or swimming in it?"

"Drinking it," I said, answering her rhetorical question.

Sara smiled at the quip, but then responsibly wiped the smile from her face. "You need to get off this floor before I have to call somebody," she said as she headed back to the open door of her dorm room. "Lydia's not there. Go back down stairs and go to bed, Sam."

I remember wondering where Lopez was if she was not in her room, and I remember wondering how Sara knew she wasn't in her room. However, not wanting to cause any more trouble, I was already walking towards the stairwell. "That didn't go well," I announced to myself as the angry women went back to their rooms one by one, and for some reason I continued to talk aloud to myself on my way down the stairs. "I wonder what has happened to my little Texan friend. Where have they taken her? Those rat bastards, I'll find you Lopez! God damn it, if it's the last thing I ever do. They'll never get away with this. I'll hunt them dow…" But my tirade came to an abrupt stop as I rounded the last corner of the third-floor hallway and was able to see through the open doorway to my room.

Taking into account the weirdness of the night so far, I should not have been as surprised as I was when I saw Taylor sitting in the Big Chair, smoking a cigarette, dressed only in his plaid boxer shorts and the familiar cape and cowl of Gotham's Dark Knight. Still in my makeshift beer stained Jesus costume, I walked into the room and stopped a few feet from him. He looked at me, raised an eyebrow beneath the mask, and took a drag of the cigarette. I remember wondering what brilliant debauchery had he been up to. I narrowed my eyes and pulled my chin back and to the right, bracing myself for whatever I might be about to hear. We stayed that way for a long, pregnant moment, and then he took another drag from his cigarette and said in a deep, gravelly voice, "I'm Batman."

Wednesday

It didn't even occur to me at the time that Elwood had not been in the room that night. We had the windows open, and I thought I heard a church bell ringing at midnight. I remember thinking that was odd, church bells ringing in the middle of the night. I wondered if it had anything to do with the end of Halloween or the beginning of All Saint's Day, or if I had imagined the sound entirely.

"Did you hear that?" I asked Taylor, who was still wearing the cape and cowl.

"Hear what?" he said. He suddenly looked very nervous.

"I thought I heard church bells…"

"Church bells?" he said, "ain't it just like the night to play tricks when you're tryin' to be so quiet?"

"What?" I said.

"Nothing," he replied.

"Take your mask off, Bruce," I said. "What happened to Rudolph?"

"Hmm…about that," he said as he pulled the rubber mask off of his head, his closely cropped brown hair falling back into place miraculously. "I suppose you're going to find out sooner or later…"

"Find out what?" The anxiety was suddenly starting to make me feel sober again.

"Audrey and I sort of traded costumes," he said as he held up the Batman mask and nodded towards it.

I was confused. "That's none of my business," I said trying to convey the idea that I would never hold him in judgment for such a deed. "Hell, that's brilliant!" I added.

"Thanks," he accepted the compliment, "but, um, she's asleep in your bed."

48

"What you talkin'bout, Willis?" I said as I gave him an *are you serious?*-smile.

"She said I was snoring..." he said as he slowly followed me to the curtain hanging in the doorway of my sleeping chamber. Sure enough, when I pulled the curtain over, there she was on her belly with one leg under the covers and the other one curled up by her side as if she were some sort of drunken and passed out hurdler. I was more shocked than aroused by the sight of half of her bare ass as I realized that she was wearing only the silly foam rubber Rudolph mask.

Trying to be clever, I asked, "What happened to Robin?"

"Alyssa?" he said, clarifying that we were talking about the roommate and former crime-fighting partner of Audrey, the naked girl asleep in my bed.

"Yeah," I answered.

"Where do you think I was last night?" he said.

"Clever," I said. "Who would've expected that you'd go after the sidekick first?"

"I'm an evil genius," he said in a peculiar monotone.

"You're like the Riddler," I replied as I shot him a fabricated look of approval. The motivations behind Taylor's random acts of debauchery were, at times, a mystery to me, but I felt that I would be perceived in the best possible light if I pretended to understand. Yet, there were times when I was quite confused. My first instinct concerning his sexual conquest of two relatively sexy and possibly bi-sexual roommates on successive nights was awe and envy, but his divulgence had sounded more like a confession than braggadocio. I wondered sometimes if he had any control over his deplorable and wickedly delicious behavior. It occurred to me as I walked across the room and usurped the Big Chair, that I had lived with Taylor for three months and still knew very little about him. I fought through the momentary queasiness I had just caused by sitting down too fast and took out a slightly mangled cigarette. I lit it, inhaled deeply, and leaned back in the chair as I considered the strange case that was my roommate, Taylor Beckett.

I knew he was from Louisville and had graduated from St. Xavier before matriculating to the University of Kentucky, and, in spite of his recent carnal adventures, he had mentioned a girlfriend, Jenny, waiting back in Lexington. Taylor was a writing major, but, in contrast to Kat, he would have been better suited for acting. He had never mentioned what his parents did for a living, but he had talked about working on a thoroughbred farm when he was a kid. It was obvious from the beginning that Taylor enjoyed the finer things, gourmet foods and well aged Scotch. He was aware of the arts and fine culture and had even talked me into attending the London Symphony Orchestra with him a few weeks earlier. He reminded me of Gatsby though despite my speculations I really didn't know anything about his socioeconomic background, and, if he came from money, he didn't flaunt it as Gatsby might have. The only exception to this had been the last weekend of September.

Most of the Harlaxton student body had been preparing for the four-day, school-organized bus trip to Ireland. I had been planning on spending the weekend at home in the all-but-deserted manor house. I was still dealing with bad vibes from the bus trip to Paris and was in no mood for another guided tour. Also, I was broke.

"Do you know what this weekend is?" Taylor asked me that Thursday evening.

"No, dude," I said.

He put his hands on my shoulders and looked right into my face as he said, "The largest party in the world."

"What are you talking about?" I asked. I had become somewhat used to the hyperbole with which Taylor introduced these adventures.

"Oktoberfest," he said. "Munich."

"Sweet," I said. Knowing that I wouldn't be going anywhere other than the Greg, I was feigning interest at this point. "Are you going?"

"Nope," he said. "We're going!"

Flattered that he had invited me, I smiled as I shook my head. "No cash, dude," I said.

"So you're just staying here this weekend?" he asked.

"I haven't gotten my housing loan check for next month yet," I said.

"Fuck that," he said as if he were angry with me, "you're going with. Get packed. It's on me."

Fifteen minutes later we were in a taxi headed for the train station in Grantham. We traveled by rail to Heathrow and were able to get two standby tickets on Lufthansa arriving in Munich at 11:30 local time and returning from Nuremburg three days later. However, the trip had been poorly planned. We landed in Germany just in time to take the last train to Munich, and it was well after midnight when we actually started looking for a place to stay. Being that it was Oktoberfest, we had no luck and ended up sleeping in an alcove by the front doors of a public library. We spent most of the next day waiting in line to secure a couple of beds at the youth hostel, and the rest of the day exploring the city. Hiking through the nice Bavarian neighborhood near our hostel, we began following a canal and, quite by accident, stumbled upon Nymphenburg Palace. We climbed one of the bell towers and surveyed the city from the top of the Frauenkirche and wondered awkwardly through a memorial to the victims of the Allied bombings during WWII.

Later that afternoon, secure in the knowledge that we had a place to stay, we headed for Oktoberfest. We found that many people spoke English, and Taylor spoke enough German to get us by when they didn't. As we got closer to the festival we saw the lederhosen and heard the polka and dodged the puke on the sidewalk, and the anticipation began to swell. We began the evening cautiously, eating bratwurst and drinking beer from giant mugs in the *Winzerer Fähndl* tent, but in a matter of hours we were smoking pot at the base of the Bavaria Statue with an exiled immigrant to Canada who had been deported back to Germany for, of all things, selling drugs. We parted ways with him when he cut his finger on an aluminum can while rolling a second joint and subsequently invited us to share the bloody doobie.

The next day we made our way by train to Nuremburg where we spent the night in the hostel at Nuremburg Castle and flew back to London the day after that. Throughout the course of the weekend, Taylor had paid for everything. Exhausted from our travel, we sat silently fighting sleep on the train back to Grantham. I thought about thanking him for the trip, but it proved too awkward and, for some reason or another, I never did. I should have. Taylor had been my best friend the entire time I had been overseas. We had the same sense of humor, and we worked well together in a social setting. We didn't really know each other that well, but our mutual respect had been enough for us to be able to get along. For the most part I liked Taylor just fine, but there was a strange, secret part of me that kind of hated him. I had watched in awe over the last three months as he charmed his way through everyone around us. It was fascinating how effortless it seemed for him. In most ways he was a very likable fellow, and most people very much liked him. Perhaps, I had just spent too much time with him. His flaws reminded me of my own, but that was not the source of my secret loathing. When I saw him at his best he was everything I wanted to be. He was my Phineas, and sometimes I wanted to push him out of the fucking tree.

Of course, in our room on Halloween night with his naked conquest passed out in my bed, there was no tree. There was a window, but it probably would have been too narrow for him and there definitely would have been a struggle. So I just asked him about his girlfriend, but that didn't work either.

"Dude, Jen's in Lexington," was his reply.

1:53 AM Wednesday (Hour 13:57)

Lying in my bed I heard the clock tick and thought of her. Once again, I was wide awake. I was too young and ignorant back then to truly understand the concept of love, but my relationship with Kat, however ambiguous, was the first thing that I thought about when I woke up in the morning and the last thing that I thought about before I went to sleep. Taylor and I had carried his date back to his bed, and I had tried to call it a night, but I felt caught up in circles, my mind reeling as I tried to get to sleep.

Confusion was nothing new. It seemed like I had done this every night for a month or so. Averting me from slumber, my mind would flashback to warm nights when we would walk together out on the moors and talk about all of the fantastic things we hoped to someday accomplish. Time after time I would roll the conversations over and over again in my head, dumping out a suitcase of memories until I drifted off to sleep, almost leaving them behind.

Most nights sleep did come, but with it came dreams, vivid dreams that I could not always tell from reality. Sometimes I would picture her out in the English countryside somewhere walking too far ahead of me. She would be calling to me, but I couldn't hear what she was saying. The day after I had first kissed her under the ancient gatehouse out on the mile-long drive I woke up abuzz with rabid excitement about this new woman in my life. I was high. My mind was numb with good vibrations as I gleefully daydreamed about all of the wonderful places that our relationship might go. It hadn't even been noon on the day after when I had gone up to her room, salivating for chapter two of our courtship.

She said, "Go slow." At the time, I didn't know her well enough to understand why. A scarred and sacred beauty, she had already lived through tragedy at her tender age. This trip overseas was to be a new beginning for her, but a serious relationship was not something for which she was ready. She had interpreted my enthusiasm as pressure, and the last thing she needed was pressure. I wanted to tell her that it was fine, that I could slow down without falling behind. I wanted to tell her to take all the time she needed to find her way and that if she ever got lost, she could look and find me waiting for her, but, as it turned out, none of that was true. I swear to God I had tried to be patient, but I just didn't have it in me. I had been a stupid and ungrateful child tearing through his packages on Christmas morning. I had been a fool, and the realization might have come too late to change anything.

Most nights sleep did come, and I would dream of a world in which it had not been too late, a world in which there was still time to do things right. I dreamt of a picture, a photograph that I had never seen. I saw the distant outline of France on the horizon of the night sky and the green suds of the Channel, but the picture faded and the darkness turned to gray, and when I would wake up the next morning, the song would still be playing in my head.

Yet, unlike all of the nights before, sleep did not come on that night. Through the thin wall to my right I could hear Taylor and Audrey. They were both snoring, but I just stared into the darkness between myself and the ceiling. Reality had set in though the dream did not exactly end. Consciousness meant fear and anxiety, and I knew that they would turn the dream into a nightmare in which I was locked out of her life, watching through windows and wondering if she was okay. I dreaded that fear, the evil masochistic fantasies to which I would subject myself during the long and excruciating time before I fell asleep, and, lacking the conviction to tough it out, I sat up in bed and began searching for Taylor's little brown bottle. I took a couple of numbing hits and everything began to feel better. My perception of the world having shifted just enough, I tightly gripped the bottle, secrets stolen from deep inside, the drum beat out of time, but the song was still playing in my head.

2:01 AM Wednesday (Hour 14:05)

I was lost in deep, intellectual thought about the philosophical schools of Determinism and Fatalism as I aimlessly walked the silent halls of the sleeping castle…

Yeah, right.

I was thinking about Kat, running through the highs and lows of our brief history, our weekend in Paris, that first night together at the Greg and all the little moments in between. She had come heavy with the mixed signals right from the start, and I had been reeling ever since. As I wandered through the quiets halls, I remembered how we kissed under the gate house, and how she had blown me off the next day. Perhaps too eager, I had climbed the stairs to her floor and knocked on her door the following afternoon. I remembering sitting in an uncomfortable folding chair in her room as she told me that she didn't want things to get too serious between us and that she wasn't interested in having a boyfriend while she was in England. Suddenly, I was embarrassed to even be there, and I couldn't get out of that room fast enough.

It all seemed simple at first. It wasn't as if I had never been through anything like that before, but then Paris happened and it all got complicated again. I began to wonder if I had taken a wrong step somewhere, and that was what had led me to thoughts about Determinism and Fatalism.

At the time, I had only recently come to understand the difference. Fatalists believe that all events and actions are subjugated to fate or some other inevitable schedule of predetermination. Determinists don't share this view exactly. They believe that the extent to which human beings have influence over their future is dependent upon and therefore limited by present and past events. They accept that there are things we cannot control, but they still feel that we have some influence. Perhaps my mind was now wandering aimlessly, but the inner debate became suddenly significant when I entered the library and saw Kat studying in solitude beneath the humming fluorescent lights.

I was relieved that I had changed from my sacrilegious costume to an everyday tee shirt and pajama pants. In order not to startle her, I purposely exaggerated my movement as I approached so that the extra noise would send advance warning of my arrival. As I walked up to her, she looked up and said, "Hey, Sam."

"Hey," I said back as I watched her set her pencil down and take off her glasses. "What are you doing up?" I said.

"British Studies paper," she said as she motioned towards the open books and stacked papers in front of her, "How about you?"

"I heard some screaming," I answered, "but when I got up to investigate I discovered that it was coming from inside my head."

"You're so weird," she said, but she smiled as she said it.

"No, seriously," I continued, "if you hear a bunch of crazy rumors tomorrow about some drunken guy dressed as Jesus wondering around and screaming up on your floor, I don't know anything about that. In fact, the whole episode will probably turn out to have been some sort of group hallucination."

"Sam," she exhaled. "What did you do?"

"It's the voices, Kat," I said. "I have to do what they tell me."

She looked up again and smiled at me, but she didn't say anything else. As she did, I looked into her eyes and held her gaze just a second too long, tipped my hand, and became transparent again. Awkwardly, she looked back down at her work and an uncomfortable silence came over the room. As the lights hummed above us, I renounced Fatalism and tried once again to influence my own destiny.

"Listen," I said trying to convey with the tone of my voice that I was serious now, "I know I've been weird over the last couple of weeks."

She looked up at me, but she didn't speak.

"I'm sorry. I know what you've said, but I don't believe you. We still laugh together..."

"Sam, don't..." she interrupted, putting her hand on my chest to get me to be quiet. She turned her face down and away from me, but she didn't say anything else. I was frozen, afraid I had made the wrong decision. I just wanted to get out of the situation. I wanted to blurt out how much of a loser I was, and tell her that it was okay because I never should have expected someone as interesting and as lovely as her to end up with me. I just wanted that moment, that dot on the timeline, that bad memory in progress to be over.

Then I noticed that she was crying.

Without thinking about it, I touched her shoulder, and she looked up at me and smiled. I was confused. The crying had caught me off guard, but the smile seemed positive, maybe just gracious. I questioned myself as I watched a tear run down her porcelain cheek, and I silently cursed myself for causing her pain. She leaned into my chest and I put my other arm around her as the crying subsided. She hugged me back, and after a few moments said into my chest, "I never wanted to hurt you, Sam."

"What do you mean?" I said as I leaned back and looked down at her.

"I just didn't want it to get like this," she said as she withdrew her arms, releasing me.

"Like what?" I asked.

"Sam, I'm sorry," she said, "I'm not ready for this."

"Neither was I," I said, "but that's the beauty of life, isn't it? All of the best stuff is unexpected. Don't you ever want to just quit thinking about it and live?"

"No," she said in a quiet and sure voice that made me a bit uneasy, "all of the worst stuff is unexpected too." She looked down and away, and there was silence for a moment.

"Where do you go?" I said.

"What?" she said.

"Where do you go when you drift off like that?"

She looked at me and chuckled. "It drives me crazy too," she said. "It takes me hours to get to sleep sometimes."

"I hate to see you cry," I said.

She smiled at me again and said, "Sit down with me, Sam. There's someone I need to tell you about." Dreading the forthcoming content, I furrowed my brow as I slowly sat down with her. "I had a boyfriend back home. His name was

Donnie." My heart sank as she began her story, but her eyes stayed focused on mine and that kept me listening. "We started dating when I was a junior in high school. He just came up to me in the hallway one day and asked me if I wanted to dance. There was no music, and my friends were all staring at us like we were morons, but I said yes and he took my hands and we danced right there in the main hallway, like some sort of waltz or something."

"That's cool," I said truthfully.

"Yeah," she said, "He was a Pisces too. You would've liked him. He was definitely a free spirit. We were in drama class together, and he was an amazing painter."

"Sounds cool," I said.

"So anyways," she continued, "He asked me out a few days after that, and we started dating. It was so storybook; he was like my first real boyfriend. The first time that he came to pick me up for a date he showed up with two long stem roses, a red one for me and a white one for my mom. How sweet is that?"

"So," I said, "I guess he's waiting for you at home, right?"

Her eyes dimmed a bit and she said, "Don't guess. Just listen, okay?"

"I'm sorry," I said and I reached for her hand. To my surprise, she met me with hers and continued to hold on to me.

"So, like, the longer we dated the more serious it got, right? I mean we're talking serious first true love. It was codependent almost. We were literally around each other all of the time; I quit hanging out with all my other friends. He was it."

"So what happened?" I asked.

"We were making out on my bed. It was after school and my parents weren't home from work yet. And we hadn't even gone all the way yet, so it was still exploratory and adventurous. I was on top of him and we were kissing and sliding our hands all over each other, up under each other's clothes and I felt these scabs on his chest."

"Scabs?" I said.

"Yeah, I was totally freaked out," she said. "I asked him what had happened, at first he wouldn't tell me, but he finally did. He did it to himself!"

"What, like he cut himself?" I asked.

"Yeah," she said, "He had done it with his shaving razor. Said he just pressed it into his chest one morning and worked it back and forth until the blood ran all the way down to his pants."

"Wow," I said.

"Yeah," she shook her head. "Turned out that he did it all the time, whenever he was feeling bad enough."

"Did he ever say why?"

"I guess so," she said. "I pushed him and pushed him about it, told him to stop, asked him why he did it, and one day he finally broke down and opened up to me. He told me everything once he got going. His real dad had been hit by a train when he was like two, so he had never really known him, and his mom got remarried when he was like nine. Apparently, his step dad was some kind of pervert. He had abused Donnie, you know, sexually."

"Damn," I said somewhat stunned by the turn in her story.

"He said it only happened a few times, but it must have been enough to…" she started crying again as she tried to finish her sentence, "… mess him up…you know?"

I put my arms around her again and she wept into my chest for a moment. When she had regained her composure a bit she said, "I just never knew how bad it was, you know? I think I could have helped him if I had known how bad it was..."

"What do you mean?" I asked, "What's he doing now?"

"He's gone," she said shaking her head slowly and pressing her lips together. There were still tears hanging in her eyes. "He killed himself the summer after we graduated. His mom heard the gun go off. She totally freaked, I can't even imagine. I didn't find out for like three days, but I understand. How do you call somebody up and tell them that, right?"

"Kat," I shook my head, "I...I don't know what to say."

"You don't have to," she said. "I know I should've explained...I know it wasn't fair to you..."

"Oh my God," I interrupted, "Don't worry about me. I mean, I never would have asked you...no one would expect you to be, you know..."

"Okay," she finished. "I guess I'm not."

3:16 AM Wednesday (Hour 15:20)

I sat on the massive cedar staircase in the main hall of the mansion and lit a cigarette. A few moments before, I had said "Goodnight" to Kat after walking with her from the library. I watched her walk up to her floor as if I was standing guard, and then I sat down on the bottom step. It was dark and quiet, and I stared at one of the motionless cherubs in the clerestory above. I think he was staring back at me; I think he wanted a cigarette. Sugar is one of the components of the Camel Lights blend, and every once in awhile you get one that's just a little bit sweeter than the rest of them. I was

61

savoring one as that little bastard looked down, no doubt he would have rather been on a Van Halen album cover.

"Fuck you," I said to him as I took out my little brown bottle, "you don't get any of this either."

As I inhaled the sour vapors and the blood rushed to my face, I realized that I no longer had any realistic expectation of sleeping that night. Kat's story had been upsetting; I had not been expecting it. I had no idea what she had so recently lived through, and, after the long day of aimless partying, I was not emotionally prepared to hear about it. I wondered how close they had actually been. I tried to imagine what it would have been like to lose a girlfriend that way. Before I could stop it, my mind wandered to what it would be like to lose Kat that way, and I had to shut it down.

I thought a shower might do me good so I stumbled to my feet, took another hit of the Amyl, and headed back to the Vortex.

3:56 AM Wednesday (Hour 16:00)

The architecture of Europe had been fascinating to me over those months. The antiquity of it alone was astounding. The keep at York Castle had stood on the motte for over seven hundred years. There weren't any buildings in Indiana that were 700 years old. The hundred year old manor house in which I had been living would have been considered ancient by American standards. I suppose it should have been no surprise that the plumbing was bad.

The showers for our floor were right down the hall from our room, but we had discovered some months earlier that, for some reason, they were incapable of delivering anything other than magma hot, scalding water. At first I tried, as most of the other men did, to endure this inconvenience in a civilized manner. We filed formal complaints with resident assistants and the school administration while learning to clean the dirtiest parts of our bodies as quickly and with as little Hades water as possible. Taylor, however, was not one to *endure* anything.

Early in the semester he had deduced that the fourth floor showers, which were for use by women only, were directly above the third floor showers, and, since the stairwell was directly outside our door, they were actually no further from our room than the showers on our floor. Also, a preliminary reconnaissance mission had informed us that the women had individual shower stalls within the shower room complete with shower doors, an amenity that men living in communal housing almost never had. What this meant was that it would be fairly easy for us to slip out of the Vortex, up the stairs, into the women's bathroom, and behind the closed door of one of their shower stalls without being seen. Once we heard that the women had hot *and* cold water available, it was only a matter of time. Taylor tried it first and was successful. Upon his return he told wondrous tales of the forgotten pleasures of washing oneself at a leisurely pace, the risk seemed worth the reward, and it was not long before sneaking up to the women's shower was as regular a practice for the three of us as leaving the door open and peeing in the sink had become. The threat of detection was even less at four in the morning, so I felt quite comfortable heading up to the fourth floor for a shower that night.

During daylight hours there was always a bit of an adrenaline rush that accompanied showering on the fourth floor. Not only were we not allowed and in constant fear of being caught, there was also the possibility of a young lady showing up as my shower was in progress and slipping into the stall next me to begin her own. It was a drag any time this happened because I had to wait for her to finish and exit the bathroom in order to remain undetected. However, I would be remiss not to admit that these occurrences were every bit as exhilarating as they were frightening. Despite the fact that I never knew with which of the female students I had just shared the bathroom, I had sneaked back down the stairs on more than one occasion with a bulge under my towel.

But in the predawn hours of this All Saint's Day, such adventures were of no concern to me. I had the bathroom to myself so I was able to take my time and be comfortable. A relaxation that I had not felt in hours came over me with the water falling off of my head, my long hair, and down over my shoulders. It was as if all of the emotions and anxious thoughts were being washed down the drain with the grunge of the day. For the first time in many hours, I wasn't thinking about anything. Nothing at all. As I washed my body, my mind seemed to empty, and, quite in contrast to my initial inclinations, the physical pleasure of being clean suddenly became apparent down below.

Although I am not ashamed to admit that I did succumb to temptation that night, I found it interesting all that flooded my head as I did so. It's amazing how important visual images are to male sexuality, and it's even more amazing how many of them we collect during the course of a day. I closed my eyes and leaned forward against the stone wall, supporting myself with my other hand as they flashed before me, dirty snap shots edited from the context of everyday circumstances. It was no surprise that most of them had come from the Halloween party. The crowded Bistro had been a jumble of legs and cleavage, a red vinyl devil, white lace and smeared mascara on a fallen angel, thick stripes on the knee socks of a wicked witch, and of course Batman and Robin. And, as always, there were surprises, images that I didn't even remember noticing, Audrey's half moon from under my own bed sheets and annoying Sara's flat stomach as she chased away the drunken Messiah. I didn't really want to have sex with any of them; I was just looking at the photographs that my mind had taken.

Yet, on my way back down to my room, I couldn't help but think it strange that I had not allowed myself to enjoy one single image of Kat. In all of my recent waking hours I had only been able to think about one woman, and as the natural urge overcame me in the shower that morning I found it necessary, for some reason, to bar her from my mind.

5:02 AM Wednesday (Hour 17:06)

British Studies was at 8:00 AM; there was no reason to try to sleep before then. I wanted a cup of coffee but the refectory did not open until six. Weary of wandering the uncanny halls of the manor in the quiet hours while everyone was sleeping, I eventually found myself back in the library curious about my "last chance lifetime". It should have been no surprise that I would find myself reading about my astrological compatibility with Sagittarius.

At first, it seemed serendipitous. I learned that Pisces and Sagittarius have a common ruling planet, Jupiter. The two signs share an immediate understanding of each other and often have similar patterns of thinking. The dreamy, sensitive, mystical Pisces can be very appealing to the Sagittarian idealism. Pisces and Sagittarius may both spend a great deal of time looking for the deeper meaning to life, and it is not uncommon for them to build a relationship on this common pursuit.

As I read I began to wonder if there really was any meaning to this star-gazing bullshit. I had never before given it much thought. In the flickering fluorescent light I read on:

Sagittarius is fiery and outgoing and may push the easygoing Pisces. Ever flexible, Pisces can adjust to almost any surroundings, but he needs to be allowed to dream and to do things at his own pace. Sagittarian likes to get things done, to put dreams into practice rather than just dream them. Getting together with a Pisces may not appeal to Sagittarius at first. Pisces wants to settle down, create a family and get on with the job of living a nurturing life. Sagittarius is not ready for that so soon. She wants to travel and pursue success and fame.

The Pisces man is difficult to pin down, he keeps most of his true feelings hidden. He is attracted to anything stress free and without a competitive edge because he hates restriction. On the other hand, he is also attracted to things that stir his emotions, including women. Pisces man is notorious for choosing the wrong woman.

When confronted with complicated issues he tends to retreat into his dream world and may pretend there is nothing wrong when his relationship is on rocky ground. When life is not going so well, he can be very hard on himself and very self destructive so it is better for him to live in denial. The Pisces male needs a firm, strong woman to guide him because he is very indecisive. This need for nurturing is often very attractive to women.

The mystery of the Pisces man makes dating him unlike dating a man of any other astrological sign. There is always the element of the unknown and a slight unreachable quality that keeps a woman's interest. To be invited into the Pisces man's mind is like being invited into a secret realm, where he experiences things and plans ideas that no one on the outside will ever know about, and he will protect his woman and cherish her. He has an amazing ability for love.

I closed the book, and sat there fascinated. So much of it seemed to be true that I immediately suspected my mind had been playing some sort of trick on me. I imagined astrology as the literary version of a Las Vegas stage magician, preying off the naiveté of an audience that desperately *wanted* to be amazed. I know I had always wanted to believe that there was some rhyme or reason to the universe, but, so far, it had seemed that complete chaos was much more likely. Yet, I found myself flattered as I read about the way I was supposed to be, according to the stars. Perhaps I shouldn't have been.

7:50 AM Wednesday (Hour 19:54)

When I first heard that University of Evansville students could go to England for a semester for the same tuition that we were already paying I knew there had to be some sort of *catch*. As it turned out, British Studies was the catch. A six credit hour survey covering everything from 1066 to WWII, it was the one course that was required of every American student at Harlaxton. 8 AM, Monday through Thursday, like roll call at an internment camp. I could almost hear them playing *Revelry* as we all filed into the long gallery and suffered through it together.

This was an unusual morning because I was early. Being there on student visas, none of us were allowed to have jobs, and the result of the excess free time had been overindulgence in local nightlife. Most days, I found myself hung-over and unenthused, and I usually sneaked in the back of the lecture hall just as Dr. Wallace was saying, "Okay, people let's get started," in his thick Scottish accent. In fact, most of my circle of friends, Taylor, Lopez, Elwood, were usually sneaking in late with me. But I had been early that day, a result of my insomniac walkabout. I had just run out of things to do. So I sat there in the empty lecture hall, watching my comrades come in one at the time, and trying to assess whether or not I had cheated an extra day out of life or merely given up a night of sleep.

I had finished my reading assignment on *James I* for that class, but I had a short story due at 1 PM that I had yet to begin writing. Then, of course, there was the play. I was pretty comfortable with my lines at that point, but I really hadn't put anything else into it. The production hadn't touched me on any kind of artistic level yet, I felt like my character was peripheral to the theme of the presentation, and, to be honest, I was just going through the motions for loyalty to Lopez and an excuse to be around Kat.

And at that moment she walked into the long gallery, short hair tousled, baggy pajama pants hiding her delicate hipless frame. I had spent many minutes over the previous few hours trying to digest what she had told me in the library and trying to decide what to say to her at class in the morning, and I was quite surprised when she only nodded slightly as she walked past me and sat down next to her perky friend, Sara. I was momentarily distracted as I saw Lopez and Elwood slip into the room just ahead of Dr. Wallace, who sauntered up to the lectern in his former soccer player's gait, opened his notes, and said, "Okay, people let's get started." I turned back toward Kat, but she never looked back at me so I stared at the back of the head in front of me and decided that I had merely given up a night of sleep.

9:08 AM Wednesday (Hour 21:12)

"Right," Taylor said as he and I, Lopez and Elwood strolled back into the Vortex, "the year is 1610. You're a peasant in a feudal agriculturally driven society so life pretty much fuckin' sucks already." He plopped down in the Big Chair as we all followed him into the room and he continued, "What do you think it would do to your state of mind..I mean how would it affect what you thought about your place in the world to find out that your king was a homo?"

"I'm gonna say that would do it," Elwood said. "Game over. Start the revolution. Give me liberty or give me death."

"Just because the king is gay?" I asked.

"Well, not just because of that," Elwood said. "I gotta tell ya, I really ain't buying in to that whole *serf* thing already. Then I gotta find out that the king, my king, the ordained fuckin' sovereign leader of my people is a God damned peter puffer!"

"They don't even know if he was gay or not?" added Lopez. "It's sheer speculation."

"No thanks anyways," said Elwood. "Not my king. Not now, not never."

"You're an American," I said, "You don't even have a king."

"Just one minute my friend," Elwood retorted, "I'll have you know that I happen to be a red passport carrying citizen of this united kingdom of Britons!"

"No way!" said Lopez. "Seriously?"

"Seriously," he answered. "My mom's from Wales. My parents still have a lake house there."

"Well," said Taylor, who had up until then been only a spectator in the conversation he had started. "There is more to you than meets the eye Elwood."

I put a cigarette up to my lips, lit it and said, "You still don't have a fuckin' king."

Because I fancied myself a writer, one of the things that I did back then was keep a journal full of scribbles and musings, short descriptions of people and things that made an impression on me and other observations that I feared I might forget before inspiration drove me to do something with them. It seemed like a good idea, but it had never really worked. Most of the time I just found myself re-reading it and fantasizing about how brilliant and insightful everyone would think I was someday.

However, on that day, with my 1 o'clock deadline looming, I was scurrying through it furiously trying to find something about which to write. Taylor and Lopez had gone for an early tea and Elwood was the only one left in the room. In desperation, I began to bounce ideas from my journal off of him.

"What about this?" I asked. "A kid loses faith in God when his parents tell him the truth about Santa Claus,"

"Are you serious?" he asked.

"Yeah," I said. "That really happened to *me*!"

Elwood shook his head and laughed. "You know," he said, "For such a big strong guy, you really are a pussy sometimes."

"Fuck you," I said.

"Hey, call 'em like I see 'em."

"Okay," I went on to my next note, "How the modern news media might cover the second coming of Christ?"

"You're gonna get through that in the next three hours?"

"You're right, that's a whole fuckin' book!" I said.

"Maybe a series," Elwood added.

"How about this? A guy feels guilty about cheating on his girlfriend with the girl that he is *actually* falling in love with."

"I don't even get that," he said.

"Nothing?" I said.

"Nope," he shook his head.

"How about a college student who is forced to come to terms with his alcoholic father after dealing with his drunken roommate?"

"Easy, fella!" Elwood objected, "Let's not make this personal!"

We looked at each other and got a good chuckle out of that one. We were still laughing as Taylor and Lopez walked back into the room behind us.

"What are guys doing?" Lopez said as she set her tea on the desk.

"He's trying to think of something to write a short story about," answered Elwood.

"Oh, yummy," she said as her face lit up. "What've you got so far?"

"Nothing," I said, "and it's due at 1 o'clock."

"C'mon," Elwood said, "what's next?"

"Let's see," I looked back at the page in the journal. "A man must overcome the shadow of his great father to compete in the National Lumberjack Olympics?"

"Now we're talking!" said Elwood. I think he was serious.

"Lumberjacks have Olympics?" Lopez asked.

"Yeah!" Elwood said. "Oh man it's fucking great! They do log rolling and spar pole climbing and the hot saws!"

"What's a *hot saw?*" she asked.

"A shining example of the white man's genius," he said. "It's a chainsaw, right. But then they put an expansion chamber off of a dirt bike on it to give it like nine times the horsepower so's they can rip through a three foot log at like Mach Jesus. It's fucking super!"

"That's definite white man shit," Lopez said. "Build big fire; sit way back."

"Guys," I interrupted. "This isn't helping. I'm running out of time, and I'm really starting to worry here!"

"Why?" Taylor asked as he swallowed a sip of his tea. "I've read your stuff, Sammy. You're good. All you need is a prompt, and you'll be fine."

His interjection rendered me silent. I didn't know what to say. I was not only stunned by the compliment but also by the nonchalant way in which it had been delivered. Taylor didn't seem to notice the effect. He just took another sip of his tea and said, "I've got a story for ya."

10:09 AM Wednesday (Hour 22:13)

The enthusiasm of youth can on occasion be more than enough fuel to pull an all-nighter, and skipping sleep the night before had been no bother to me so far. However, as I sat in one of the hard plastic chairs in the less-than-palatial Harlaxton College writing lab, the first signs of physical fatigue surfaced. My lower back was tight, and the muscles in my arms and legs ached as if I had worked out the day before. I wasn't in pain; I was just annoyed. There was no way to get comfortable in that tiny chair, but I vowed not to let that discourage me. The blue glow from the monitor of that sleek, new IBM 486 was all the comfort that I needed. I had a story to write.

There are people who claim that writing is hard work, and most of the time they are correct. Often it takes skill and discipline to string together a coherent narrative logical enough to be understood and entertaining enough to discourage sleep. However, sometimes it is automatic. Sometimes you find your muse. It is as if your wakened mind falls asleep and the collective consciousness just flows out of you, off the top of your head, no effort at all. It doesn't feel like you are creating a new story, but rather remembering one that you had known all along. Despite the discomfort of my fatigue, my eyes were narrow and my fingers danced across the keyboard. My body was an antenna receiving a signal from the ether and transmitting it into English on the glowing blue screen of the 486 in front of me. My deadline was still looming, but there were no worries now.

Back in the room, Taylor had told me about something that happened to him as a child. It was a simple little anecdote, but as he had predicted, it proved to be the prompt that I had needed. Salman Rushdie once said, "Fictions are lies that tell the truth.", and I had always felt like I understood what he meant. Everything that I had ever written was actually true. The plots had been contrived and the names had been changed, but all of the tiny little details remained just as I had seen them. I felt it happening again in the writing lab that day, and, as Taylor's anecdote changed ever so slightly, it became a working story with a tone and a theme and a catharsis that were all mine.

Taking a moment to feel good about myself, I reread the last few lines I had typed, and I really liked them. My chill was not riffed until I saw perky Sara enter the lab and take her place two computers down. She was dressed like a 15 year-old in pajama pants and colorful socks that fit each toe individually like the fingers of a glove, but she looked as cute as she did silly. In spite of myself, I watched her a little too long and her eyes caught mine before I looked away. She smiled and waved at me in the same perky way that I thought she would have smiled and waved at anyone, but I didn't acknowledge her. I didn't mean for that to be as rude as it must have come off; it's just that I was on a roll. The writing gods had smiled upon me and I didn't want to anger them by stopping.

Sara turned the computer on, but she didn't get right to work. In retrospect, I think she was just sitting there simmering, because, after a bit, she turned away from her monitor and said, "You know you're the one with the problem!"

"What?" I said. I was taken aback by her declaration, but not stunned.

"You know, I have tried to be nice to you," she continued, "and I just don't understand what your problem is!""

I squinted my eyes a bit and said, "You're upset with me for some reason?" I was genuinely surprised by the confrontation she had initiated.

She shook her head as if in frustration and said, "No Sam, I'm not upset with you. I just don't understand the animosity."

"What animosity?" I asked. All I had done was ignore her. I honestly never expected my indifference would seem malicious.

"Sam," she said as she half-heartedly threw her hands up. "It's pretty obvious that you hate me." The truth was I hadn't formed a very passionate opinion about her one way or the other. Actually, I knew very little about her. Her last name was Walters and she was from somewhere in Connecticut. I never caught the name of the town, but I heard someone say that her parents lived next door to David Letterman. She had long blonde hair and the body of a dancer or an Olympic gymnast, muscular, shapely legs and striations in her deltoids that were visible whenever she wore a tank top, which was quite often. Her constantly upbeat personality was a little much for me, but I didn't think that I had ever done anything to make her think I hated her.

"What makes you think I hate you?" I asked.

"Forget it," she said.

"No, when did I say that I hated you?"

"You say it," she said.

"When did I say that?"

"Whether you know it or not…"

"When did I say that I hated you?"

"You say it every time that you scoff at one of my comments in class, every time you talk down to me, every time that you ignore me when I say hi." She looked me in the eyes as she spoke, and I remember realizing how rare that was at our age.

"What difference does it make?" I asked.

"Huh?" she said. She threw her hands up a little higher and then crossed her arms.

"Why do you want me to like you so much?" I knew that wasn't what she was saying, but I couldn't resist the jab. After all, she had started it.

"I don't want you to *like me so much*," she said. "I just don't understand why you are always ugly to me. There's nothing wrong with me, you know. I've never done anything to you. I'm a nice person! People like me!" She was near screaming as she finished.

For a second, I thought about what she had just said. She was right. She was positive and upbeat, full of hope and faith, one of those people that genuinely believed they could make the world a better place. In retrospect, any ugliness I had shown her was probably just an ill-conceived shield. I was intimidated by her old-money upbringing, her Barbie Doll good looks, and the fact that everyone seemed to like her. I was aware of how different we were, but I couldn't remember anything else that she had done to deserve my disdain. In fact, at that moment I might have been close to realizing that I *was* out of line, but I had been awake for too long and I had not all my wits about me.

Sara also might have recognized how close I was because she softened her tone before she asked, "Why do you always look at me like you don't like me?"

But then I said, "Well, because I don't like you."

"Oh my God!" she said. Her voice was rising again, "What kind of a thing is that to say to a person?

"What?" I said. "You asked."

"Seriously!" she yelled. I'm fairly certain she was pissed off at that point.

"I'm not trying to hurt your feelings," I said "I'm just answering your question."

"Just answering my question," she mocked. "You are just impossible!"

She wasn't buying it so I decided to tell her what I actually thought. "You know, maybe you shouldn't dig around for the truth until you're sure you can handle hearing it. I've just never really liked you Sara. I find you about as interesting as every other ex-cheerleader, dean's list, clueless little daddy's girl that I've ever met. It's the ignorance that I can't get past. You've been given everything your whole life because you're pretty and your family has money, and you're completely oblivious to the fact that there are people with real problems. You're just in love with yourself and your own good intentions as the real world goes on all around you. Well, not everybody loves you. It's not the end of the world. I'm sure loads of people don't like me. I'm okay with it."

"People don't like you because you're mean," she said.

"I'm not trying to be *mean*, Sara," I said. "You said you wanted to understand it."

"No I didn't, Sam!" she said loudly. Her face was very close to mine and I could feel the heat coming off of her flushed skin. "Is that it? Did you just assume that I'm so dull that I needed it explained to me? I mean, Lord knows you would be the perfect person to do that for me with your superior intellect and all. I should be thanking you for helping me to see the light. But you didn't listen very well smart guy. What I said was that I didn't understand it. I never asked you to explain anything to me!"

I nodded my head and then smiled a bit as I said, "You're a crazy person, aren't you?"

"Of course," she answered. "That explains it. I must be insane because there couldn't be any faults in your personality. God forgive the rest of us for not seeing the world so perfectly. Well here's some news for you, I know I have faults, but I still like who I am just fine! "

"I would expect you to," I said.

"You don't know half of what you think you do," she said. "I can't believe I ever defended you."

"What are you talking about?" I asked as my forehead wrinkled.

"Oh my Gosh, there's something else you didn't know!" she said sarcastically. "You mean you didn't know that Kat came back from the library last night and cried on my shoulder for an hour before she finally got to sleep. What did you say to her?"

"Nothing," I said, and at that moment I couldn't really think of anything that I had said to her.

"Why'd you bring up all of that stuff about Donnie? What is the matter with you?"

I just looked at her. I couldn't really think of anything to say.

"Do you know what she told me last night? She told me that she never wanted to see you again because it's too painful to be around you. You remind her of Donnie and she doesn't want to be reminded of Donnie right now. You put too much pressure on her and she just can't take it anymore."

"I love her," I said. I think I was trying to defend myself.

"And do you know what I told her? I told her that if she didn't care about you then it wouldn't be painful. I told her to give you a chance because I could tell that you really care about her. What was I thinking? You're wandering around like a drunken fool all night, waking us all up, upsetting my friend, and I still had your back..."

My mind was reeling as I digested what she had said, and as it all sank in I began to feel hurt and angry. "Why are you telling me all of this shit?" I asked.

"I don't know?" she said as she began to pack up her books and papers. "I don't even know how this got started."

"I do," I said seizing my chance to turn it back on her. "You started it."

"Whatever," she said. She slung her book bag over her shoulder and started to walk towards the door.

"Yes, I remember it," I said as she continued her exit. "I was sitting here working, minding my own business. You came in, sat down, and, out the blue, started telling me all the ways that I'm an asshole!"

Sara stopped in the frame of the doorway and half-turned around back toward me. "I didn't call you an *asshole*," she said. "I said that you were the one who *had the problem*. You like to look down at everybody else and point out everyone else's flaws, but we're all fine. Yes, we are imperfect, but we're all fine. There's nothing wrong with me. There's nothing wrong with Kat. You're the one who has the problem!"

"Oh, yeah?" I said. Now I was pissed off.

"Yeah," she said.

"What's my problem?" I asked.

I saw her knuckles turn white as she clinched her fists, and as she stormed out of the writing lab she yelled back over her shoulder, "You're problem is you're an *asshole!*"

11:25 AM Wednesday (Hour 23:29)

Despite the lack of sleep and bad vibes from my confrontation with Sara, I arrived back in the Vortex in peculiarly high spirits. When the fatigue had first started to report a few hours before, I figured that I was going to need a nap that afternoon, but I was still on a high from my success in the writing lab. Though disturbing, the confrontation with Sara had been somewhat exhilarating, and I still didn't really feel like sleeping. Of course, in retrospect I realize that it hadn't even been 24 hours yet.

In 1964 a kid named Randy Gardner stayed awake for eleven days as part of some sort of military experiment. That was the longest scientifically documented period of time a human being had intentionally gone without sleep. He did it without any pharmaceutical stimulation and was under medical supervision the entire time, but I was unaware of that at the time of my little experiment. Recently, I read about a study that showed sleep deprivation to have some potential in the treatment of depression. The researchers claimed that about 60% of depression patients, when sleep-deprived, showed immediate recovery, with most relapsing the following night. The physicians recommended treating the incidence of relapse by combining the sleep deprivation with medication. Of course, if medication was the answer, it seemed to me that they could've just skipped the sleep deprivation, but maybe that's why I'm not a physician. In any event, when I look back on the events of those days in

England, I can't help but wonder what I was thinking. Even in retrospect, it is hard to nail down the motivation. I certainly had made no conscious effort to conduct any sort of experiment; I just didn't feel like sleeping.

"You look like hell on a stick," Lopez said to me as she walked into the Vortex and unslung her book bag onto the desk.

"I haven't slept," I said.

"I don't get you people," she said, "I needs me sleep."

"I'm on a mission," I said.

"Whatever," she rolled her eyes, "Listen, we only have one more rehearsal before show time. Are you going to do any practice today?"

"Play practice?"

"No, football," she said sarcastically, "Yes, play practice you silly git!"

"Wasn't planning on it," I said, "I'm golden."

"Whatever!" she said as she smacked me on the shoulder. "You better not let me down on Friday!"

"What are you so worried about?" I said, "I'm sure you're getting' an *A* in that class regardless."

"It's not just about the grade, Sam. This project could be really cool," she said. Then I saw her heart sink a little as she added, "I think I've got something to say here…"

Empathy sneaked in behind her words and I felt compelled to say, "I'm sorry, Lydia, I know it's important to you. Trust me, it'll be fine. Everybody's going to be great."

"I know," she said. "I'm just nervous."

"You've seen Kat in rehearsal," I added. "The biggest part of it is on her anyway."

"Yeah, she's been great, but I'm the director, you know. There's a lot on me too!"

"I know," I said as I realized my *faux pas*. In an effort of damage control I added, "Lydia, you've worked your ass off on this and you've done a good job. It's going to be great."

"Thanks, Sam," she said, "You're the best."

"…there is at what I do, but what I do best isn't very nice."

"What the hell are you talking about?" she asked.

"Nothing. Did I mention that I'm on a mission?" I said, and I saw from her confusion that the distraction was working. She shot me a questioning glance, but I only raised an eyebrow back at her as I produced my little brown bottle of Amyl and took a soft wiff.

"What the fuck is that?" she said. Mission accomplished; all discussion of our upcoming presentation was on hold for now.

"Rush," I answered. "Taylor got it somewhere. Wanna hit?"

11:56 AM Wednesday (Hour 24:00)

"Come on!" Lopez giggled, "We're almost finished!"

"Okay," I agreed. I was laughing too at this point. "Ready?" I asked.

"No, give me another hit," she said and reached for the bottle. Her caricature inhalation made me giggle as her face grew flush and serious. I watched her eyes glaze a little as she buzzed. Then she gave the bottle back to me, took a deep breath, and began. Speaking as fast as possible, she ran the words together as she said the next line, "I-hope-better…"

"Sirrah-Biondello-go-and-entreat-my-wife-to-come-to-me-forthwith…" I added much faster than I thought my memory would allow.

"O-ho-entreat-her-nay-then-she-must-come…"
Lopez rattled back even faster; she was reading.

"I-am-afraid-sir-do-what-you-can-yours-will-not-be-entreated-now-where's-my-wife," I said and, as I slammed my fist onto the desk in emphasis of the last few words, we both burst into laughter. "I'm done," I said as my laughter dribbled away.

"Come on," she prodded. "You're almost there!"

"Nope," I said as I lit a cigarette, "We ran almost the whole play in like a half an hour! I'm done; I got class at one."

She whined some sort of unintelligible response but decided not to fight me. She dropped my copy of the play on the floor next to my bag and rustled out one of her extra-long *Benson and Hedges*. In my memory it seems like all of the artistic, interesting young people during the mid-90s were smokers, and it was common for girls in that group to assert their femininity by smoking 100s. Lopez strove to be the most artistic and feminine of them all, but I did notice that she spent more time burning cigarettes, expertly flicking the ash by kicking the butt with her thumb, than she did smoking them.

"So where did you end up last night?" I asked her as the buzz of running lines subsided.

"Yeah," she answered vaguely, "You never did get to see my costume!"

"Well, you never got to see mine," I retorted.

"No, but I sure heard about it," she chuckled. "Fucking Catholic blasphemy," she teased.

"What?" I teased back. "I thought all you Mexicans were raised Catholic!"

"I was," she answered, "but I'm not a blasphemer."

"Huh," I grunted, "I thought all Catholics were."

"Just you big guy," she said as she crushed out her cigarette, jumped up, and grabbed her book bag. "I gotta get ready for class, Sammy. I'll see you there." With that she was up and out the door, a tiny half-breed squaw full of charisma and hope and vehement contradictions.

1:41 PM Wednesday (Hour 25:45)

I wrote my first short story in the fourth grade. It was a five page crime novel, an imitation of the first book that I could remember reading, a *Hardy Boys* novel that my grandmother had given to me. The entire work consisted of about six paragraphs written on lined notebook paper, illustrated in colored pencil, and stapled together along the left-hand column. I had no thoughts at that time of ever being a writer; I was just a kid doodling, but the thing that always stuck with me was the fuss that everyone had made over it. Even though the story was not part of any assignment, I had finished it up at school, and when my teacher saw it he gave me 10 bonus points for English. When I took it home my mother and father were so impressed that they kept it out on the coffee table in the living room for weeks and showed it to everyone who came over. That might have been the first time in my life that I ever felt like I was capable of doing anything special.

Fueled by the adoration, I kept pumping them out all throughout my school years. As I grew and matured so did the stories. The plots became more complicated and the characters became more detailed, but the only source I had for any realistic conflict was the observations from my actual life. This created a bit of a conundrum for me. My main motivation for writing had always been the accolades of the people who enjoyed my stories, but, as I began to write about emotions and ideas that were relevant to my actual life, I became apprehensive about sharing my work with others. I had always tried to camouflage the sensitive information, but I could never really tell how much I was exposing myself.

I was dealing with these same mixed emotions when I went to the podium to share my hastily done short story in writing workshop that day. I never questioned whether I could have done a better job on it, and it never crossed my mind that I maybe should have started more than a few hours before it was due. As I began to read, I was just curious about what people would think of it, what Kat would think of it…

One time, back when I was only four years old, I got up in the middle of the night because me and Ralph had to go pee. Well, looking back, the real tragedy is the fact that Ralph didn't really have to go pee at all. Ralph was a stuffed monkey.

Actually, as I found out much later in life, Ralph's name really wasn't Ralph at all. His real name was Curious George, you know – the monkey in the books who gets in all the trouble. My mom gave me a whole bunch of those books that used to be hers when I was born. I loved those books. Even before I could read I would just flip through the pages and look at all the things that crazy monkey did. Come to think of it, I should have figured out Ralph's true identity a long time before I did. But I didn't; I called him Ralph.

Anyway, me and Ralph (Curious George) both went to pee that night because I never went anywhere by myself after dark. Of course now I can walk all over the house myself at night, but when I was little, I always wanted Ralph to go with me.

I had to wedge Ralph into my armpit when I got there to pee because I needed both hands to hold my pajamas down and pull my thingy out. So I did, and I started to go. It felt good because I had to go real bad, and I started to hum and pretend like I was shooting bad guys, because I often started to hum and pretend like I was shooting bad guys when I peed at night after the initial stress of traveling all the way from my room to the toilet had passed.

So there I was in the dark humming and shooting bad guys when all of a sudden I felt Ralph slip away from the grasp of my armpit and plop into the toilet. My heart raced as I finished peeing – I had to – you can't really stop once you've started. Then I pulled my pajamas up and struggled to reach the light switch. Out of sheer determination I switched the light on and stood dumbfounded at the sight of Ralph, my beloved stuffed monkey, laying all contorted at the bottom of the toilet like a guy who fell off a really tall building in a TV show.

I reached down into the dirty water and pulled Ralph out by one of his huge ears. I had to save him before I flushed the toilet. So I pulled him out and flushed and was going to go back to bed when I discovered Ralph was all squishy and soggy wet. I didn't want Ralph to have to go to bed wet so I let him stay in the bath tub the rest of the night, and I went back to my room by myself to sleep (that was the first time I walked down the hall after dark by myself!).

I went to bed, hoping that Ralph would be okay by himself all night.

The next morning, when I went to get him, he was all dry and looked the same as ever, but when I picked him up I found out that he was kinda stiff and crusty and he smelled really bad, kinda like Jake's doghouse. It was at this point I first realized something was horribly wrong.

I decided to take the problem to Mom as quickly as possible (of course I was four so I took all my problems to Mom as quickly as possible). I found her in the laundry room sorting clothes and told her all about the adventures and misfortunes that had occurred the night before. I knew that if anybody could save Ralph, Mom could.

Mom told me that no one could save Ralph. What she knew and I didn't find out until I was much older was that

Ralph was just as old as all those books that Mom gave me. In fact, he too used to be hers when she was little. If he were still alive he would be even older than me.

And Mom said back when Santa Claus and other toy companies made stuffed monkeys like Ralph they put sawdust in them instead of whatever they put in them now. I didn't really know what that meant, but Mom said that Ralph would never come clean right because the dirty toilet water had soaked into the sawdust.

I began to panic as I first realized the implications of this. I didn't want Ralph to have to live the rest of his life all crusty and smelling like pee. Surely there should've been something we could do, I thought! I pleaded with Mom to do something to save Ralph until she agreed to try and wash him in the washer machine.

I waited for what seemed like my whole lifetime for that washer machine to finish washing Ralph. It made me mad too, because every time it would finish one part of the washing I thought it was done, and then it would start right back up with another part of the washing.

And the washer did help Ralph. It made him all soft and cuddly just like he was before he fell into the toilet, but mom said he had to go away anyway because he still smelled too bad for me to play with. I didn't really care. I would have played with him anyway. I just didn't want him to have to leave.

Mom made Dad burn Ralph in the fireplace not long after that. They didn't think that I knew because they did it late at night when I should have been asleep, but I did.

I got up to go pee (I did that by myself all the time now), and I heard the fireplace crackling like when you wad up a Fruit Roll-up wrapper. So I went into the living room to see what was going on, and I saw Ralph burning. His little monkey head had the same big smile on it that he had had all *his life. Mom put another piece of wood on the fire, but she looked real sad. She didn't want to have to do what she was doing. I thought maybe Ralph had even helped her find her way to the bathroom when she was little and that was why she was sad.*

I was sad a little, but not sad for myself. I was only sad that Ralph wasn't going to be with any more kids after me like he had before. I really wish I didn't pee on him.

As I finished reading, I gathered my papers, looked around the room, and was intoxicated. There had been laughter while I was reading, but there was none now. There were a few smiles and a few sad faces, but what really told me that it had worked was that the whole class was engaged. I didn't see one person gazing out the window or scribbling on their own story. I stood there for a moment, basking in it, all attention still on me as if everyone was waiting to see if I was going to continue. I searched my audience until I found Kat's smiling face. I smiled back at her before I left the podium, and the high followed me back to my seat, where I concentrated to restrain my jubilation as the class began to discuss my story.

3:25 PM Wednesday (Hour 27:29)

On a dreary Midland day, as classes were coming to a close, the pull of the Vortex was almost irresistible, and there was quite a crowd in Room 333 when I returned from writing workshop that day. Elwood had just got out of bed and he was at the sink preparing for his afternoon stroll down to the pub. Jerry, a neighbor from down the hall was strumming his guitar, while his stoner roommate, Ben, clapped and swayed along. Lopez was sitting on the window sill smoking a long, feminine cigarette, and sitting in the Big Chair was Taylor, presiding over it all.

"How'd it go?" asked Taylor as I walked through the open door into the room.

"It went well," I said as I surveyed the afternoon guests. Jerry and Ben hadn't stopped by in a while, and it usually turned into a pretty good party when they did.

Jerry was a good ol' boy from Salem, Indiana who always seemed to have a grin on his face and a guitar in his hand. He was, like me, a bigger fella, but his thick glasses and flowing mullet kept him from being intimidating. He was a very talented singer and songwriter, but he was too laid back to ever want to be a star. It takes a certain desperate insecurity to draw that kind of attention to oneself, and I just don't think Jerry cared that much what anyone else thought. When I saw him walk into my writing workshop class months ago with his Harley-Davidson tee shirt and his out-dated hair style, my first impression had been less than favorable. He looked like a hundred other 4-wheel-drivin', AC/DC crankin' rednecks from my hometown. I certainly didn't expect him to be as interesting as he was. As I got to know him better, he impressed me with his confidence and his straight forward curiosity.

Coincidentally, a tangent of the conversation that very day had led us to an interesting discourse about first impressions. I think we had been talking about song lyrics when I wandered off about how stereotypes existed because, for the most part, they were accurate.

"Man, stereotypes aren't always true," Jerry had said.

"No, but they're true enough to be useful. Otherwise, we wouldn't use them," I retorted.

"I don't go by them," he said.

"Yeah you do," I said. "We all do. Look, take Ben for example," I said as I nodded toward his stringy-haired, tie-dyed roommate. "When you first met Ben, how long did it take you to make the assumption that he might be the kind of fellow that enjoys smoking a bit of cannabis every now and again?"

"Not long, man" Jerry laughed.

"That's my point," I said. "Ben fits a certain stereotype, long hair, puka shells, *Grateful Dead* apparel…"

"But not all pot smokers look like that," Jerry interrupted.

"You're right," I conceded, "but enough of them look like Ben that you made an assumption before you ever knew anything about him."

"Hell, I guess I did," Jerry said.

"That's fucked up, man," Ben said as he shook his head in disgust.

"That's prejudice," I added "You pre-judged Ben, man."

"Yeah, but he was right," Ben piped up. "I do love the ganja!"

"That's what I'm saying," I said. "There are five and a half billion people on the planet; we don't have time to get to know them all. So why do we consider prejudice to be morally wrong when most of the time it's just a matter of efficiency?"

"That's fucking interesting, man," Jerry said as he idly fingered his guitar strings. As always, I had put a great deal of thought into my argument long before I ever chose to speak, so I was not surprised when Jerry began to see things my way. However, I was surprised when he then said, "So what was your first impression of me, man?"

When sharing my opinion about stereotypes, I was always careful to point out that there were exceptions to the rule, and that of course, was the inherit problem with prejudice. Yet, I couldn't remember ever being personally challenged with such an obvious example of this, and I hadn't put any thought at all into how to answer his question. Realizing that my decision had to be made quickly, I gave into the ebb of my fatigue and the flow of the hash buzz and decided to go with the truth.

"I thought you were going to be a bit of a tool," I said.

"What?" he said. "Why do you say that?"

I was relieved to see him smiling so I smiled too. "Man, I don't I know? The mullet, the tee shirts, you just looked like a lot of people I used to know."

"It's not my fault you used to hang out with tools, buddy" he said.

"That's true," I said. "Besides, I was wrong anyway. You're one of the coolest dudes here."

"Yeah, right," he said. Then he turned to Ben and said, "Did you hear what Sam said about me? He thought I was a tool!"

"That's fucked up, man," Ben said as he shook his head in disgust.

"I never thought you were a tool," I said, "that was just my first impression."

"So *at first* you thought I was a tool?" Jerry asked.

"Yeah," I said. "I mean no...I mean...yeah, I guess so."

"Man, you're a real asshole," Jerry said facetiously as he passed me the pipe.

"Yeah, I guess so," I said as I took a hit and passed it on to Ben.

"Did you hear what this asshole is doing?" Ben said and pointed at me as he took the pipe.

"No, what's he doing?" Jerry said as he went back to his idle strumming.

"He's going to try to stay awake forever, man," Ben said. "Isn't that fucked up?"

"Seriously?" Jerry asked.

"Not really," I said

"No, it's true," Lopez said from her perch on the window sill. "He hasn't slept in like two days."

"It hasn't been two days," I said.

"Well, how long has it been?" Jerry asked.

"Well, I don't know exactly," I said, "just last night really."

"So why aren't you sleeping?" Ben asked.

"I don't know," I said.

"That's nothing, man," Jerry said, "My brother cranked for like fourteen days once."

"You need to get some sleep before the play," Lopez said.

"How long could you make it?" Jerry asked.

"I don't know," I said.

"Well, how long has it been? We'll start keeping track," he said.

And so it came to pass that my lack of sleep became a matter of documentation. To the best of my memory, I had been awake since a little after noon on Tuesday, so we decided to call it *12:04* when we set my wrist watch to tally the forthcoming hours. Twenty-nine and counting, the race was on.

5:31 PM Wednesday (Hour 29:35)

There were hundreds of places in London to get fish and chips, crunchy breaded cod all soggy with salt and malt vinegar, wrapped in newspaper and then devoured. Bangers and mash was also quite good, and the influx of immigrants in the city had made it easy to find a variety of curries from India and Bangladesh and delicious Chinese and Thai stir-fries. It wasn't even that hard to find a *McDonald's*, but fifteen minutes outside Grantham in the tiny village of Harlaxton the dull horror of traditional British cuisine could seldom be avoided.

When asked why British food was so bad, the renowned British person, John Cleese, once said, "We had an empire to run!" England's Puritan and utilitarian heritage had spawned a menu vastly devoid of bold flavors like garlic, tomato, and other complex sauces which were commonly associated with those filthy Catholics from the mainland. English meals have ancient origins, and are likely to consist of simpler ingredients like bread and meat. Dinner in the quaint English countryside wasn't exciting, but it was hot and brown and there was plenty of it.

I could not adequately identify the particular dish being served in the refectory that night as I waited in line, inching my plastic tray down the stainless steel bars. It appeared to be some combination of bread and chopped meat, baked together in a steaming black pie, similar to American meatloaf but darker in color and thicker in texture. However unappealing it may have appeared, it didn't last long. I must have been burning more calories than usual due to my lack of sleep because the disgusting mass, along with the accompanying sprouts and rock-hard scones, disappeared from my plate quickly.

I had sat to eat with the theater majors for two reasons. Obviously, I was hoping that Kat might walk up and set a tray down beside me, but that didn't happen. The other reason was a conscious effort to avoid the English majors. Too many English majors want to be writers. Even if they plan on teaching literature or grammar or going into journalism or editing, they all really want to be writers, and writers are thinkers. And thinkers are talkers, and I had no energy for conversation at that moment. I just wanted to eat my hot, brown *whatever* and get on with the night. Theater majors have nothing to say. They have no personalities of their own. They are much more comfortable mimicking the personality traits of others.

Of course, conversation could not be entirely avoided, but, for the most part, the chatter at the table had been uninteresting and I was able to go through the motions without really paying attention to any of it. However, my interest was aroused when I heard Ian, one of the few students at Harlaxton that *was* from England, discussing his evening plans and making mention of a pub in Grantham called The Blue Pig.

7:24 PM Wednesday (Hour 31:28)

About fifteen minutes away, Grantham was much larger than the village where the college was located, but that did not change the fact that all of the pubs closed down at eleven. Time was of the essence.

"Taxi's on the way," I said to Taylor as I entered the Vortex. The only telephone to which we had access was two flights down, and I had just jogged all the way back up to the room.

"Sweet," he said. "What's the count?"

"Thirty-one and a half," I said after looking at my watch.

"How you feeling?" he said.

"Good, bro," I said.

"You still hittin' that amyl?" he asked.

"I haven't had any since Lopez was here this afternoon," I said. "I was hitting it pretty hard last night, but once the sun came up I got my second wind."

"Cool, man," he said. "Just take it is easy on that stuff."

"Why, is it dangerous?" I asked.

"It can't be good for you," he said. Then he held out his hand and said, "Give us a hit real quick." I handed him the bottle, and he opened it and inhaled the invisible fumes. He held his breath while the rush washed over him, and then he gave it back to me and said, "So who's going to be there?"

"You know Ian? He's a theater major. He's from here, Liverpool I think," I said.

"Yeah, I think," Taylor said, "Kinda pretty?"

"You could say,"

"Who else?"

"His roommate, Michael, Jerry, Ben, maybe Lopez, maybe Paul, and Elwood's probably been there since like four," I said as I zipped up my trusty Gortex hiking jacket.

Taylor slid into a fashionable black leather coat and said, "Let's do it."

Graham, the taxi driver, was already waiting when we burst out of the service door onto the circle drive in front of the old manor house, but we were regular customers and good tippers and he smiled when he saw that it was us. "Where to this evening, gents?" he said as we climbed into the back seat.

"The Blue Pig, sir," Taylor said.

"Right," Graham said. "Off we go."

It was much easier to get around in England without a car than it would have been in the States, but I still missed that American sense of freedom in being able to travel medium-to-long range distances at one's own leisure, no fares, no schedules, the independence of having my own wheels. In England, it seemed like I was always waiting on a taxi or a train or the tube. Yet, the public transit system there was really quite efficient, and in a matter of minutes Graham was saying, "You lads stay out of trouble now," as he pulled away from the curb and disappeared around the corner between the old buildings on the narrow street.

The Blue Pig was a classic English pub in the center of the oldest part of Grantham. The ancient two-story building was a character itself. Exposed stone on the first floor with a half-timbered cottage above that, the old inn had neither a straight wall nor a level surface to be found. Marked only by the bright blue, sow-shaped wooden sign that hung above the sidewalk, the old pub creaked its welcome as we pushed open the heavy oaken door and ducked through the crooked door frame. It had been dark outside, but it was somehow even darker inside the pub. My feet slowed as my eyes adjusted and scanned the room for a familiar face. In the last few months I had enjoyed a handful of good nights there, but I knew that, in contrast to the Gregory Arms, The Blue Pig did not *always* welcome American students from Harlaxton College and it would be in our best interest to locate some friendlies as soon as possible.

After a few more steps, I recognized Michael, Ian's roommate, sitting at the bar with Ben the stoner, and I adjusted my path in their direction.

"What up Sam? What up T?" Ben said as he stood up to greet us. When meeting Ben out, it was obligatory to slap hands in at least one of a variety of different combinations of finger snapping and high-five-type gestures. I had always felt ridiculous doing that kind of shit, but it was a matter of etiquette so I did not hesitate to comply before taking my place at the bar. Taylor completed the ritual after me and sat down as well.

"You guys know Michael, right?" Ben said as he sat back down with us.

"Yep," I said. "What's goin' on?"

"Yeah, what's up?" Taylor said.

"Cheers," Michael said.

"Yo, Michael, this is that dude I was telling you about, man!" Ben said as he half-hugged me and slapped my back. "He's gonna try and stay awake for as long as he can."

"Not really," I said. "I just didn't sleep last night, and these assholes are trying to make some sort of game out of it."

"Brilliant," Michael said.

"What you having, mates?" the bartender said as she walked up to us. Her name was Susie; I recognized her from my last trip to the Pig. We were in good hands.

"Pint of the black stuff," Taylor said as if he were speaking his native language.

"McEwen's," I said, "one pint of, please." I was trying, but I failed to sound as cool as Taylor.

"So where is everyone?" Taylor said as he turned back toward Michael.

"You just missed your mate, Dan," Michael said. "He left here with a lady not five minutes ago!"

"How do you like that?" I said to Taylor.

"Didn't know Elwood had it in him, did you?" Taylor said.

"Ian and Jerry are playing a snooker match with a couple of blokes in the back room there," Michael said as he motioned in that direction. "Waste of a good buzz, snooker," Michael said as he raised his glass, "if you ask me."

"And here we are, gentlemen," Susie the bartender said as she set down our beers. For the first time, I noticed that she was very cute.

"Thank you," Taylor said as he smiled into her eyes. "We plan on keeping you busy tonight."

9:31 PM Wednesday (Hour 33:35)

Ian and Jerry had returned from the snooker table, and our group now occupied an entire end of the bar. Susie the bartender had indeed been busy, and the conversation had gradually gotten louder and less conservative. There had been no sign of bad vibes until Ian and Jerry started talking about royalty.

"So what do you still have a Queen for anyway?" Jerry had said. I really don't think he meant to be offensive; by nature he was curious in a fearless and childlike sort of way.

And I don't think Ian was offended really. He chuckled a little, paused a moment, and then said, "I guess it's just something about people. It's like the culture needs someone to look up to, and the Royals have kind of always been there so why do away with a good thing, right. We all need some kind of royalty."

"We don't need any royalty," Jerry said.

"Yeah, of course you do," Ian said. "What about Elvis Presley?"

"Taylor did hang a picture of him up in our room," I admitted.

"Elvis wasn't a real king though," Ben said. "He was just a singer."

"He wasn't *just a singer*," Taylor said.

"That's right," said Ian, "He became an icon representing American culture."

"What about the American culture did Elvis represent?" Jerry said.

"More than anything else, economic and social mobility probably," Ian said. "That really is one of the greatest things about your country. A bloke can start out dirt poor and become a millionaire if he plays his cards right."

"If he gets dealt the right cards," I said.

"No, I'll buy that," Taylor said. "especially in the 50s."

"So that's the Queen's job," Ian said to Jerry.

"What do you mean?" Jerry asked.

"Well, what Elvis did, sort of by accident, the Queen does as her duty," Ian said.

"Right," Michael added, "It's her duty to remind us of the very best of England."

"Right, I get it," said Taylor.

"That's fucked up, man," said Ben.

"We still don't have any royalty, buddy" Jerry said. "Elvis is dead."

"Well, if it's not Elvis it's someone else," Michael said.

"Right," added Ian, "It's Madonna or Michael Jordan or whoever else."

"Jerry Garcia for Ben, probably" Michael said as he nodded toward our tie-dyed comrade.

"Damn right," Ben said.

"So you're saying that celebrities are our royalty?" Jerry said.

"Of course they are," Ian said. "You practically worship them."

"...and you don't?" Jerry asked sarcastically. "Lennon's as much of an icon as Elvis."

"Maybe, but we don't call him *The King*. We already have a queen," Ian said. "We don't need to make kings out of the Beatles."

"You made knights out of them didn't you?" I said.

"No," Ian said.

"Yeah you did," I said, "back in the 60s. I remember reading about it."

"Knights used to be heroes," Ben said. "That's fucked up, man."

"Entertainers are our heroes now, Ben," Taylor said.

"Actually," Michael said, "They were only made *members,* not knights. There *was* quite a lot of controversy made of it though."

"Members?" I said.

"Right," Michael said, "Members of the Order of the British Empire."

"Well that's still some level of royalty isn't it?" I said.

"Not really," Michael said "I can't imagine they'd ever actually make knights out of the Beatles."

"They will," said Taylor.

"I doubt it," said Michael.

"To be quite honest," said Ian, "I could see it."

"Fucking Illuminati," said Ben.

10:03 PM Wednesday (Hour 34:07)

Fueled by the drinking, the conversation continued, and, in all fairness, our tendency toward growing louder and less conservative may have been approaching the level of nuisance. Up until that point, the mood had been light and jovial, but I first recognized potential danger when I noticed a group of townies, also growing more raucous, at the other end of the bar. I know there was no good reason to suspect trouble, but my fear was not paranoia. Two unaffiliated groups of young men ought to be able to enjoy the same pub without an escalating cold war of snide remarks and uneasy stares, but, alas, man is not that far removed from his reptile brain. I understood this, and I could hear the echoes of our warring, tribal ancestors growing in the murmurs that began to pass from one end of the bar to the other.

I noticed two of them in particular. A slim, toe-headed fellow in a black leather jacket seemed to be unusually interested in us. He was establishing a pattern of looking in our direction, leaning over to talk into his friend's ear, and then snickering wildly. His big, brown-bearded friend caught my eye because of his size. Years of lifting weights for football had made it so that I was usually the biggest guy in the room, but there's always somebody bigger. This fellow looked like he was part grizzly bear and my initial evaluation was that we should, if at all possible, try to avoid a physical confrontation.

However, my hopes of this began to wane as the night evolved. An audible increase in snickering washed through their group as tie-dyed Ben staggered by them on his way to the water closet, but I was not able to confirm that we were the focus of their fun until I saw Toehead nod our way, lean over to Brownbeard, and say, "Another lot in from the colonies." I remember wondering how it was going to play out. It was like I was outside of myself, watching the situation unfold, as if it were happening to someone else. I think I knew that there was going to be trouble before anyone else in either group, but I did nothing to stop it, nothing to avoid or diffuse it. I was just overwhelmed with curiosity; I had to know what was going to happen next.

"How you Yanks enjoying our hospitality?" Toehead finally said loud enough that it would not be ignored. I nodded to myself as I watched it happen. Those pointless, barroom altercations always started with a similar gambit, an open-ended question delivered with just enough zest to let everyone know that it was a bit left-handed. The feigned purpose is to solicit a simple response, but the overall goal is to establish territorial dominance.

"Immensely," Taylor said as he raised his glass in the direction of the local boys.

"Brilliant," the Toehead said sarcastically.

"Aye," Brownbeard said.

"Enjoying themselves *immensely!*" Toehead quoted Taylor.

"Aye," his friend said.

Taylor's diplomacy had been stellar, not aggressive but too cute to be mistaken as acceptance of the other party's dominance. The tactic conveyed little desire for confrontation but also showed no inclination towards surrender, and the aggressors were left almost completely stifled. Their only options were to either end the campaign or repeat the initial gambit in hopes of provoking a different response. Obviously having chosen the latter, Toehead turned back to us and said, "From where in the colonies are you, mate?"

Jerry, who had been drinking imported Budweisers since before we arrived, took the bait. "I'm from Salem, Indiana, and it ain't no goddamn colony," he said.

"Not a colony?" said the Toehead in feigned surprise. His tribe giggled in response.

"Naw," Jerry said, "We kicked your ass in a war remember?"

"They don't teach history at Hartlaxton?" Toehead said. "How many battles did the yanks win in that war? They hardly kicked anyone's arse. If it weren't for a few strokes of luck you would all *still be* colonies today."

"Actually, Indiana never was a colony," I said. I could never resist correcting factual details.

"Cheeky Yanks," Brownbeard said. There were four of us involved now.

"We're not all yanks over here," Michael said. Now that was five.

"Apologies, mate," Brownbeard said. "Cheeky Yanks *and* dirty Scousers."

I had never before heard that word, *Scouser*, but I would say that Michael had. Furthermore, he didn't take too kindly to it, at least, not the way that it had been delivered. He set his pint down on the bar, and stood up slowly and with purpose. Realizing that I would need to be mobile very shortly, I dropped enough money on the bar to cover my tab as I watched Michael walk toward the yokels. I couldn't make it out, but he said something to Brownbeard as he approached. I remembering glancing at Taylor, trying to telepathically tell him to get ready to move, but when I jumped off of my stool I saw that it had already started. Brownbeard shoved Michael in the chest with his broad, open hands, and I saw Michael grab the big fella by one wrist and use his own momentum to pull them both to the ground.

"Shit, here we go," I said as I started moving toward the fight. Obscuring my line of sight, Toehead jumped on the two of them, and I glanced behind me quickly and noticed that Jerry was the only one of my party moving toward the pile with me. When we got there I saw that Michael was already cut and bleeding above one eye, but he still had a hold of the big man's wrist. He had wrapped his legs around Brownbeard's arm and the larger man was grimacing in pain. Toehead and another townie were stumbling around the two of them, trying to grab and punch at Michael.

From behind, I wrapped my arm around the neck of the guy that was closest to me, and pulled him off of the pile. However, he spun around much quicker than I expected and let a wild punch fly that was aimed directly between my legs. I felt him miss, but the proximity had startled me, automatically kicking up the intensity of my aggression. I grabbed the back of his head and squeezed his neck between my left hand and right forearm. At the same time I pulled him forward and allowed my body weight to push him down flat on his belly. I held him that way until he quit struggling, and then I got back to my feet in time to see that it was all pretty much over. Jerry was helping Michael up, and most of the formerly unruly group of locals had dispersed. Brownbeard was on his feet, but he was still holding his arm and trying to catch his breath. Toehead was out cold on the floor, and the fella that I had grabbed was beginning to regain consciousness on the ground by my feet.

"Come on, they've called the police for sure!" Ian said as he pulled on the sleeve of my rain jacket. I followed him out of the front door of the pub. Michael and Jerry were right behind me. Many of the patrons had already gone outside, and there was quite a congregation in the street lit cobblestone drive. Wondering where we had lost Taylor and Ben, I headed into the crowd at first, but I immediately began to feel like that was a bad idea. People stepped away quickly whenever I got close to them, and they looked at me with wide eyes like I was the monster in some horror film, like the madness was contagious.

When I turned back around, I realized that I had lost track of Ian and Michael and Jerry. I thought I saw them disappear into the darkness down one of the narrow streets, but before I could follow them I saw the guy that I had choked exit the pub and point in my direction. There were two others with him that I didn't recognize. I saw Toehead and Brownbeard walking away meekly behind them, but this second wave seemed rejuvenated with bad intentions. I was trying to decide whether to stand my ground or evac in the direction I had last seen my friends when I heard a voice behind me say, "What the fuck've you got into tonight, Sammy?"

A thick mist hung above the tops of the old Grantham buildings, and the reflections from the street lights made it feel like a ceiling above the road. Even at night, it was brighter in the street than it had been in the bar. I stood sweaty, eyes widened. The adrenaline was still pumping and my heart rate and breathing were still slightly elevated. My half-drunk, fatigued mind was trying to formulate an efficient defensive strategy, when I saw Paul Patmore step in front of me and address the three men coming my way.

"Cheers, Tommy," he said to the guy that I had wrestled with in the pub. "What's the SP here, mate?"

"Why don't you ask him?" the guy said and motioned at me. "He's the one what sucker punched me inside." He still seemed quite upset, but he and his friends did stop walking when they reached the place where Paul was standing.

"Right, okay," Paul said. He took out a cigarette and lit it. Using body language to communicate that he was now the presiding mediator in this matter, he turned his body perpendicular between us and said, "Sammy?" But before I could say anything, he stole my opportunity to answer and said, "I'm sorry, Sammy this is me mate, Tommy. We went to primary school together." Then he turned back to the other guy and said, "Tommy, this is me mate, Sammy. He's up at the college, not a bad fellow for a yank." Paul winked at us when he said *Yank*.

"He's a fat cunt, what he is," said Tommy. I wanted to choke him again.

"Yeah, he's a bit of a palooka, but he's not a bad guy," Paul said. Then he turned to me and said, "So what'd you sucker punch me old schoolmate for?" Then, once again stealing my opportunity to reply, he turned back to Tommy and said, "This ain't over some bird is it?"

"I wish," Tommy said, fighting back a smile. "All blokes in this place tonight, mate."

Paul executed a very genuine sounding laugh and then said, "Sounds like that may have been the problem, eh?"

Tommy smiled, almost laughed, then pointed back at me and said, "No, this fucker here is the problem." I really wanted to choke him again.

"He's not your problem," Paul said. "Your problem is you're fucking pissed." Then he turned to me and said, "and so are you, and by that I mean you're bloody drunk. You likely don't even know about what you're fighting, do you?"

"He was kicking my friend in the head," I said.

"Your friend started the whole fight," Tommy said.

"Who's that, Taylor?" Paul said.

"No," I said, laughing at the idea of Taylor starting a fight. "He's talking about Michael, Ian's roommate."

"From Liverpool?" Paul said.

"Yeah, I think so," I said.

"Well, there's another piece of the puzzle," Paul said, winking at his friend, Tommy. "Look, you two don't want to waste the rest of the night rolling around out here on the stone like a couple of poofs. Besides, you both seem to have a rather larger problem anyway."

I cocked my head at Paul, and Tommy said, "Yeah, what's that?"

"You've both left your pints somewhere," Paul said. Then he checked his watch and said, "and you've only got about ten minutes to get another one."

I saw the tense muscles in Tommy's neck relax as he looked down and shook his head smiling. Paul pursed his lips in a strange way, raised his eyebrows comically high, and tilted his head toward the pub. I couldn't help but laugh. I no longer wanted to choke anybody. He was a fucking genius.

"Come on, man," I said to Tommy. "I'll buy you one."

"Alright, mate," Tommy said. "I'll let you."

Tommy and his two buddies waited for me to go first, and then we walked back towards the crooked door of the Blue Pig. Paul Patmore, legendary dilettante of social diplomacy between the locals and the Americas, followed the four of us like the good shepherd that he was. As we entered the dark pub I heard him say, "Why is it that no one ever offers to buy me a drink?"

Thursday

As it turned out, Tommy was a pretty decent fellow. After making last call at the Blue Pig, he and Paul and I left on foot, wandering through the deserted streets of Grantham until we reached his parents' house. The house was a small but very nice two-story stone cottage situated snugly among a row of other small but very nice stone cottages. Very different from the suburban neighborhood in which I had grown up, the street had a large sidewalk, and the houses were very close together with tiny, manicured lawns. Tommy's house was one of the most manicured. The path to the front door was a winding brick walk lined with trimmed hedges and marigolds and phlox, but we walked around to the back where Tommy jumped the wooden fence and unlocked the gate from the inside.

Paul and I sat down among the potted ferns and rubber plants at a round, glass table on the back patio as Tommy sneaked through the French doors on his way to retrieve three more pilsners. Paul took out two cigarettes, offered one to me, and then lit it as I leaned over above his tarnished brass Zippo. Sitting back in his chair, he lit his own cigarette and then said, "So where did all your mates get off to?"

I made a sort of Robert De Niro face and shook my head slowly. "They're probably all in bed by now," I said.

"No rest for the wicked, eh Sammy," Paul said.

"I never thought of myself as wicked," I said and we both looked up as a light came on inside the house. There were some muffled voices and then the light went off, and Tommy slipped back out the door carrying three bottles in his arms.

"Woke up me mum," he said as he passed out the beers and sat down at the table with us. "She don't like it when I'm out this late. Afraid I'll get in trouble."

"You did get in trouble," Paul said as he twisted off his cap.

Tommy smiled and pointed at me. "The Yanks started it!" he said.

"I thought you said it was the bloke from Liverpool," said Paul.

"Yeah, right," Tommy said. "It was. He actually called us *wollybacks*. Haven't heard that one in a while."

"Silly Scouser," Paul said.

"Man, I have no idea what either one of you are talking about," I said.

"*Scouser* is a name for a person from Liverpool," Paul said, "and *wollyback* is what a Scouser calls someone who isn't."

"Scouser, huh," I said. "Where's that come from?"

"From speaking fucking Scouse," Tommy said.

"It's an accent, a dialect, like a regional thing," Paul said. "It's like English mixed with Irish and Scottish. Sort of like the Beatles."

"So, *Scouser*, is that like, pejorative and shit?" I asked.

"Not necessarily," Paul said.

Tommy laughed and said, "It's like being a Yankee!"

"Can be," Paul said as he nodded his head.

"No, it is!" Tommy said, and the three of us laughed at the expense of the people of Liverpool, none of whom had ever done anything malicious to me.

There was no answer when I called for a taxi. I suppose they were closed too at that point. Left with no alternative, I bid my hosts farewell and departed on foot. The first bit of the trek was exhilarating, trying to navigate the small, deserted city, looking for the bus stop or the train station, moving from landmark to landmark until I found A607, the two-lane highway that led back to the village of Harlaxton. However, the going got tough as the lights of Grantham slowly faded behind me. Each farmhouse looked the same as the last, and I passed the same trees and the same hedgerows over and over. I even lost interest in the lovely dry stone fences, and I was still about two miles away from the manor when I began to think.

Much like insects, we live our lives in stages. The only difference is that our stages aren't as clearly defined, and the most ambiguous of them all is adolescence. The physical part is simple, secondary sex traits and wet dreams, but that is just puberty. There is a reason we have the two separate words. Adolescence encompasses the period of psychological change that takes place as we develop from juvenile to adult, that murky gray limbo of eggshell stepping, learning the behaviors and expectations that we should have of ourselves when we become grownups, and for some it takes longer than for others.

In our culture, Western culture, American culture, it seems to take the longest. Holding on to sovereignty as long as possible, the older generations mete out responsibility in conservative rations. We are granted the freedom to risk our lives behind the wheel at 16 and to share the responsibility of electing our leaders at 18, but alcohol consumption, by inference the most dangerous and sacred of adult activities, is not allowed until age 21. The entire process is devoid of logic, and it is a wonder that any of us has the patience to endure it, questioning authority and rebelling against convention. No doubt it would be more pleasant to sleep though it in a cocoon.

Perhaps that is why teenagers and young adults are such creatures of the night. After eleven, the world is ours. The grownups need to sleep. They are tired, worn down by their jobs and their kids and their nagging spouses. Youth is truly wasted on the young; we have no idea where we are going but we are making killer time. Earth becomes a different planet, empty streets and sidewalks, deserted parking lots that glow like the surface of the moon. It's all ours when the sun goes down. While our parents sleep we research and rehearse and plot our revolution for the time is coming when we will take over, and then, finally, we will do things our way. At least until we have to sleep...

And for the first time, I had a horribly depressing vision of our life together, me and Kat, older and fatter, grayer and balder, slowly dying and trying to remember what it was like to be alive in the days before we ruled the world. Until that moment I had only seen her as a river, endlessly flowing with passion and vigor as I tumbled along, caught up in her current. I was suddenly so scared. What happened to Wendy when she got home from *Neverland*? Did she meet a nice man and settle down? Did she trade her dreams for a good job and a few cute kids? Did she ever stop thinking about her ex-boyfriend who shot himself one day when she was just a girl?

For a few moments, in between heavy steps on that dark country roadside, I saw the error in my naive world view. She could never be mine. Not in the sense that I had thought about up until that point. She was angelic and precious, as if she had wandered down from Olympus and then humbly forgotten from whence she came. Everyone who came in contact with her was aware of the invisible, divine aura that surrounded her. Curious and compassionate, she explored our world, enriching it haphazardly. She was an Immortal, and it was her singularity that made her so. I realized for the first time, as I marched across the fairytale bridge, through the gatehouse, and up to the steps of the manor, that no man was worthy of her, and I indulged in a new fantasy. I renounced the notions of possession and love ever after, and appointed myself her noble guardian, vowing to protect her from any man who may try to taint the rare beauty of her life with his own. I wanted to protect her from any man like me.

4:10 AM Thursday (Hour 40:14)

Once inside the manor, I headed for the service stairs. In addition to the fact that I had been awake for over 40 hours, I had just hiked nearly five miles from Tommy's house in Grantham, down the old Melton Mowbray road, up the drive to the manor, and my feet were getting heavy. Similar to the Baroque cedar staircase in the main hall of the manor, the service stairwell was a wide wooden right-angled staircase that spiraled up the floors of the house. It was not nearly as ornate as the main stairway but was actually quite impressive on its own. The main difference was a lift that had been installed in the center of the existing stairwell some years after the house was built.

    The old gondola rattled down its chain and the unnatural metallic sound echoed through the empty halls. I waited at the bottom of the creepy steel cage until the noise stopped. Then I slid open the collapsing lattice door and shut it behind me as I entered the lift. Slowly, the old contraption began to haul me up to the third floor. I had never noticed how loud the thing was, but I had also never heard it run at night. The lift noise probably just blended with the rest of the cacophony of activity around the house during the day. Actually, no one ever used the lift. It was much faster to take the stairs, but fatigue was catching up with me and I needed to save steps.

The elevator jolted to a stop when it reached the third floor. It was very dark and I struggled for a moment with the latch holding the lattice gate closed. When I got it open I stumbled out of the gondola and headed for the Vortex. Down the hall, around the corner, down the steps, damn this was some archaic architecture, up the steps, watch your head, and, for some reason, I never expected to hear the voice of a giggling girl coming from my room at four in the morning.

As I rounded the final corner and stepped up through the open doorway into room 333 I saw Taylor sitting in the Big Chair. He had his glasses on and there was a cigarette burning in his hand, and his closely cropped hair was being tousled by the girl wrapped up in the comforter and sitting on his lap. "It just can't be messed up," she said, and it took me a moment to recognize her as Susie, the bartender from the Blue Pig.

"You're on quite a tear," I said to Taylor as I walked past them into my sleeping chamber and kicked off my boots.

"What's he on about?" I heard her ask as I took off my jeans and my jacket and slid on a pair of gym shorts that I had picked up off of my bed.

"Nothing ," he said to her, "Not enough sleep." Then he raised his voice slightly and said, "What's the count now?"

I looked at my watch as I walked back out into the common area. "Little past forty," I said.

"Nice," he said. "You remember Susie, right?"

"Yeah," I said. I smiled at her and she smiled back. "So did you see the fight?" I asked.

"Fight?" Taylor said.

"Yeah," I said. "Michael from Liverpool, Grizzly Adams, the fucking fight, man!"

"I'm just kidding, dude," Taylor laughed. "Looked like you guys were doing fine, so I took it upon myself to make sure that Susie here got out of there safely."

"Right," I said. "Did everybody else make it back?"

"Yeah," Taylor said. "Dr. Wallace took Michael down to the clinic. I think he got a couple of stitches above his eye. Everybody was worried that *you* never came back."

"Everybody except you," I said.

"I knew you'd be fine, brother," he said. "Where the fuck did you go anyway?"

"I hooked up with Paul outside the Pig," I said. "We had a couple with a friend of his."

"That was like four hours ago!" Taylor said. "Wallace was fucking pissed, man."

"Taxi place was closed. I had to walk back," I said.

"Fuck, man," he said. "You walked the whole way back?"

"Yeah," I said and I shot a glance towards Susie. "What have *you* been doing for the last four hours?"

Taylor raised an eyebrow at Susie and said, "Should we show him?"

Her face turned red and she smacked Taylor on his bare chest with her open hand. "Cheeky boy!" she said.

"Never mind," I said. "I'm gonna go break into the refectory and make some coffee."

"Suit yourself," Taylor said as I turned to leave the room.

"Cheers," Susie said.

"Yeah, cheers," I said sarcastically, and I continued to talk aloud to myself as I sauntered down the hall. "It's always *cheers*. It's like Sam Malone's wet dream in this country. How 'bout a *nice to meet ya* or a *see ya later* or something that makes sense? How about a cup of god damn coffee instead of your fucking hot tea!"

4:56 AM Thursday (Hour 41:00)

We used to run stadium laps at football practice, up one row of stairs all the way to the top of the stadium then down the next row and so forth. Jogging up the stairs was the hard part; going down the next row was always fun. If you kick your feet out at just the right rhythm gravity does all the work for you, pulling you down the steps, 9.8 meters per second. It was like snow skiing except without the snow or the skis. Going down, three laps around the old lift and I was back on the first floor of the manor, headed for the kitchen.

I really did have intentions of breaking into the locked refectory just to make myself a cup of coffee, but that proved to be a little more challenging than I thought it would be. The main entrance was a set of those industrial double doors like you might find in a hospital hallway or at the exit of a school gymnasium. I don't know if they were dead bolted into the floor or just each other, but I found them impervious to my advance. I was contemplating a flanking maneuver, going out into the courtyard and trying to squeeze through one of the narrow windows when I heard a voice say, "Sammy, what are you doing up?"

"Hey Lopez," I said when I saw that it was her.

"Jesus, you're not *still* up are you?" she said.

"Maybe," I said. "I was going to break into the kitchen and make a cup of coffee."

"Why?" she said.

"Because I really want a cup of coffee," I said.

An exaggerated look of sympathy appeared on Lopez's face. "Sammy, you're a danger to yourself and others, you know."

I looked at the floor.

"Follow me," she said. She started walking away from me, toward the faculty offices, but I just stood there. "Come on," she said as if she were talking to a cute little puppy. "Come on, boy!" I followed her and she continued to speak, "Haven't you been in any of the academic offices?"

"Nope," I said.

"You haven't talked to your advisor?"

"We have advisors?" I said.

"Yeah," she seemed confused. "How'd you sign up for classes?"

"I did that at Evansville, before I ever left," I said.

"Oh," she said, "and you haven't been sent to see the Dean yet?"

"Believe it or not," I said as I shook my head.

"Well check it out," she said as we arrived. What must have been some sort of sitting room in the old manor house had been converted into the lobby of the Harlaxton academic offices. The individual office doors were all locked, but the lobby had high arched, ornate entry ways and there really was no way to seal it off from the rest of the house. I followed Lopez into the lobby, past a few of the locked office doors, to a small painted door with a brass sign on it that said *Faculty Only*. I noticed the double action hinge on the door as Lopez pushed it open. "There's no lock," she said, "but you have to get here early…before any of the professors get to work."

The room was tiny, probably an old broom closet or pantry, but to my delight I saw that it had been turned into a makeshift break room complete with individually packaged snacks, a small icebox, and a coffee maker. "Lopez, you're the man!" I said.

She looked at me, made a sour face, and said, "Thanks...I guess." It became apparent as she produced the filters and the coffee that she had done this before.

"How long have you been making coffee down here?" I asked.

"Since like the second week of school," she said.

"Fantastic," I said. "You have no idea how happy I am right now."

She smiled at me as she poured the water into the machine and turned it on. Then her smile went away, and she said, "Sammy, can I ask you a question?"

"You just did," I said.

She ignored my remark. "How do you think of me?" she said.

"We're friends," I said. "What do you mean?"

"Seriously, a minute ago you called me a dude," she said.

"I did?" I said. "Right, sorry."

"Is that how you think of me?" she said. "Like a dude, like a buddy?"

"Not exactly," I said.

"Do you think that's how Taylor thinks of me?"

"As a dude?" I said. "Have you slept with him yet?"

"No," she said.

"Hmm...maybe," I said.

"That's not funny," she said.

"I'm not really joking," I said.

"Listen," she said. "I guess it's probably obvious that I've liked him, right?"

"Yeah, probably," I said.

"And I guess it's probably obvious that he never liked me the same way that I liked him?"

"Lydia, I don't think Taylor is capable of liking *anybody* the same way that you liked him," I said.

"Yeah," she said. "I mean, I knew he had a girlfriend and everything…"

"I'm not sure that's even relevant," I said.

"Yeah, well," she said. "That's what I thought at first too."

There was silence for a moment. I didn't really know what to say. Then she spoke again.

"Do you think it's ever perfect?" she said.

"What do you mean?" I asked.

"Like, love, you know," she said. "Do you think it can ever be perfect?"

"You're not talking about Taylor still are you?"

"No, Sam," she said. "I'm not talking about Taylor at all. I'm just talking about love, you know…between anyone. Do you think it can ever be perfect?"

"I want to," I said.

"I know you do," she said and she smiled up at me as she handed me a Styrofoam cup of steaming American style black coffee.

"I guess I'm probably pretty obvious too, huh?" I said.

"Yeah, probably," she said. She poured a cup for herself and we left the tiny break room and strolled toward the great hall as we talked.

"That's what the play is about, you know," she said, "accepting your role, taking what you can get. Look at your character. Hortensio is just as in love with Bianca as Lucentio is, but he dosen't bring as much to the table so he ends up having to settle for the widow. "

"Bianca wouldn't have married Hortensio," I said.

"Oh yes she would have," Lopez said. "It's never *just* about love."

"Well, of course it's never *just* about love," I said, "but that doesn't mean that the love part of it can't be perfect."

"Perfect?" she said.

"Well, close to perfect." I said.

"How close?" she asked. "Perfect is an absolute. *Close to perfect* is the same as *not perfect*."

"So what about your reading of Kate, then?" I said.

"What about it?"

"Ok, correct me if I am wrong," I said. She nodded and I continued, "In your production Kate delivers her final monologue sarcastically, right. She's not been tamed at all; she's just playing along, saying what Petruchio wants to hear, and everyone knows it except him?"

"Right," she said.

"So Kate never settles," I said.

"Well, yeah she does," Lopez said. "She doesn't really love Petruchio."

"Yeah, but *love* was never what she wanted in the first place," I said. "It's everybody else that wants her to get married. Bianca wants her to get married so she can get married. Her father wants her to get married so he doesn't have to support her anymore. And Petruchio doesn't love her either; he's just in it for the money."

"Well, right, but it's not like it works out perfectly for her," Lopez said, "She's *the Shrew* because she's not interested in her social role as an upper-class lady-in-waiting. Her perfect situation is ruined when everybody starts putting all the pressure on her. That's why it's a tragedy instead of a comedy. The turning point is when she realizes that she can never have that back."

"Never have what back?" I said.

"Solitude, independence," Lopez said. "She's perfectly happy to be on her own until they all start fucking with her about it."

"So she gets married just because everyone else wants her to?" I said.

"She has to," Lopez answered.

"So why go along with all of Petruchio's games?" I said.

"It's purely utilitarian," Lopez said. "It's the lesser of two evils. She figures that she'll be happier with a husband than she will be with everybody constantly riding her ass for not having one."

"Well, then that's my point," I said. "She gets what she wants."

"No she doesn't," Lopez said. "She is forced to settle. She only chooses the better of two lives that she didn't want anyway."

I didn't say anything. I thought for a moment about what she had said.

Then she said, "Do you think people like Taylor have to settle?"

"People like Taylor never even think about settling," I said.

"Well what about you?" she said. "What about Kat?"

"I don't know?" I said. "How are you even supposed to know if someone's settling? That's not how it's supposed to be. It's supposed to be...mutual, you know?"

"So you *do believe* that love can be perfect then," Lopez said.

"I don't know," I said. I swallowed the last bit of my coffee and I carried the empty cup as we came to a stop and sat down on the bottom step of the old cedar staircase.

"So what's going on with you guys?" she said.

"Who, me and Kat?" I said.

"Yeah," she said. "Are you guys like still an item or what?"

"I'm not sure," I said and I noticed Lopez look at me in a strange way.

"Don't worry about it Sammy," she finally said. "It's all going to be fine. Not perfect... just fine."

6:33 AM Thursday (Hour 42:37)

Having temporarily given up the more exotic drugs in favor of caffeine, I was the first one to hit the coffee pot in the refectory that morning. I hadn't thought that I was hungry, but as I sipped my coffee I began to be aroused by the mingled smells of bacon, eggs, sausage, and beans. Deciding that food might be a good idea, I moved to the end of the line and advanced along the stainless steel rails as the kitchen marms filled my tray with hot steamy goodness. I looked around the cafeteria trying to choose the appropriate company for the morning meal. The table where the theater majors sat was sparsely populated at this early hour, and the English majors weren't especially well represented either. However, the nursing majors were already bustling with bright eyes and energy conspicuously absent from the rest of the room.

Except for British Studies, the nursing students at Harlaxton College were subject to an entirely different curriculum than the rest of us liberal arts kids. As a result, they had become quite a close-knit group, type A personalities all organized and professional in their smart little scrubs. I realized as I headed toward their table that I hardly knew any of them. I recognized Amy because she was dating my friend Jerry, and I remembered Audrey from Halloween night. On average, they were older than the rest of us, and

123

that was apparent in the utilitarian manner in which they spent their time. So many of us were logistically challenged, immature, too young for college, wandering through our educations without any real sense of where we wanted to go or what we wanted to do with our lives. The nurses were different; they had it figured out.

"Good morning ladies," I said as I sat down between Amy and Audrey.

"What are you doing up this early?" Audrey said.

"I'm on a mission," I said.

"I hear you're not sleeping at all," Amy said.

I shrugged.

"Seriously?" Audrey asked. "You haven't slept?"

"It's only been like two days," I said as I began to work on my eggs and sausage.

"Jerry said you're keeping track," Amy said.

"That was his idea," I said. Perhaps I should not have agreed to keep time on my excursion of sleeplessness; the endeavor was beginning to draw attention.

"So how long have you been up?" she asked.

Stilling chewing, I looked at my watch and said, "Forty-two hours and fifty-one minutes."

"Why?" Audrey said.

"No good reason whatsoever," I said.

"No seriously," Audrey continued. "Why are you not sleeping? Are you cranking or something?"

"Nope," I said. "These breakfast beans are delicious!"

"Have you been sick?" she said.

I shook my head.

"Have you ever been diagnosed with depression?" she said.

"No, I just haven't felt like sleeping," I said.

Being a newcomer to the nurses' breakfast table, I had garnered some attention when I first arrived, but, after I sat down and began talking to Amy and Audrey, most of them went back to their routine, morning conversations about internships and finding veins, oblivious to me and my sausages and my beans. However, as I began answering Audrey's questions about my recent sleep deprivation, the nursing students gradually became interested in the interview.

"Are you on any medication?" said one them, I think her name was Christy.

"Nope," I said. I assumed she had been asking about something other than Amyl Nitrite.

"Are there any other symptoms?" another one asked.

"I'm not sick," I said. "I just haven't slept in a couple of days."

Audrey chuckled. I don't know if she was laughing at my silly waking marathon or the interrogation from the other nurses, but she smiled at me and said, "What do you do all night?"

"Loiter," I said and she laughed again. "I've been playing a lot of snooker. I wander around the estate, talk to the ghosts?"

"Yeah, I heard about you wandering around the fourth floor!" she said.

"A little harmless peeping," I teased.

"I'm telling your girlfriend!" she teased back.

"Girlfriend?" I said.

"Yeah," she laughed. "You and Kat are still together aren't you?"

"I don't know," I said.

She cocked her head at me. She might have raised an eyebrow; I don't remember. I didn't say anything else. Then she said "I swear you're crazy!" and she slapped me playfully on the shoulder.

"Do you really think so?" I asked.

She shook her head and said, "Sometimes. Jeez, you need to get some sleep today!"

"I don't feel like sleeping yet," I said.

"That can be really dangerous, you know," she said.

"It's a *dangerous* mission!" I said.

"I'm serious," she said. "I just did a research paper on hormone imbalances and brain function abnormalities. Sleep deprivation is one of the most common causes of those."

"I was dragging pretty hard around the 30 hour mark," I said, "but I actually feel pretty good right now."

"That's because you're past the point of simple fatigue," she said. "You've actually been awake long enough for it to start affecting your normal brain function."

"Is that right," I said.

"It is!" she said. "It all happens gradually so you won't notice it at first, but simple brain functions like decision making slow down. You start making decisions that are out of character. You'll be more prone to depression and mood swings. You may even start hallucinating."

"Don't you think you are being a bit of an alarmist," I said. "How's not sleeping going to cause hallucinations?"

"I'm not kidding, Sam," Audrey said. "Your body uses the time when you sleep to reorganize all the chemicals in your brain. If you don't give it a chance then the neurotransmitters can get all imbalanced and all kinds of stuff can go wrong."

"You nurses really know how to make it sound bad," I said as I pushed my empty plate toward the center of the table.

"It is bad, Sam," she said. "You really can't just stay awake. You body will start microsleeping if you keep it up."

"What's a microsleep?" I said.

"If you've been awake long enough," she said, "the brain automatically shuts down for like 10 or 15 seconds. You actually fall asleep but you don't know it. It's like a blackout."

"Well, thank goodness I haven't had one of those yet!" I said.

"You're not listening," she said. "You wouldn't know it if you have had one!"

"Well, thank goodness for that too," I said as I kicked my chair back and stood up to leave. However, when I reached for my half-full Styrofoam cup of coffee, I misjudged the distance and knocked it all over the Formica table top. "Oh Jesus God, I'm sorry about that," I said as I dammed the spreading liquid with napkins and tried to keep it from reaching any of the edges of the table.

Audrey helped me contain the spill, but after we had cleaned up my mess she looked at me like a den mother and said, "You *need* to get some sleep Sam!"

"Thanks for your help, Audrey," I said, "but what I *need* right now is to go outside and have a cigarette."

7:03 AM Thursday (Hour 43:07)

The sun had been up for over an hour, but the grass outside still glistened with droplets of dew. Mist hung above the courtyard, but the air was warm and comfortable. The focal points of the elaborate landscaping at Harlaxton Manor were two oversized stone lions that sat watch over the grounds atop giant pedestals on each side of the front drive. I leaned against one of them, one foot on the ground, one foot on the pedestal behind me as I smoked a Camel Light and watched a taxi from Grantham coming up the long drive.

When the taxi passed me I turned around and noticed Taylor and Susie coming out the front door of the manor.

Wearing the same clothes that she had worn to work, the bartendress didn't look as cute as she had the night before, and, in the morning light, I realized that she was more than a couple of years older than us. Taylor, too, looked a bit disheveled in his pajama pants and sweatshirt, but his hair was still perfect.

As I finished my cigarette, I watched the awkward dance of their body language as she prepared to get in the taxi. I couldn't hear what they were saying, but I could see it. They were standing very close to one another, almost snuggling, until they saw the taxi. As the car pulled up they moved apart. I couldn't tell if she had stepped away or if Taylor had pulled back. Their hands touched for a moment, but neither one of them held on to the other. They both smiled, but they did not kiss. Then the door was shut and she was on her way back to town.

"That was mighty gentlemanly of you," I said as I walked over to where Taylor was still standing.

"Give me a fag," he said.

"They're called *cigarettes*," I said as I produced one for him.

"What's wrong with you, dude?" he said as he lit the cigarette with his own lighter.

"Just grumpy I guess," I said.

"What's the count?" he said.

"Like forty-three hours," I said.

"Doing okay?" he said.

"I'm fine," I said. "The nurses tell me I'm flirting with disaster, though."

"Audrey?" he said.

"How'd you know?" I said.

"I saw the way you were looking at her the other night," he said.

"Whatever," I said.

"I'm fuckin' with you," he said. "I saw you sitting next to her at breakfast."

"Question is," I said, "did she see you with the bartender?"

Taylor shot me an odd glance and said, "Why's that?"

I wrinkled my brow as I thought. When I didn't say anything, he raised his eyebrows, cocked his head to one side, and walked off.

7:50 AM Thursday (Hour 43:54)

The halls of the manor were crowded with the morning migration to British Studies lecture. I had felt fine when I left the room, but an odd feeling came over me as I walked slowly down the halls of the old mansion. I felt disoriented, not lost, just a bit hazy, dreamlike. My head was swimming, and I remember wondering seriously if I had finally fallen asleep. I looked down and saw my feet moving, but I felt like some other force was propelling them. It was as if I wasn't really there, like my consciousness had stowed away inside someone else's body and I was eavesdropping on them as they walked to class. For the first time in two days, I was sleepy.

I thought about going back to the Vortex and lying down, but I had already missed British Studies lecture too many times that semester. That would have looked especially bad since I had been AWOL the night before. I decided to power through and was doing fine until I got to the great hall.

The great hall was one of the most impressive rooms in Harlaxton Manor. Inspired by medieval banquet halls, the room was wrapped in lush oak paneling and crowned by the same kind of Jacobethan stone carvings that covered the outside of the manor. There was a large crystal chandelier suspended above the center of the room, and an ancient stained glass window on the southeast wall. As I walked into the room that day the light bleeding through the stained glass and dancing off of the shimmering crystal painted the room. The spectrum of colors floating in the aquarium air amplified my already dreamy state, and I remember chuckling as I saw myself lie down on the marble tile.

The cold marble was surprisingly comfortable. I curled up in the fetal position and used my book bag as a pillow. As other students stepped around me on the way to lecture, I closed my eyes. My breathing slowed, and I was almost gone when I heard the thick Edinburgh accent of Dr. Wallace saying, "Well, I've never seen this before, Thompson."

My eyes snapped open, but I did not move. I knew I was in trouble, but I just stared up at him waiting to see how bad it was going to be. His hands were on his hips, but he wasn't looking down at me. His head was on a swivel, surveying the grand room as the passing students furrowed their brows at us.

"I was a bit worried when you didn't return from battle last night," he said, "but initially it appeared that Michael and his split skull were the worst casualties of the skirmish. Now that I see that you lack the strength for bipedal locomotion I'm no longer certain."

I looked up at the bottom of his chin and noticed that he had a tiny bald spot in his beard. His tone was very serious, but he did not sound angry. Finally, he looked down. Slowly, he squatted next to my prone body, perfectly keeping his balance as his hamstrings came to rest upon his calves. He lowered his voice a bit, as if he didn't want anyone else to hear, and then he said, "I won't sugar coat it. You did well last night soldier. I didn't think you were going to make it back at all, but this war is not over. Now I need to know straight away…can you go on?"

My ambition strangely roused by Dr. Wallace's facetious monologue, I looked up at him and said, "Sir, I think so, sir."

"Excellent," he said as he stood back up and back into his regular character. "Your next mission is to get up and get to class. I've prepared a riveting lecture on the trial and execution of Charles the First, and I'm quite sure you wouldn't want to miss that!"

9:14 AM Thursday (Hour 45:18)

Under normal circumstances, I might not have made it through Wallace's lecture without nodding off, but his battlefield pep talk on the cold tile of the great hall had inspired me. In fact, I was wired, afraid that if I let him down by lowering a lid that the Scotsman's full fury would be unleashed. Of course, it didn't hurt that his *Charles I* lecture actually had been entertaining. England had survived a civil war and then another, and at the end of it all they had blamed the king, the beginning of the end of the monarchy's absolute sovereignty. Charles felt that, as king, his power had been granted by God and he could therefore do no wrong. The 59 cats that signed his death warrant did not agree.

They cut his head off on a public scaffold, but I was distracted from the gory details by Kat who kept writing in the margin of her notebook and then sliding it over to my desk. As Dr. Wallace talked, I would read what Kat had written and then add to the story and pass the notebook back to her. We took turns trying not to laugh as our tale progressed, and the fate of *Charles I* became more and more obscured as we quietly added details to our story about a lonely spinster who falls in love with the pervert that has been masturbating onto her refrigerator door.

I don't remember whether or not our tale had a happy ending. The important thing seemed to have been the process by which it was written. The story was silly and satirical, but, as with most stories, it was somewhat based in truth. I remembered Kat's reoccurring fear of spinsterhood from a conversation we once had, and I wondered how many of her quirky character's traits were based on her own. Perhaps none were. The pervert was obviously based on me, but I don't think I would ever actually have jerked off onto anyone's appliances. The whole thing was probably farce, but there was one image that Kat had added that I just couldn't get out of my head. She had described how the spinster could tell her lovers apart without seeing them, by only feeling the distinct shapes of their bellies against the small of her back.

10:04 AM Thursday (Hour 46:08)

Kat closed her notebook and slid it into her canary yellow book bag as Dr. Wallace closed his lecture and dismissed the class. She was wearing her glasses and the light in the long gallery hid her eyes as she smiled up at me shyly. We had been writing back and forth for over an hour, but we had not spoken. It proved more awkward than I thought it would have to get the first words out.

"So," I said as I motioned toward the yellow book bag, "Do you think it's ready to publish?"

She smiled again, and I saw her eyes that time. "For sure," she said. "I'm thinking *The New Yorker.*"

"Huh," I said, "I was thinking *Playboy.*"

"You would be," she said. She got up to leave the room and I followed her. "Do you have your poem finished?" she said.

"Poem?" I said. "Oh, yeah…I remember that assignment now."

"You're crazy, Sam," she said. "You haven't even started it yet have you?"

I pressed my lips together and shook my head. As we walked next to each other through the great hall I said, "Did you finish yours?"

"Yeah," she said. "It's called *Spinster*. How funny is that?"

"Autobiographical?" I said.

"They tell me that *Sagittarius* is the sign most likely to end up a spinster," she said, "I wonder sometimes."

"Not you," I said.

"Sara says it's our destiny," she laughed. "Lonely old biddies with our cats and our crossword puzzles."

"What does she know?" I said.

"Yeah," Kat smiled. "I heard you two tussled."

"Yeah," I said. "Any idea what that was about?"

"She's convinced that you hate her," she said.

"I'm gettin' there," I said.

"She's just being protective of me," she said. She jokingly poked me in the chest as she said, "She thinks you're no good for me!"

"That's not exactly what she said."

"Yeah, well," Kat said, "She doesn't exactly know what she thinks of you."

"And you don't either," I said. "Do you?"

"I liked your story," she said as she smiled sheepishly. She even made avoiding my question cute.

"Thank you," I said, "What'd you like about it?"

"It was sweet," she said.

"Sweet?" I said.

"Yeah," she said. "It was funny and then it was sad, but not too sad. The little boy was very real. I want to be a mom someday."

"My story made you want to be a mom?" I said.

"No silly," she said. "It just reminded me."

She smiled at me again. I walked with my head turned sideways so that I could look at her. We both stopped when we reached the base of the cedar staircase.

"What?" she finally said.

"You're beautiful," I said.

"Whatever," she said. "I got out of bed like five minutes before class."

"I'm not just talking about what you look like," I said.

She looked at me. Then she looked down. Then she looked at me again and said, "Thank you Sam."

I took a step closer to her. I held out my hands, palms up, and she took hold of them with hers. "I've missed hanging out with you," I said.

"I've missed you too," she said. She shifted her weight back and forth from one foot to the other, but she never let go of my hands.

I didn't know what to do next, but when her eyes made contact with mine I decided. Holding her hands, I gently pulled her towards me. She looked up at me, our hands held by our legs, and as I leaned down toward her face she leaned up to mine.

I remember that moment very well. It felt like we were in a bubble. The noise of the world became silent; the fatigue in my tired body was gone. The only things that existed were me and her at the base of that giant stairway. We kissed in slow motion, lightly but seriously, and I remember the feeling of her cheek against mine. Her skin felt softer than a woman's, soft like a child. Our mouths were slightly open, but our tongues did not touch. I could feel her softly breathing into me. It was very different from our first, tipsy kiss under the gatehouse on the drive, very different from the kisses in Paris, and when it was over she hugged me tightly, pressing the side of her head into my chest.

We stood that way for a moment as the world, which had disappeared around us, gradually came back into existence. I hadn't planned on kissing her that morning, and I certainly had no plan for what to do after the kiss. I wanted to say something about how wonderful it had been, but I couldn't come up with words to describe it. It was as if it had happened in another language and there was no direct translation. When the silence became too awkward for me, I resorted to honesty. "I don't know what to say," I said.

"I know," she said. "Me neither."

"I want to say something," I said.

"You don't have to," she said.

"But I want to," I said.

"Please don't," she said. "Can't we just let it be what it is?"

"Kat, I love you," I said.

"Sam," she said with a deep exhaled breath. "How do you know?"

"I know," I said.

"You don't know that," she said. "Why would you say that to somebody when there's no way that you could know that?"

"How do you know I don't know that?" I said.

"Because you're only twenty," she said.

"So are you," I said.

"Right," she said.

I looked at her with a furrowed brow, and she suddenly seemed very sad.

"That's the problem with humans," she said, "the world is full of so many beautiful experiences, beautiful things and beautiful moments, but we don't know how to enjoy them. We just collect them, put names on them, and file them away into categories. Love is something that shouldn't have a name. It's too big."

"What are you talking about?" I said.

"Sam, you're a really sweet guy and I like you a lot, but you're impulsive and you're rash and you don't have your head on straight yet."

"I have my head on straight," I said.

"Really?" she said. "How long have you been awake now?"

"I love you Katherine," I said.

"Will you stop saying that," she said. "You don't know what love is."

"I've never felt anything like this in my life," I said.

"I believe you," she said, "but when you love someone, it stops being about *you*. I was in love with Donnie, and when that happened I gave a part of myself to him. I didn't think about what it meant, I just trusted him with myself. And when he died, that part of me, the part that I had given to him, died too. And I realized that he never really loved me. He could have never done that to me if he had. I'm not mad at him anymore; we were just kids. But I'm still mad at myself, and I don't know if I'll ever be able to trust anyone like that again."

I watched her as she spoke, but I couldn't decipher her motivation. She was frustrated, but she wasn't angry. I had let her down, but she wasn't through with me. I closed my eyes when I said, "Kat, I don't know what to say."

"That's why you shouldn't have said anything," she said.

"I want you to know how I feel about you," I said.

"I already know that," she said.

"So why not say it?" I said.

"When you name it, it becomes whatever name you give it," she said, "and it stops being what it was."

"Everything changes," I said.

"I liked what it was," she said. "I'm not ready for it to change."

"Kat," I said. "You're the only girl I've ever thought about this way. If you don't want me to call it *love*, fine. I won't. I'm not ready to get married yet either, but I don't think it's weird that I want to call you my girlfriend. That's what you are to me, you know, whether you want to name it or not."

"I don't want to be a *girlfriend*, Sam" she said. "I just want to be me."

I couldn't think of anything to say. I just looked at her, memorized her, her blue eyes behind the glasses, her cute boy haircut, and her tiny elfin ears.

"I need to go," she finally said. "I'll see you at rehearsal, okay?"

She started up the stairs, but she stopped for a moment when I said, "Kat..."

She turned and spoke before she headed back up the stairs. "I like you a lot, Sam," she said as she smiled down at me. "Just let it be what it is."

10:36 AM Thursday (Hour 46:40)

Frustration began to manifest as anger as I walked back to the Vortex, and I decided that I didn't want to deal with that circus at this moment. Searching for solitude, I found myself in the garden behind the conservatory sitting between the lions on the steps in front of the fountain. Perhaps it was the fatigue, but my mind was cloudy and sluggish, trying to digest my latest encounter with Kat. I couldn't stop thinking about it, but I couldn't focus on it either. I just wanted a distraction, so I sat there smoking a cigarette and thinking about the past.

A couple of months earlier, I had signed up for the group bus trip to Paris that the Evil Student Activities Committee had organized for the first four day weekend of the semester. In theory, it seemed like a good idea. Going with the group was less expensive and probably safer than traveling alone, but there were certain limitations that could not be avoided. Chief among them was the fact that the social structure of the college ended up following us to Paris; people shared rooms with the same roommates from school, cliques walked abreast down the *Rue de Rivoli* the same as they did in the halls of the manor back at the college. It was amazing, even in Paris, how easily they fell back into their routines.

It was dark when we reached the English Channel, and we all had to get off of the bus when the driver parked on the ferry. As we made our way from the car park up to the observation deck, I made a conscious effort to separate myself from my fellow students. The boat was huge, like a floating airport terminal with commercial grade carpeting and gift shops and tourist information booths, and it was easy to lose my classmates, to disappear into the crowd of strangers. We waited at dock for a long time as the huge ferry was loaded, and I was standing outside by the railing where I could barely see the white cliffs as we motored out of port.

Enjoying the smell of the salty wind, I waited there until the silhouette of England had vanished, and then strolled back inside to check out the midway. The observation deck had the feel of a Las Vegas casino; the only things missing were the slot machines. It was the middle of the night, but everyone was wide awake, changing currency, buying snacks, parents scolding half-heartedly as their children played hide-and-seek among the legs of strangers. It was all gloriously distracting until I saw her standing there.

Kat was wearing the same woolen jacket that she had been wearing the night that I met her. Looking a bit queasy, she was leaning against the brightly colored wallpaper near one of the cash changing machines. She saw me coming and tried to straighten her posture a bit, but it was obvious that she was not feeling good. "Are you alright?" I said as I approached.

"Yeah," she said. "I just feel a bit light headed. I don't think I've had enough to eat today."

I offered her my forearm as I came to a stop next to her. "Do you want to sit down somewhere?" I said.

"No," she said. "I think I'd throw up."

"Do you want to go out on deck," I said, "get some air?"

"No. I need something to drink," she said.

"Like a water or Sprite or something?" I asked.

"I actually came up here to get a Coke, but then I realized that I left all my cash on the coach," she said.

"You want a Coke?" I said.

"I would trade my body for a Coke right now," she said.

"I'll be right back," I said. "You okay here?"

"Yeah," she said. "You're so my hero right now!"

I walked up to one of the snack windows, but I kept an eye on her the entire time that I was in line. I bought two large *Coca-Colas*, walked back to her, and offered one to her. She took it with both hands, raised it, and grasped the straw between her delicate lips. I smiled at her exaggerated glee and again after she swallowed and said, "Oh my God, that is the best Coke that I have ever had in my life!"

"Yeah?" I said as I took a sip of my own.

"Yeah," she said. "Thank you so much!"

"You're welcome," I said. She seemed a little steadier on her feet, and I thought it would be a good idea to get her away from the crowd. "Do you want to try to walk outside?" I said. "The air might feel good."

"Yeah, okay," she said, and I offered her my forearm again.

As she took hold of it and followed me out on deck I said, "You were kidding about that *trading your body* thing weren't you?"

She said, "Yeah," and then she laughed.

The Channel was very dark that night, and we looked out into the darkness as we leaned against the steel railing of the ferry. There was nothing to be seen in any direction; we might as well have been floating in space, but it was warm that night and the cool air over the Channel felt good. The rhythmic sound of the hull cutting through the waves was soothing, and I couldn't think of any place on earth that I would rather have been.

"It's so cool," Kat said, "the smell, the feeling of the ship moving. I've never been out on the ocean before!"

"It's not really an ocean," I said.

"Don't ruin it," she said. "Here, take my picture." She handed me a cardboard incased disposable camera that she had pulled out of her coat pocket as she turned around, leaned against the railing, and faced me. She put one foot up on the bottom rail, both hands out to the sides on the top rail, and turned her head toward the invisible shoreline of France. The wind lifted her short bangs and they danced like a bird's feathers during flight. I took a step back to get her entire pose in the frame. I knew that the photograph was going to be beautiful, but when I pushed the button on the little cardboard camera the *click* was anticlimactic.

"Thanks," she said as she slipped the camera back into her pocket and stepped down from the rail. "This is awesome out here! I'm going to get Sara. She'll love it!"

"So you're feeling better?" I said.

"Yeah," she said. She smiled as she stood still. Tilting her head toward one shoulder, she wrinkled her nose and said, "Thanks for the Coke, Sam. I owe you one."

"You're welcome," I said. "I'm just glad you're feeling better."

"Thank you," she said as she pulled her jacket shut and began walking away. "You really are my hero, Sam!"

I watched her disappear into the crowd inside, and then I took out a cigarette and learned against the rail. The wind made lighting it difficult at first, and I remembered a public service announcement I had once seen about how that was a sign from God telling us that he didn't want us to smoke. The orange ember glowed as I inhaled, and I thought I saw the outline of France appearing on the horizon.

At dawn we all filed back onto the bus, and a few hours later we were rolling into Paris. As a group, we checked into an old hotel in the middle of the city, and I ended up sharing a room with Ben the Stoner. Taylor had decided to fly to Paris because he didn't want to endure the long bus trip, and we had made arrangements to meet that afternoon under the Eifel Tower. After we dropped our gear in the room, I invited Ben to tag along, and we walked to a Metro and took the train to the *Champ de Mars* station. As we walked up I remember thinking that the tower was a lot smaller than I had pictured it, and, since Taylor was nowhere to be found when we arrived, Ben and I decided to pay the admission to go up and check it out. The wind whipped through our long hair at the top of the tower, and we took a few humorous photos of each other. Then we laughed again as we hypothesized how we might have arrived an hour early for our meeting with

Taylor because he was still on England time. When we came down from the Tower, we found a spot on the lawn in the park across the street and watched the lights of Paris come alive as the sun slowly set. Dissatisfied with merely waiting, Ben walked off deeper into the park with hopes of scoring some weed. I stayed on the lawn and watched the lights and the traffic and the people visiting the Tower and wondered if I would ever be back there again.

We met Taylor a little while later, smoked some of Ben's newly acquired marijuana under the lighted Eifel Tower, and then the three of us had diner and drinks at a sidewalk café off of *Rivoli*. We sneaked Taylor into our room that night so that he could avoid paying for a room of his own, and the three of us made plans to go sightseeing together the next day. In the morning we walked to Notre Dame and then spent a few hours at the Louvre. Around noon, we took a train up to *Sacré-Cœur*, smoked up again on the steps in front of the cathedral, and then wandered through the surrounding neighborhood, taking in the aura of the narrow stone streets and the peddling artists. We decided to go back to the room and clean up before going out that night, and that's where I ran into Kat again.

She was dropping off a letter at the front desk of our hotel. I smiled at her as Taylor and Ben and I walked into the lobby. She smiled back and walked over to me before the elevator door opened to take us upstairs. "Where've you been, stranger?" she asked as Taylor and Ben stepped onto the elevator.

"Walkabout," I said after a bit of a pause, and I realized that I was still a little high. I motioned for the guys to go ahead without me and turned back toward Kat as the elevator door closed behind me.

"What are you doing now?" she asked.

"We've been out all day," I said. "We were just going to chill here awhile before we headed back out for the night."

"Well come chill with me," she said. "There's a cute café right down the street and I owe you a Coke."

I walked next to her in the shade of the trees that lined the sidewalk until we ducked into the little café on the corner. We sat in the back by an old Wurlizter jukebox and the garcon followed us to our seats and said, "*Bonjour, bienvenue à Cafe Bruno.*"

To my surprise Kat answered him in French, "*Bonjour Monsieur, avez-vous une glacée Coca-Cola?*"

I followed as well as I could as the waiter said, "*Non, je suis désolé. Je peux vous offrir quelque chose d'autre?*"

"*Oui,*" she said, "*un café s'il vous plaît.*"

"*...et pour votre ami?*" the waiter said.

"*Oh, il n'est pas mon ami,*" she said. "*Il est mon amant!*"

"*Oui, mademoiselle,*" the man said as he smiled slyly at her. "*Je vais faire deux cafés.*"

"I didn't know you spoke French," I said as the waiter left the table.

"How would you have known that?" she said.

I raised my eyebrows and nodded at her as I took out a cigarette and lit it.

"Can I get one of those from you, cowboy?" she asked.

"I've never seen you smoke," I said as I handed her a Camel Light and held out my burning Bic so that she could light it.

"I guess I'm just full of surprises," she said.

"I guess so," I said as I watched her exhale the smoke through her tiny nostrils.

"I wanted to thank you again," she said. "I was really out of it on the ferry. You totally came to the rescue."

"Don't worry about it," I said.

"Seriously," she said. "That was the best tasting *Coca-Cola* I've ever had in my life!"

I laughed and said, "It was a damn fine *Coca-Cola*."

"But seriously," she said as she reached across the table and took my hand in hers, "thank you."

Before I could say anything, the waiter returned with two steaming cups of coffee. He asked Kat something in French and she shook her head. When he had gone she said, "I'm sorry. They didn't have Coke. We'll have to settle for coffee."

"I love coffee," I said.

"I love coffee too," she said.

"What else do you love?" I said and she looked up at me quickly and smiled slyly.

"Chocolate!" she giggled.

"What else?" I said.

"Hmm…" she said. "I love to sleep in a very cold room with loads of covers wrapped around me."

"Very cool," I said as I pictured her snug as a bug.

"What about you?" she said as she rolled the ember off of her cigarette in the glass ash tray.

"What?" I said as my little daydream abruptly ended.

"What else do you love?"

"Women," I said.

"All women?" She cocked her head as she asked.

I grinned at her and said, "Women who love coffee."

"…and chocolate?" she added for me.

"Yeah," I smiled, "and especially women who sleep in very cold rooms with tons of covers wrapped around them!"

"I love men who listen," she said.

"I love women who think," I said.

"I think too much," she said.

"It's very becoming," I said.

"It's very distracting," she said. "Sometimes I wonder if it wouldn't be simpler to just be blissfully ignorant."

"Like a *Chi Omega*?" I joked.

"Oh my God, yes!" she sarcastically gushed as she fell into character, "I was a *psych* major but now I'm taking a semester off to follow Dave Matthews and work on my tan!"

"That's so hot," I laughed.

"You'd love that wouldn't you?" she said.

"I don't think so," I said.

"No?" she said.

"Nope," I said.

"So you like the smart girls?" she said.

"Pressure's on now," I smiled.

"What makes you think it even matters to me?" she asked coquettishly.

"I can see you trying to figure me out," I said.

"I like to try to figure people out," she said.

"I know," I said. "I like that about you."

We talked for a while longer, and then she ordered two more cups of coffee for us. When the waiter left again she excused herself to the restroom, and I got up to check out the Wurlitzer. The jukebox gods had smiled upon me, and when Kat returned to the table she noticed the ethereal recording of Cyndi Lauper's *Time After Time* gliding along with her back to her seat.

"Awe…" she said as she sat down, "You played our song!"

I smiled from behind my raised mug. "Yeah," I said. "This *should be* our song."

We finished our second coffees and then went for a walk in the neighborhood around our hotel. We had only been walking for a couple of blocks when we came upon the *Seine*, and we followed its banks down to the *Ile De La Cite* and held hands as we walked across *Pont Neuf*. We discovered a secluded little park next to the ancient bridge just on the tip of the island. Triangular with water on two sides, the park was surrounded by small shade trees with iron park benches lining the triangular walk that traced the parameter of the area. It was one of the most beautiful places that I had ever seen, but I never caught its name.

Kat and I walked down the steps, around the little walk, and sat on one of the benches listening to the river as the sun set on the city. We talked a bit, but I don't really remember what we talked about. The moon was visible in the dusk sky when I finally leaned over and kissed her. She kissed me back enthusiastically, and it occurred to me that she might have been waiting for that kiss for a while. She fell back onto the park bench and pulled me with her, arms around my neck, one of my knees between her thighs. I supported my weight with my arms posted against the bench, my large body hovering above her delicate frame. She ran her fingers through my long hair as we kissed. The sensation on my scalp was amazing. The rhythm of our kissing increased and I was shocked when I felt her start to rock her hips against the bench, grinding her blue jean covered mound against my thigh. Instinctively, I dropped my hips closer to her writhing body, and when she felt my enthusiasm against her leg she stopped kissing me and smiled up into my eyes.

I looked down at her. I probably smiled. It was dark by then and the lights of the city cast shadows across her glorious countenance. We were both very still for a moment. Then she pushed her hips into me one more time, closed her eyes, tilted her head back, and whispered, "Yes." Then we were kissing again, hands exploring, our breathing was heavy. I unbuttoned the top of her blouse and was awestruck by the contrast of her black bra against the ivory white skin between her small breasts. She shivered when I touched them, and I did the same when I felt her hand on the front of my

146

trousers. With one hand, I reached down between us, unbuttoned and unzipped her jeans, and slid my hand between her cotton underwear and the smooth skin underneath. I felt her softly thrust up to meet my hand as my fingers discovered her for the first time, but the sensation reminded me of a fumbling backseat encounter with my high school girlfriend and I suddenly stopped.

"What's the matter?" Kat said as I withdrew my hand and sat up beside her.

"Not here," I said.

"C'mon nobody's around," she said as she gently tugged at my shirt. I looked into her crystal blue eyes and she said, "Sam, I want to."

"God so do I," I said, "but I've thought about this moment for too long. I've thought about you for too long. It can't be like this."

I winced as the words left my mouth. I was sure I had just blown it. She was going to think I was calling her a slut, telling her that I was too good to fuck her on a park bench, but she just looked up at me with those pale blues and whispered, "Oh my God, Sam."

"I'm sorry Kat," I spoke quickly. "It's not that I don't want to. I do. I want to *so much*, but I want it to be perfect. You're so special, Kat. I've never felt this way about any other girl. I just want it to be *right*."

"Oh my God, Sam," she said again and she sat up and hugged me.

A few minutes later we were walking arm-in-arm back to the hotel. I don't remember us speaking to one another at all, and we didn't kiss again until we were inside the elevator. She giggled and held onto my hand tightly as we walked down the hall toward my room. I knew that Taylor and Ben had planned on being out late that night, and I expected that Kat and I would have the room to ourselves for at least a few hours. However, the familiar smell of cannabis wafted over us when I opened the door, and I saw my two roommates sitting on the floor between the two beds playing cards and devouring two halves of a broken baguette.

"Dude, close the door. We're smoking in here," Taylor said as Kat and I stood in the doorway.

"Fucking potheads," I said as I closed the door behind me and stepped back into the hallway with Kat. "I'm sorry," I said, "I thought sure they'd be gone still."

"It's okay," she said.

"Should we try your room?" I said, but Kat shook her head.

"No way," She said. "Sara's in for the night by now I'm sure."

I closed my eyes and said, "I'm sorry, Kat."

"Don't worry about it," she said. "I had a wonderful time today. Really, wonderful."

"Yeah?" I said. "Me too."

"Seriously, Sam. You're one of the good guys. That means a lot to me," she said. Then she kissed me on the cheek, started walking back toward the elevator, and said. "Don't worry about tonight, Sam. There'll be other nights."

Weeks later back at Harlaxton in the garden behind the conservatory, sitting between the lions on the steps in front of the fountain, I thought about how there hadn't been. The weeks since the Paris trip had been excruciating. I had asked her out twice, but she had had previous plans both times. Stopping just short of stalking, hoping to recapture the magic of that night in Paris, I had scheduled my days in the attempt to be in the same places as her time after time, but my efforts had all been futile. I was beginning to give up hope. The last thing that I had expected was to be kissing her again that morning after Dr. Wallace's *Charles I* lecture at the base of the cedar staircase, and God damn it I had screwed it up again!

"What the fuck are you doing?" I actually said out loud, and I realized that reliving the memory of Paris had done nothing to improve my mood. Kat was right. I didn't have my head on straight. I thought about going back to the room and getting some sleep, but then I remembered my writing workshop assignment had to be turned in before 2:00 PM. I got up off of the surprisingly comfortable stone step and headed back toward the manor. It was time to go to work.

11:56 AM Thursday (Hour 48:00)

I had been awake for two full days. I was wandering around the manor looking for a place to write. There were too many people in the writing lab, and I didn't like to do poetry on the computer anyway. The library was depressing, the Bistro was closed, and the Vortex was completely out of the question. I thought about sitting on the cedar staircase, on the bottom step right by where we had kissed, but I ended up in a folding school desk that someone had left in the hallway outside the library.

I had never been particularly good at writing poetry. I couldn't conform to the structure of meter or the form of rhyme scheme. I had never had the patience to work that hard with the language, but I had always appreciated the art of saying a lot with very few words. On the other hand, I had always been good at describing the details necessary to create imagery, and, every once in a while, I was able to scribble down some free verse that wasn't that bad.

As I sat there at that uncomfortable little desk, I tried to come up with something clever or thoughtful, but my brain was fatigued. I was fading in and out of focus, and I was distracted by every person that walked by, every flicker of the fluorescent lights, every shift in the invisible aura of the old mansion. Surrendering, I gave in to the desire to write about the only thing that was really on my mind. I thought about our kiss earlier, and the trip to Paris, the Coca-Cola on the ferry and the coffee at *Café Bruno*. Finally, all of the distractions were gone. I focused on my tattered blue notebook, zoned out, and tried to choose a moment, a single scene to describe that best represented what I was feeling. When I thought I had chosen the right one, I began to write.

A few minutes later I closed my notebook. My first draft was to be my final draft; I didn't want to dilute it with revision.

12:40 PM Thursday (Hour 48:44)

As I approached the open door of Room 333, I could hear another riveting intellectual conversation was already in progress. Elwood's voice was the loudest.

"*Mr. Fabulous* may have played a mean trumpet, but *Mr. Wonderful* could've kicked his ass!"

"Who was *Mr. Wonderful*?" Lopez said as I walked into the room and tossed my notebook on my bed.

"*Mr. Wonderful*?" Elwood said. "Paul Orndorff!"

"Oh wow, man," Jerry said. "I remember *Mr. Wonderful*."

"*Orndorff*," Ben said. "That's a fucked up name."

"*WrestleMania*," Jerry said. "Orndorff and *Rowdy* Roddy Piper versus *Mr. T* and the *Hulkster*. That was awesome!"

"So what's that got to do with *The Blues Brothers?*" Lopez said as I sat down among them and listened. Taylor was sitting in the Big Chair, and he was just listening too.

"Nothing really," Elwood said, "just the name, *Mr. Fabulous, Mr. Wonderful.*"

"I want to be fabulous," Taylor said. "Being wonderful implies goodness."

"What about *Mr. Perfect?*" Jerry said.

"Yep!" Elwood said, "Another great protégé of Bobby *the Brain* Heenan!"

"Dude," Taylor said, "You guys watched a lot of professional wrestling."

"Watched?" Jerry said. "I still watch it."

"Jeez," Lopez said, "It's impossible to keep you guys on a subject!"

Elwood laughed. "What were we talking about?" he said.

"*The Good Old Blues Brothers Boys Band from Chicago!*" she said.

"That's funny," Ben said.

"I got one for you," I finally said. "*Mr. Perfect* versus Matt *Guitar* Murphy."

"Oh, good one!" Elwood said.

"You gotta be kidding me!" Lopez said.

"Matt *Guitar* Murphy did have the guns," Elwood said.

"Yeah," I said. "He had that whole *Apollo Creed* look going."

"Yeah," Jerry said, "but *Mr. Perfect* was absolutely perfect!"

"I don't know anything about your wrestlers," Taylor said, "but I'll wager Matt Murphy was a lover, not a fighter."

"Oh definitely," Elwood concurred.

"You better think about what you're saying. You better think about the consequences of your actions!" Lopez said in a perfect Aretha Franklin voice as she stood up and soulfully waved her finger in Elwood's face.

Everyone laughed and then Taylor said, "So what's the count, Thompson?"

I checked my watch and said, "Forty-eight plus."

"How you holding up, man?" Jerry said.

"I'm right as the rain," I said.

"You don't look so good," said Lopez.

"I have not yet begun to defile myself," I said.

"You need to get some sleep before the play," she said as she touched a greasy strand of hair that had pulled loose from my pony tail. "And you need to take a shower!"

"I will not be pawed at," I said as I got up and walked over to my sleeping chamber. I gathered up my towel and shampoo and bid farewell to the crowd in our room.

As I started up the steps toward the women's showers I heard Lopez say, "See you at rehearsal, Sammy. Two o'clock!"

2:21 PM Thursday (Hour 50:25)

Considering all the extra time I had been saving by not sleeping, it was amazing that I still seemed to be running late for everything. Lopez was right, the shower had been refreshing but I had taken too long under the relaxing cascade. Despite the fact that I had felt invigorated with a new burst of energy as I dressed and collected my script, I was still not going to make it to practice on time.

Lopez scolded me as I rushed into the great hall. They had run through the *Induction* already, but Lopez had wanted everyone there before starting the action in Padua.

Props and players already in place, they had obviously been waiting on me. Kat shot me a smile as I sheepishly took my place with her in the wings, and we both watched as *Lucentio* and *Tranio* started the scene.

In between lines, I watched Kat shine, and, as she did, I saw the frustration and anxiety evaporate from our director's heavy brow. The rest of *Act I* sped by, and by the middle of *Act II* I was a patron as much as a player. Lopez had planned an intermission after *Act III* so she allowed us a short break, and I used the opportunity to find her and apologize for my tardiness.

"You're forgiven," she said. She was still abuzz from seeing the first half of the dress rehearsal. "But you won't be if you show up late tomorrow!"

"When have I let you down before?" I said.

"You were late today!" she said.

"Yeah," I said, "Besides that?"

"You never got to see my Halloween costume," she said.

"I never even saw *you*," I said.

"Too bad," she said. "It was brilliant."

"I came looking for you that night and everything," I said.

"I know. I heard," she said. Then she winked at me and said. "Don't worry about it. It wasn't entirely your fault. I did leave the party pretty early."

"Taylor and I went as *Jesus* and *Rudolph*," I said. "What was your brilliant costume?"

"You really are oblivious, Sam," she said. "I think the lack of sleep is affecting you."

"What do you mean?" I said.

"I went to the party with Dan," she said. "I was *Joliet Jake*."

153

In my fatigued state, it actually took me a second to remember who *Dan* was. "Oh yeah," I said aloud, "Elwood." Lopez looked at me as if I was an idiot, and then my brain slowly started to put the pieces into place. "So you went to the party with Elw…er…Dan?" I said.

"Yeah that's what I said," she chuckled.

"Like, as a date?" I said.

"I guess so," she said.

"So why did you leave earl…" I asked and then it dawned on me. "You left early *with* Dan?"

She nodded, and I tried to wrap my mind around the idea of my hard-drinking Chicagoan roommate being involved romantically with my tiny half-Mexican, half-Apache buddy. Granted, my brain may not have been functioning at full capacity, but the two images just did not mesh. As I stood there stunned I realized that maybe I never *had* actually thought of Lydia as a woman, and I certainly had never expected any woman to be attracted to Dan. My thoughts were still skipping like a scratched CD when I said, "So…you and Dan?"

"I guess we're sort of seeing each other," she nodded.

"I never would have suspected," I said.

She laughed again, and I noticed a slight flush in her face. "You just missed us at *The Blue Pig* last night too," she said.

"And so I did," I said.

"So…" she said, "what do you think?"

"What do you mean?" I said.

"Of me and Dan," she said. "What do you think?"

It had also never occurred to me that Lopez might be interested in my opinion on such a matter. I was flattered that she had asked for my assessment. I had never really known that she thought of me as that kind of a friend. I smiled at her and said, "If you like him, I think it's great."

"He's funny," she said, "and I think he really likes me."

"Dan's a good guy," I said. "I wish I could've seen you two in costume."

She laughed and said, "It was pretty fucking awesome." She smiled as she walked away, and I saw her stop and talk with the actor that was playing *Petruchio*. Silently, I was proud of my little Texan friend; she had done well.

As we began *Act IV*, I was thankful that I didn't have a larger role. Simply standing had become difficult as I waited for my periodic entrances. The temporary boost I had gotten from the shower was gone and my joints were beginning to ache. Perhaps the sleep thing was catching up with me a little, for I found it difficult to concentrate on my role even as the play was in progress. I was thinking about Dan and Lydia and what she had said to me earlier about things being *fine* but not *perfect*. I was distracted by Kat every time she took the stage, lost in her grace, in thoughts about our kiss earlier and all of the kisses before that.

However, the production had come together nicely. The rhythm was good and I could tell that Lopez was happy with our collective performances. As *Act V* came to a close, all of the players watched in near-reverence as Kat delivered *Katherina's* final soliloquy exactly as Lopez had wanted it, sarcastic and bitter, in such a tone that it was obvious that this version of the play was not a comedy. Although she had never taken acting that seriously, the rest of us marveled at her talent. She was a natural, hiding what needed to be hidden and showing what needed to be shown.

I had wanted to tell her how incredible I thought her performance was, but before I had the chance, she had been surrounded by too many others wanting to do the same. Frustrated and intimidated by the attention she was receiving,

I sulked away when the rehearsal was over. I didn't want to risk having her think of me as *just* part of the group.

5:46 PM Thursday (Hour 53:50)

Leaving Kat and Lopez and the rest of the troupe behind to celebrate their dress rehearsal, I walked alone back to Room 333. As always, the door was open and I heard Jerry and Elwood discussing their evening plans as I walked in and sat down in the oddly vacant Big Chair.

"So what the fuck is a *beatnik*?" Elwood said. It was a bit surreal to hear his voice for the first time after Lopez's earlier disclosure. I just sat there listening to them.

"They were like *hippies* I think," Jerry said. "Only they were more into poetry than regular hippies."

"Is it like one of those SAT questions," Elwood asked, "all *beatniks* are *hippies* but not all *hippies* were *beatniks*?"

"I never took the SAT," Jerry said.

"Then how'd ya get into school?" Elwood said.

"I took the ACT," Jerry said.

"So why do they call them *beatniks*?" Elwood said.

"Well they used to carry these little drums around," Jerry said, "like bongos, and they used to *beat* on the drum while they were saying their poetry."

"I think you mean *reading* their poetry," Elwood said.

"Naw," Jerry said. "I think some of them were just saying it."

"Like making it up?" Elwood said.

"Naw, like they wrote it before," Jerry said, "like singing a song."

"Well that's the same as reading then," Elwood said.

I had to interrupt them there. "What the hell are you two talking about?" I said. Together, Elwood and Jerry began

156

to inefficiently explain to me that those evil bastards from the Students Activities Committee had planned another theme party in the Bistro. Perhaps they secretly had wanted us to drink. At very least it was a ruse to control our drinking by keeping us on campus. Apparently, the latest concept with which they had come up was *Beatnik Night*. As Elwood and Jerry continued to argue about what a *beatnik* was, I sat there thinking about the stupid idea of a room full of mid-nineties twenty year-olds dressed in black pretending to be Kupferberg and Kerouac. I remembered the *sock hop* theme at my eighth grade dance. That was a blast. I wondered if we would ever be trying to get our children to go to a *grunge* dance. Perhaps in another forty years it would be *Rap Night* at the Bistro, and two asshole descendants of Elwood and Jerry would be arguing about what a *rapper* was.

Nevertheless, I knew I would be there. As always, their vile ruse had worked. People were always looking for a party, and I was always looking for people. I didn't care about the party one way or the other, but I knew enough about myself to know that I would seek the audience. As Elwood and Jerry continued their discussion, I got up, walked back to my sleeping chamber, and began getting dressed for another manic night. When I had finished dressing I bid my friends farewell, walked down the stairs to the ground floor, and headed down the mile drive toward the Gregory Arms. I should've just gotten some sleep, but my mind was restless. I felt like my soul was restless, but I didn't know if that was possible. I was apprehensive about what results another night of partying might bring, so I had decided to skip supper in the refectory and treat myself to a solitary steak dinner in a dark corner of the Greg.

I remember that walk to the Greg as well as I remember my first walk back from the Greg. The days had been getting shorter, and the sky was gray. I walked

157

backwards for a bit, and admired the old manor house up on the hill. Majestically, it presided over the quaint little village below. For the first time, I realized how fleeting my time in England had been. It wouldn't be long before I was packing up and heading back to Indiana, waking up from the dream and getting on with my real life. It seemed unnatural to think that I would never be back here again, and yet I knew that logically that was quite likely. And as I walked on, my mood became very sullen. I thought about Kat and Taylor and Lopez and the rest, and wondered how the goodbyes would go. Would we exchange addresses and promise to stay in touch? Would any of it mean anything in the years to come?

It was early and the pub was still empty when I got there. I ordered my steak and quietly enjoyed it by myself in a dark corner as Andy stood behind the bar and watched the Arsenal game. But then I ordered a Glenfiddich. I drank it slowly as Andy gracefully mourned his team's defeat, and then I ordered another. I was already drunk when I started back up the walk towards the manor. Perhaps I had planned to be. For some reason I had as much dread for the upcoming evening as I did anticipation. Maybe I had known, subconsciously, where I was heading all along. Even now, I'm not sure. Maybe I had known all along that before I stumbled down to the Bistro that night I would feel the need to walk back up to my room and grab my tattered blue notebook.

9:30 PM Thursday (Hour 57:34)

Beatnik Night had been pretty much what I thought it was going to be. The theater majors had seemed to enjoy it the most. They had come in costume and in character. One of them had located an authentic bongo drum, and they took turns on stage reciting parodic verses in a manner of

158

caricature rather than homage. Tuli and Jack wouldn't have liked it, but the patrons in the Bistro that night seemed amused enough by their silly antics. Even Kat had a go at it, and her poem, *Ode to the Jerry Springer Show*, was actually quite clever.

I had noticed her arrival a few minutes before she went on stage, but I had not said anything to her yet. She had come in with her roommate, Sara, and they had been quite striking. They had both been wearing the kind of tight, featureless black pants that stage hands wear during a play. Kat had complimented the pants with a tight striped shirt with the sort of thick black and white horizontal stripes I might have expected to see on a mime. Sara was wearing a simple black top and a ridiculously pretentious beret. They had both been drinking wine and smoking cigarettes through long plastic filters like Raoul Duke or the Penguin.

I had been drinking pilsners one after the other as I listened to all the light-hearted poems and laughter. I chuckled cynically to myself as I thought of another poem I had once heard, something about *liquor before beer* and being *in the clear*. Despite that nugget of colloquial wisdom, my good senses were really nowhere to be found when I gathered up my blue notebook and stumbled up to the stage for my turn. I sat down on the stool, opened my notebook, and mumbled about how I had something to say, and then the silly theater fool behind me began to rap at the taut skin of the bongo as I read away. *"Standing next to Kat on the ferry,"* I said, *"the salt wind teases her black pixie bob as she asks me to take her picture."* I might have slurred the first word, but I quickly fell into rhythm with the drum. I saw Kat's eyes grow wide, but I just continued to read on, *"In all my attempts at photography...my shallow impersonations of Helmut Newton...I know that this is the greatest picture I have ever taken."*

159

"Her short bangs dance like a bird's feathers during flight. The Channel is in the background, the green suds, and the distant outline of France."

"Leaning against the railing of the ferry, she smiles at the camera, and I try to pretend she is smiling at me."

"I think about the coffee she bought me in Paris, and the cigarette we shared with Cyndi Lauper."

"I made it to Notre Dame and the Tower and all the other sights I was there to see, but I wish I could have spent more time with her..."

"And I wish I had that picture, my only masterwork of photography, taken with the not-very-fancy camera that she slipped back into her pocket before she walked away."

The crowd was silent as I closed the notebook, and I began to realize that I had awkwardly ruined the previously jovial collective mood. Then a few people started clapping, and the modest applause helped me feel confident enough to get up off of the stool and return to my seat. As I crossed the room, I looked for Kat's reaction. I wanted to see that same, validating smile that I had seen on her face when I read my short story in class, but I didn't. Her cream colored countenance was flushed and she looked uncomfortable, and when her eyes met mine I realized that I had made a mistake.

I sat down by myself as my inebriated mind struggled for a damage control strategy. My first thought was teleportation. Oh, how sweetly efficient it would have been to *bamf!* like Kurt Wagner and disappear from the room. By the time that I decided to go say something to her it was too late. Futilely, I got up and walked across to where she had been sitting, but I only found Sara and her pretentious beret.

"I wouldn't have done that if I were you," she said and I noticed that she was slurring her words worse than me.

"Where'd she go?" I said.

"Where'd who go?" she said and she chuckled at her own spiteful facetiousness.

"Come on Sara?" I said. "Please."

Mockingly, she put her finger to her lip as if she were contemplating my request. Then she picked up her wine glass and said, "No."

"Why not?" I said.

"Because she doesn't want to see you," she said. "Isn't that obvious? That's why she left. She just wanted to cut loose and relax tonight. Her and I are on our third bottle of wine, and we've been having a great time all night. Not one mention of ex-boyfriends or *current* boyfriends. Then you show up and read that fucking poem in front of everyone! I don't know any other reason why she would've just got up and left, do you?"

I looked at my shoes, the concrete floor, the scarred foot of the table at which she was sitting. I couldn't look her in the eyes; I knew she was right.

I recognized my words when she said set her empty wine glass on the table and said, "You know, maybe you shouldn't dig around for the truth until you're sure you can handle hearing it." She looked up at me and smiled a gleefully vindictive version of her normal perky smile. Then she got up and pushed by me on her way to the bar. "I'm sick of wine," she said. "I'm gonna get a beer."

10:32 PM Thursday (Hour 58:36)

An hour later, I was still in the bistro. I had contemplated going after Kat. I probably should have, but as my mind slowly sobered I found so many ways to talk myself out of it. I didn't know where she was, she probably didn't want to see me; I didn't know what to say if I had found her. In retrospect, I think I was just afraid. How had it all gone so wrong so quickly? That morning we had been kissing, holding hands at the base of the stairs. A few hours later I was drunk, sitting in a booth with three other drunken guys, and Kat was a long way away from me.

"Are you sure you don't want another beer?" Taylor said as he got up to go to the bar.

I shook my head. I never wanted another beer again.

"I'll have a pint," Michael said, "if you're going."

"Ian?" Taylor said to the fourth member of our party.

"Yes, please," Ian said.

"You've got some catching up to do mate," Michael said to me as Taylor walked away.

I shook my head again. "I'm way ahead of you," I said.

"Well I must tell the truth," Michael said, "you're starting to bring the mood down a bit."

"You could always start another fight," I said.

"Thank you, no," Michael said. "I've got nine stitches from the last one!" He pointed to the bandaged cut above his eye and all three of us had a chuckle.

Taylor returned to the table with three pilsners. Then he sat down and said, "So where the hell are you from anyway, Michael."

Michael grinned and said, "Why, I'm from England mate."

"No, where from in England?" Taylor said as we all three laughed again.

"Leeds," Michael said.

"Leeds?" Taylor said. "Everybody keeps saying you're from Liverpool."

"Are you joking mate?" Michael said. "Dirty scousers!"

Michael and Ian were the only ones to laugh that time. Then Ian said, "He's from Leeds. I'm from Liverpool. We met last summer at *Pleasure Beach*. We both worked the *Pepsi Max*. He's been trying to master me accent ever since."

"Oh piss off," Michael said.

"So how did you end up at Harlaxton?" Taylor asked Michael.

Ian answered for him. "It's all part of the master plan."

"Master plan?" Taylor said.

"Right," Ian said, "tell 'im."

Michael took a sip of his beer, smiled a sly smile, and then whispered, "We're here to meet your women."

"And so far it looks promising," Ian added. "They love the accent, mate."

"Ought to be easy enough," I said.

"You know we have pretty good luck with *our* accents in *this* country too, my friend," Taylor said.

"Is that right?" Michael said.

"I wouldn't know," I said.

"He's been hung up on one chick the whole time," Taylor said. "I've done just fine. You know Susie, the bartender from the Blue Pig?"

"Sweet Sue?" Ian said. "She never falls for the Yanks!"

"She did last night," I said.

"Well it's not as simple as all that," Michael said. "Anyone can have a shag. I'm lookin' for one of these birds to fly me out of here."

"What do you mean?" Taylor said.

"Don't tell nobody," Ian said, "but 'e wants to be an American!"

A bit surprised, Taylor and I looked at each other as Michael looked away. "Is this true?" Taylor said. "Are you

163

here searching for some poor unsuspecting lass to marry you away from all this?"

"Look, it's not like that. I wouldn't be with a girl *just* for that alone!" Michael said, "but it's bollocks here, mate. I'm nearly twenty-four years old and the best job I've had since primary school was running the fucking roller coaster with this arsehole!" He nodded at Ian and then said aside, "No offense, mate."

"Oh," Ian said as he shook his head, "none taken."

"Half of me class is still on the dole!" Michael said. "This country, it's old and stagnant. The economy is bollocks, the politicians are a lot of old fools still curtseying every time the royals pass by. There ain't no future for nobody my age *here*. I ain't no gigolo, but if it worked out that I got on with an American girl and the opportunity to move home with her came about, I sure wouldn't mind having that option."

"Marriage is the easiest way to get a visa, you know," Ian said.

"Or being a student," Michael added. "Which is another reason we enrolled here. It'll be a lot simpler now to transfer to Evansville at the end of term."

"So that's the master plan?" Taylor said. "You want to move to the States?"

"Land of opportunity, right?" Michael said as he smiled and raised his bottle.

"Well you should've just said so," Taylor said. "I'll sneak you home in my luggage."

"Hey," Michael said with wide eyes, "that might work for Ian here." He tapped his friend in the chest as he continued. "He certainly won't have to worry about losing any brain cells at high altitude!"

Taylor and I laughed as Ian groaned and said, "Piss off."

"Speaking of *losing brain cells*," Michael continued, "what are you gentlemen doing after they close this place?"

"Not much to do," Taylor said. "Everything around here is closed."

"Michael and Ian's hash bar is always open," Michael said. "Do you smoke?"

"Does the pope shit in the woods?" Taylor said.

"What's that?" Michael said.

"He means *yes*," I said.

"Excellent," Michael said. "We leave immediately!"

"I need a slash first, mate," Ian said.

"What?" Taylor said.

Comically enunciating the last word, Michael said, "He's going to the *bathroom*!"

The four of us chuckled at the silly difference in language as we got up from the table. Michael and Taylor walked out of the Bistro and headed up the steps, but Ian took a left down the short hall to the men's room and I followed him. Another logistical drawback of the Bistro was its limited urinal capacity. There were only two toilets in the place, one in the men's room and one in the ladies' room. Leading me by a few steps as we walked down the hall, Ian slipped into the men's room ahead of me and closed the door behind him. Many times in the past, I had just used the ladies' room, but the yellow light emitting from beneath the door told me that I was going to have to wait.

I wasn't prepared at all when the door opened and Kat's friend Sara staggered out, tripping over the threshold, and stumbling awkwardly into my arms. Instinctively, I put my hands on her shoulders, catching her before she fell. I smelled the alcohol on her breath as she looked up at me and giggled. I made a sour face and her giggling abruptly stopped. There was an uneasy pause as I held her there, her drunken body slouching against mine. By that time the look on her face had grown sour as well. She narrowed her eyes as she said, "Hey Sam, remember when you said that you just never really liked me all that much?"

At the end of her sentence she smiled a strange, twisted smile, and I couldn't tell if she was angry or if she was about to cry. I may have nodded in answer to her question, but I don't remember saying anything. I should have walked away right then, but I was fascinated by her strange expression, held like Lot's wife in a curious trance. The moment was surreal and exhilarating, but I never suspected that I was in any danger. I just couldn't move. I couldn't walk away. I *had* to see what was going to happen next. I certainly never suspected it.

"Do you like this?" she said as she reached up and pressed her lips to mine. Stunned, I stood there motionless as I felt her full lips part and her tongue push into my open mouth. I don't remember exactly what happened next. It is as if there is a piece missing. I remember very well *moment A* and *moment C*, but *moment B* is completely gone. Maybe it was one of those microsleeps about which I had been warned. Maybe it was just my inebriation and my body naturally reacting, but I suddenly felt my hand on the small of her back, her palms on my cheeks, and I realized I was kissing her back.

Friday

Alone in the dark, I was walking downhill through the woods toward the old building that used to be the stable house of the estate. My head was swimming. I had lost track of my buddies. I didn't know if I could remember my way to Michael and Ian's dorm room, and I had no idea what to make of the ladies' room encounter that I had just escaped. At least I had only kissed her...

One thing at the time! As I approached the carriage house I remembered that Michael and Ian lived on the second floor. Surely there would be a light on or a *Wailers* CD playing, I thought as I pulled the large wooden door closed behind me and headed up the steps. Built from stone in the same Jacobethan style as the manor, the carriage house was the second largest building on the estate, and, like the manor, it was used primarily for student housing. The difference was that, for some reason, the American students had priority as far as getting a room in the actual manor house. It was for that reason that most of the non-American students, Michael and Ian included, had found themselves living in the old stables.

Of course, the interior of the old building had been completely renovated, and in 1995 there was no evidence whatsoever that the structure had ever housed animals. The second floor hall was straight and very beige with the same commercial grade carpeting that adorned my own hall up at the manor, and, just as I had suspected, there was audible music coming from one end of it.

"We had just about given up on you," Michael said as he opened the door. Inside I could see Taylor sitting on one of the beds as Ian was unpacking his stash on the back cover of a text book, *Early American Classics* I believe it was.

"I was beginning to get worried myself," I said as he closed the door behind me.

"Where'd you go?" Taylor said.

"I saw 'im snogging a pretty blonde on me way out the loo," Ian said gleefully.

"Blonde?" Taylor said as I sat down on the bed next to him.

"You wouldn't even believe me, brother," I said.

"Well she's not coming here, is she?" Michael asked.

I laughed a little nervously and said, "No, I think I lost her in the woods."

"Brilliant," Michael said and then he locked the door and joined Ian on the other bed. Ian took out a small dark brown chunk of hashish and handed it to Michael. Taylor and I watched curiously as Michael held the rock with a large pair of tweezers over the open flame from his cigarette lighter. I realized that he may have noticed our befuddlement when he asked, "Scored a lot of hash around here, have you?"

"A little here and there," I said. I felt like I was lying because I had never actually bought any. Truth is, I had never even seen hash before I came to England, and I had only smoked it a few times with Ben and Jerry. We had dented an empty beverage can, poked holes in the aluminum, and smoked the entire rock just like we had seen television characters do with crack cocaine. "It's pretty rare back home," I amended. "I've mostly just smoked pot."

"Yeah," Michael said. "We don't get much green around here. I imagine it's about the same though."

"I don't know," I said. "Me and two other guys smoked a whole rock the other night and we just barely caught a buzz."

"A whole nugget in one night," Ian said as he took a pinch of rolling tobacco and began to situate it on a paper. "What for, mate? You can only get *so* high."

171

I looked at Taylor and he nodded his head. "It didn't really do that much for me," he said. "Besides, I miss the smell and feel of that green bud, all tacky and delicious."

"Well that may be," Michael said, "but if you didn't get high smoking this stuff you were doing it wrong."

I watched as Michael put away his cigarette lighter and took out a small pocket knife. Still holding the hash with the tweezers, he proceeded to very skillfully shave off a dozen or so slivers of the nugget from the side to which he had been holding the flame. When he was finished he wrapped the rest of the rock back up and put it away. As he did, Ian took the slivers that he had cut and sprinkled them evenly over the top of the tobacco he had been manipulating. Then, very expertly, he began to role both of the substances up into the same joint. When he was finished he licked it closed, held the finished product out to Taylor, and said, "Honors?"

"Why thank you sir," Taylor said as he put the joint to his lips and lit it. He handed me the joint as he exhaled a small cloud of cigar shop smelling smoke. "That tastes a lot better than the stuff we had," he said as I put the joint to my lips.

"It's the tobacco," Michael said as I drew the smoke into my lungs. "Lovely, isn't it?"

"Yeah," Taylor said. "I like that."

I passed the joint to Michael and he took a long hearty hit from it. Then he gave it to Ian who did the same. Taylor started the rotation a second time, but after my third hit Michael put his hand up and said, "I'm good, mate."

"Are you sure?" I said. I offered the half-burned joint to Ian, but he also passed. I was already buzzing but I was not smart enough to follow their cue.

I handed the joint back to Taylor. He took it from me and said to our hosts, "Do you mind?"

172

"Go right ahead," Ian smiled. "There's plenty more where that come from," he said.

There was music playing in the small dorm room; I think it may have been *Bob Marley*. Ian kicked back on the bed and Michael sat on the floor, leaning against the wall. They both watched with glassy, content eyes as Taylor and I finished the rest of their joint. When it had burned out, Taylor set the roach in an ash tray and Michael said, "Alright, I'm impressed."

"What?" I said. I had no idea what he was talking about.

Michael turned to Ian as he said, "Maybe they did smoke a whole rock in one night."

Ian laughed. Then he said, "It's quite a bit different when you roll it." Then he turned to us and said, "Have you every rolled it?"

"What, hash?" Taylor said.

"Yeah," Ian said. "D' you ever roll it with tobacco?"

"No," I said. "We just smoked it out of a pipe."

Ian laughed. I could have blind folded him with dental floss. Then we were all four laughing. Taylor's perfect hair stayed perfect as he shook back and forth, giggling energetically. I stopped laughing first when I started to think again, and then I said, "What's so funny?"

"Nothing, mate" Ian said in a high voice as he wiped a tear from the corner of his eye. "It should be an interesting night."

"I know what you're talking about man," Taylor said. He looked Ian rather dramatically in the eyes and said, "I am very high."

All four of us began laughing again and then Ian said, "Well you two have smoked quite a lot of hash just now."

Taylor raised his arms in exasperation. "Why didn't you tell us, man?" he said.

Ian was still laughing. "You were just going on 'bout smoking a whole rock in one night, mate," he said. "I suspected you knew what you were doing."

"I have some peanuts," Michael said. "You fellows want some peanuts?"

"Peanuts?" I said.

"Yeah," Michael answered. "That's one thing that's good for you right now."

"I'm okay," I said. My peripheral vision was almost completely gone, and I didn't see how peanuts were going to help.

"Really?" Ian said. He sat up as if he was trying to get a closer look at me.

"Probably," Taylor said. "He's some kind of mutant."

"What, like an *X-Man*?" Ian laughed.

"Well he can handle himself just fine in a scrap," Michael said.

I nodded toward him and said, "Thank you sir. You didn't do too bad yourself."

"Except for these," he said as he pointed at his stitches.

"Yeah, how'd that happen?" I said.

"He might've caught me coming in," Michael said. "I never even felt it."

"Well that was a big fucking dude," I said, "and you had him pretty much all to yourself. Where'd you learn that arm lock thing you were doing on him?"

"My dad was a *jiu-jitsu* instructor in the Royal Navy," he said. "I got me first black belt when I was eleven."

"No way!" Taylor said. "You're a ninja?"

Michael laughed, "Right, just like Chuck Norris."

"A ninja and an *X-Man*!" Ian laughed. Then he looked at me and said to Taylor, "So what's his secret power anyways?"

174

Taylor chuckled and said, "Well for one thing, he doesn't need sleep."

"Doesn't need sleep?" Ian said.

"Nope," Taylor answered. Then he turned to me and said, "Samuel, what's the count?"

"Like seventy-two hours," I said.

"Can't be," Taylor said.

I looked at my watch for a long moment and then said, "Sixty-two? Fuck, I don't know. I can't even do the math anymore."

"Sixty-two hours?" Ian said. "You've been awake for sixty-two hours?"

"I told you about that," Michael said to him.

"Yeah," I said. "Something like that."

"What for?" Ian said.

"Why does everyone keep asking that?" I said.

"Christ mate," Ian laughed. "You really are an *X-Man*."

"I don't feel like one," I said.

"I don't feel all that well either," Taylor said. "Do you still have that bottle on you?"

"Yeah," I said as I reached into my jacket pocket and produced the little brown bottle labeled *Liquid Karma Room Odorant*.

"I need to wake up a little," Taylor said as I handed it to him.

Taylor took it, unscrewed the lid, and inhaled the fumes deeply. As he did, I noticed Michael shoot a strange look at Ian. Then he said to us, "What you blokes doing with that?"

"Taylor got it at some head shop in Grantham," I said. "It's called rush."

"It's called a popper," Michael said. "What are *you* doing with it?"

Ian laughed and said to me, "Playing for the other team are you?"

"What?" I said. Coming down from his rush, Taylor was listening now too.

"That shite's for poofters, mate!" Michael said.

"*Poof dubs*?" I said.

"Yeah," Michael said. "Homos, what you call 'em, faggots."

"I don't call them that," I said.

"This shit's for homos?" Taylor said as he held up the bottle.

"Yeah," Ian said. He was laughing almost hysterically now. "It loosens up the muscles 'round their arseholes so they can bugger one another!"

"Holy shit!" Taylor said. "I did not know that."

"I told you it was going to be an interesting night," Ian said as his laughing began to come under control.

Michael straightened his face facetiously and then said, "Is there something you two would like to tell us?"

Our hosts erupted again in laughter and I began to laugh with them. Even though I was the butt of the joke, I still genuinely enjoyed the coincidence of the situation. Foolishness was just funny to me even if I was the fool. However, as I took the bottle back from Taylor and put it in my jacket I noticed that he was not laughing.

"How the hell was I supposed to know that stuff was for fags?" he said. His face was a little flushed.

"Everybody knows that, mate," Michael said.

"Well I didn't," he said. "Did you know that, Sam?" he asked me.

"Nope," I giggled.

"Where did you say you got it?" Ian said.

"That shop on Newton Street," Taylor said, "the one with the all the glass pipes and incense."

"Oh, I wouldn't go in there," Ian said and he winked at Michael.

"Yeah," Michael said, "did you get any telephone numbers?"

"You could do quite well with your American accent in that place!" Ian teased.

"Like I said," Taylor scoffed. "I took the bartender from the Blue Pig home last night."

"Old Stanly?" Michael said.

"Who's Stanly?" Taylor said. "Fucking Susie. That hot bartender from the Blue Pig, *Sweet Sue* I think you called her!"

"Right," Ian laughed, "did you shag her proper or did you put it in her tea towel holder you fucking poofter?"

Michael and Ian erupted with laughter again, and I could tell that my roommate was becoming uneasy. We were all high but Taylor was becoming uncharacteristically agitated by their ribbing. I remember deciding that it would be a good idea to get him out of there, but then my mutant powers failed me as a second, more intense, wave of the hash buzz came over me. I looked down at my hands and realized that they were numb. A strange cousin of grogginess began to set in and I made the mistake of closing my eyes. My equilibrium failed completely as I did. In the darkness created by my eyelids, I was thrust into a different dimension where I was held suspended in space as the sum of all existence spun violently around me. I could hear Taylor raising his voice, but I could no longer make out every word of the conversation. I was only getting snippets here and there every time they spun by me.

"...Audrey the night before..." I heard Taylor say.

"...classic overcompensating..." I think that was Ian's voice.

"...nineteen sixty-six, blonde on blonde..." I heard Michael's voice from the floor.

177

"…Alyssa with the curly hair…" Taylor's voice again.

"…he takes himself so seriously…" I think that was somebody singing, "…he brags of his misery, he likes to live dangerously…"

"…they kept me up past the dawn…" Dr. Wallace? That sounded like a Scottish accent. All the words began to melt into an unintelligible cacophony. I was very dizzy and the threat of nausea was imminent. I knew I needed to open my eyes, but the centrifugal force of the spinning universe was holding them shut. Then I heard Kat's voice. "…I don't want to be a *girlfriend*…" she said. Urgently, I opened my eyes and looked around the room, but she was nowhere to be seen.

The panic had temporarily calmed my trip, and the light in the room began to reveal the strangeness within. No fanfare was made of my return to reality. It was as if none of them had even realized I had been gone. Michael was diligently sorting through his small collection of compact discs. He seemed oblivious to the rest of us. Ian had quit teasing Taylor about the amyl nitrite and the two of them were deep in some sort of profound-ish, THC-induced conversation about sexuality. Taylor was visibly distraught, perhaps near the point of breaking down, and I listened as Ian looked at him intently and compassionately like some sort of pothead therapist.

"You know I think it was my mom," Taylor said. Ian closed his eyes and nodded his head as if he actually felt the other's pain. Jesus, how long had I been gone?

"I mean, nothing was ever good enough for her, you know," Taylor went on. "It was like by omission, man. She never said anything all those years that I was on the Honor Roll every semester. Nothing, not 'good job', not 'fuck you', nothing! Then the work got harder and I just didn't work that hard anymore, and then she was pissed all the time because I was an average student. What's wrong with being average, right? I mean, she didn't seem to give a shit when I was above average!"

I watched the three of them like I wasn't even in the room. Michael kept studying his CD covers, and Taylor kept talking as Ian listened and nodded.

"So it's that validation, you know," Taylor said. "That feeling that this woman wants me, this woman loves me, you know? And I'm good at it, too. I mean, it's easy for me so I can get it pretty much whenever I want it. It's like I'm trying to make up for not having that approval from my mom, man."

"Right," Ian said, "because you don't think your mum loved you."

"No. I mean, I know my mom loved me," Taylor said. "It's just like she never told me she loved me, man. She never showed it."

"So you want all these women to love you?" Ian said.

"Yeah, sort of," Taylor said. "at least to act like they love me, you know? That moment when their defenses melt away and they become totally giving. It's like they just want to take care of me, to please me, like nothing could make them happier than to do whatever I want them to do. I'm fucking addicted to it!"

"You're talking about sex, mate," Ian said somberly, "and it ain't the same as love."

Taylor shrugged his shoulders and said, "Its close enough."

Even considering the drugs and alcohol we had consumed, I was surprised that Taylor was speaking that frankly in front of us. He had always been very observant of others, but I had never known him to say anything that betrayed reflective thinking of his own. Then I remembered that he couldn't see me, and with that realization the portal to the other dimension opened again.

2:37 AM Friday (Hour 62:41)

My eyes focused on the mildew stains in the grout of the tile floor on which my head was resting. I remember noticing at that very moment that the light was on and thinking that odd because it had been so dark just a few seconds ago. I wondered where my friends had gone. How long had I been there? I tried to locate my watch. It should have been on the end of my arm, but I couldn't find that either.

My mind began to function before my body, and it slowly started to come back to me. I remembered the room spinning, and I remembered Taylor talking to Ian about women. I remembered that horrible wave of nausea and the feeling that my legs were made of jelly when I got up to leave. The hallway had been swaying back and forth as the entire carriage house threatened to list to one side or the other. I knew something was wrong; I had had too much, and I didn't want anyone to see me like that. I had been near a state of panic as I made my escape from Ian and Michael's room, and I had been quite relieved when I found that tiny lavatory at the end of the hall and locked myself inside it.

When I first closed the door I had been glad just to be in hiding. I had leaned forward resting my head against the inside of the door and tried to breathe deeply, hoping the sickness would pass. But it hadn't, and it wasn't long before I was on my knees, pressing my sweaty forehead against the toilet seat in preparation for an explosive purge that never came. I remembered from the few times I had overdosed on alcohol the immediate relief that came with vomiting, getting that evil substance out of your belly. But the hash was already in my blood. I had knelt there waiting for some time, hoping, praying, until I felt the very sudden signs of an impending emergency evacuation of the bowels. Moving quickly, utilizing energy that I did not know was still in me, I had clambered off of the floor, dropped my pants, and spun around and down to a sitting position on the throne. Again I had waited, and again nothing happened.

At that point I was still dizzy and nauseous but I was struggling with consciousness, and I was quite content to sit there and rest. Then I suddenly felt like I was going to throw up again. Without taking the time to pull up my pants, I had jumped off the toilet and back down to my position of worship in front of the device. I labored for a bit, even stuck my fingers in my throat trying to expedite the process, but nothing happened. Giving up, I had gone back to resting, laying my head on the white plastic seat and trying to catch my breath. I was startled once by a knock at the door, but I did not respond and whoever it was eventually went away. Then I was urgently clambering to be back in a sitting position on the toilet, but still nothing came out of that end either. I sat there for a while and then I had to get back on the floor again because I felt like I was going to throw up. With the rhythm of an Irish reel, the cycle had been repeated several times, but I had had no idea, until I finally found my watch on the end of my arm, that I had been in there for nearly two hours.

Lying there on the cold tile floor, I realized how ridiculous I must have looked. What devious forces could have brought this all-American kid across the Big Pond to his ethnic homeland only to have him kneeling before a filthy fucking toilet with his pants around his ankles, bare ass in the air, praying to whatever gods might be listening to rid his system of some horrible drug that those assholes from Liverpool had promised him would be better than any pot he had ever smoked back in the States? Good Lord what had gone wrong?

2:56 AM Friday (Hour 63:00)

The cold November air felt good on my face as I staggered out of the carriage house dorms. The nauseous, sick feeling had gone away, and that had allowed me to pull my pants up, exit my tiny hideout, and make a push for my room on the third floor of the manor. My peripheral vision was still gone, but I could see far enough in front of me to make walking possible. I had the course memorized, out the carriage house, uphill through a small tract of woods, through the gates of the manor, and up the steps to my bed, and I was gambling that would be enough. Whatever end might have come to Taylor or Michael or Ian was irrelevant at that point. I was in survival mode; I just needed to keep walking. I thought that if I could make it to my bed that everything would be alright.

Initially, the cold air had given me a jolt, but that had worn off by the time I reached the woods. It had rained recently or perhaps the dew was very heavy. The moonlight became shrouded as I entered the woods and the trees made a sound like faint applause as they swayed in the wind. The small section of woods was just wide enough to have a point in the center at which neither the lights from the carriage house nor those from the manor could be seen, and that is where I realized that I was still very high. For some reason, I assumed that I was probably being followed so I decided to limit my exposure by standing quietly still until I was able to identify my pursuer. After a moment I crouched down into a more tactical position, but all I ever heard was the trees.

When I was satisfied that I was alone I stood up to continue my trek, but the world began spinning again as I did.

But I didn't feel dizzy or sick this time. My stance seemed very steady; it was everything else that was moving. I looked around the near horizon and saw the terrain in a very different way than I had ever seen it before. All of the straight lines disappeared as I noticed how the limits of my vision curved the edges of the only small, flat piece of the earth that I could visually verify existed at that moment. I watched in gleeful awe as the trees began to rotate around me, gaining speed, until each of them blended with the others into a spherical, revolving cocoon that held me aloft in whatever dimension we were floating. And as I floated in the spinning bubble of trees I suddenly became aware of the curvature of the earth, and the two spheres became one. The spinning stopped and I could see myself standing there among the trees.

I started walking again, and before long the lights from the front of the manor came into view. Thinking about the illusions of up and down that gravity created on our spherical planet, I laughed to myself as I completed the steepest part of the uphill journey. I thought about how the world *did* look flat if one was too close to it. It was easy to visualize my current trip as a finite line on a two-dimensional map, *point A* to *point B*, but the surface of the planet did not begin at the carriage house and it did not end at the manor. I thought about the fact that if I would have been able to keep walking indefinitely on my present course, through the poles and over the oceans, I would quickly pass the manor and eventually end up back at the carriage house, and I wondered if the same principle could be applied to how we thought about our time in this world. Perhaps if our lives were longer, we would see the curvature of time.

Bullshit or not, it was the mental stimulation of this new idea, this cyclical view of time, which pulled me back to reality as I emerged from the woods and continued up the drive to the manor gates, and by the time I reached the front door I was actually feeling much better. While I had been wise to be apprehensive about the evening, I had not foreseen how bad it was really going to be. I was going to have to put some work into fixing things with Kat, but all things considered I had come out of the storm in pretty good shape. I made a mental note to never again smoke hash with Michael and Ian and headed for the service stairs. As I walked up the steps I decided that the experiment was over. The risk of self destructive behavior had gotten too great. I felt confident that I had made it through the worst of it, but I knew better than to press my luck any further. As I turned the corner and walked toward the ever open door to Room 333, I was looking forward to finally getting some sleep.

3:16 AM Friday (Hour 63:20)

I was amazed that night by the human body's ability to heal itself, to rid itself of infection or poison. Back in the carriage house bathroom I was so deathly nauseated and dizzily ill that I had contemplated suicide by drowning myself in that old toilet. I had almost given up hope that I would ever make it out of there. A few hours later I had sauntered up the service stairwell with the enthusiasm of a prison escapee who had vowed to turn his life around if he could just make it to the border. I had been awake for sixty-three hours straight, and my recent adventures had convinced me that it was time to pack it in. I wasn't thinking about why I had done it; I was just ready to get it over with, to sleep for eighteen or twenty hours and then try to get back to the normal routine of my life. To sleep, ay, there's the rub...

Then the search lights came up and I heard the dogs barking behind me as I entered the Vortex only to find that the Big Chair had been usurped and was still occupied by Kat's perky roommate, Sara. Perhaps we should have closed the door to our room as a matter of regular practice.

She was still dressed in her *beatnik* garb from the party earlier, her black top slightly disheveled, her tight black pants clinging to her fit body, but her silly beret was nowhere to be found. She had Elwood's guitar across her lap and she smiled at me nervously as I walked in the room. I wanted to ask her what she was doing there, but my brain couldn't get the message out of my mouth. I was too stunned, too disappointed, for I knew immediately what was to come.

She held the guitar out to me and said, "I just wanted to hear you play."

"I don't play," I said. "That's Dan's."

"Oh," she said as she awkwardly set it down against the wall beside her. A good deal of her earlier boldness had vanished, but it hadn't gone away completely. She was still there.

"It's three in the morning," I said as I idly leaned against the desk close to where she was sitting. "What are you doing here?"

She smiled at my question, and shifted her weight in the chair. Then she looked up at me and said, "I just wanted to come tell you that I was sorry." Maybe I was still high, but I swear she even batted her eyelids. "I was just a mean ol' bitch to you earlier," she said. Then she paused and her smile went away. She uncrossed her legs and leaned forward in the chair, resting her elbows on her parted knees and said, "I'm not mean."

I narrowed my eyes and cocked my head to one side. "How long have you been sitting here?" I said.

"I don't know," she said. "Everybody else is asleep, and I just wanted to talk to somebody. I was too drunk to

185

sleep. I've been sitting here getting sober, thinking about what happened between us earlier."

"Which part?" I said.

She smiled nervously and said, "All of it, fighting with you, kissing you…"

"So what do you want?" I said.

"I want to know what you want," she said.

"What are you talking about?" I said.

"We were drunk earlier, but you kissed me back," she smiled. "I know you liked it."

"Sara," I said as I closed my eyes and shook my head. "I think you should go."

Her grin returned when I told her to leave. She stood up and slowly walked over to me. Looking me in the eyes the whole time, she smiled as she prowled right up into my comfort zone. Her full lips were very close to mine when she said, "Are you sure?"

I was the one that was nervous at that point. Certain parts of my body were beginning to respond to her in ways I didn't want. "Sara, come on," I said. "We were drunk earlier, like you said. We weren't thinking straight."

"Oh, I was thinking straight," she said as she began running her fingers along the sides of my torso. "Do you know how long I've wanted to kiss you?"

"What?" I said.

"Since the first time I ran my fingers through your hair," she said as she raised her hands and did it again.

"You took me to meet Kat that night," I said. I tried to back away from her, but I had pinned myself against the desk and there was nowhere to go.

Sara closed her fingers lightly as she wove them into my long hair. She made an exaggeratedly pouty face and said, "I didn't know you were never coming back."

"Sara," I said as I closed my fingers around her wrists and gently forced her hands away from my head. "We've never even gotten along…"

"I know!" she said, and her eyes grew wide. "I guess it's probably unhealthy that that turns me on so much. Do you have any idea what I did to myself back in my room, under the covers, after we fought in the writing lab that day?"

My jaw dropped wide open as my mind constructed a visual image of what she had just described. I had never in my wildest dreams imagined that Sara would be attracted to me. She had always reminded me of my ex-girlfriend back in Paradise, Indiana, one of those all-American, vacuous, cheerleader types from which I had tried to distance myself. In truth, I had always been rather rude to her. I had never liked her and the fact that I had kissed her in the Bistro had not changed that. I wanted to tell her to get the fuck out of my room and stay the fuck out of my life, but it was too late. Her boldness had prevailed, and I stood there like Hamlet doing nothing as she unfastened my pants.

When she had freed the evil appendage, she held it in her manicured hand, smiled up at me, and said, "Now you like me, don't you?" I didn't answer her, at least not with words. But over the course of the next hour or so, I regretfully told her everything that she had wanted to hear.

4:26 AM Friday (Hour 64:30)

Staring into the darkness between my bed and the ceiling of my dorm room, I was vexed by the thin film of sweat in all of the places where Sara's naked body was touching mine. The single bed was really too small for us now that we were lying next to each other, and I was surprised at how quickly she had fallen asleep. I had heard Taylor return to the room before we were finished, but, respectfully, he had paid no attention to the commotion behind the hanging curtain door of my sleeping chamber. Now I could hear him moving around out there as I tried to get to sleep, and, for some reason, that only added to my anxiety. My body temperature began to rise, beads of sweat from my forehead trickled excruciatingly down my temples, and Sara's sweet smell festered on me.

The first clothes I found on the floor in the dark were my gym shorts, and I threw them on as I hopped out of bed. Sara barely stirred. The contentment I saw in her sleeping face mocked me as she rolled over and conquered the rest of my bed. Surrendering my room, I slipped around the hanging curtain door and joined Taylor in the common area of the Vortex.

"Got a fag?" I said as I sat in the vacant lounge chair. Recently, Taylor had taken to sitting on the oversized window sill. It occurred to me that I hadn't seen him in the Big Chair for days.

"They're called cigarettes," he said as he picked up the pack next to him and handed me one.

"Thanks," I said. "Got a light?"

"Yeah," he said as he tossed me his Zippo. "Do you want me to smoke it for you too?"

"No, I got it." I said as I inhaled and tossed the lighter back to him.

We sat there smoking in silence for a minute or two, and then he said, "Fuck, dude, what a night, huh?"

"Yeah," I said.

"How badly did that shit tear you up, man?" he said as he crushed out his cigarette.

"Pretty bad," I said. I took the final drag from mine and half-smiled at him.

"Dude, I got fucking lost on the way back to the manor," he said. "I think I was half way to the Greg before I realized I was going the wrong way."

I thought about my trip in the woods between the manor and the carriage house and said, "Yeah, I got lost too."

"I have to be honest," Taylor said, "the way you looked when you bailed out of Michael's room I didn't know if we were ever going to see you again!"

"Yeah," I said. "I was pretty bad."

"But when you're bad you're still good my brother," Taylor said as he motioned toward my sleeping chamber.

"I don't know about that," I said as I shook my hanging head.

"Who's the lucky girl?" Taylor said.

"Man…" I said still shaking my head.

"C'mon," he said. "This is Harlaxton. Everyone's going to find out sooner or later."

"Sara," I said and waited for his response.

"Sara Walters?" Taylor said.

My face contorted, and I inhaled deeply.

"As in..Kat's roommate?" Taylor asked.

"Fraid so," I said.

"Nicely done my friend!" Taylor grinned. "She's a gymnast or something, isn't she?"

"I don't know," I said, "fucking cheerleader probably."

"She's fucking built," he said. "I've been watching *her* walk up and down the halls since the first week of school, man, I can tell you that. How was it, brother?"

I nodded my head slowly. "She's fuckin' built," I echoed.

"That's it?" Taylor said. "Dude just got laid and you look like you just lost your best friend."

"I think I might have," I said. "Kat's gonna find out."

"What?" Taylor laughed.

"I don't know, man," I said.

"Wow," he said, "are you really worried about how what you just did might affect the never ending saga of you and the imaginary love of your life?"

"Maybe she won't say anything," I said. "I mean, she and Kat *are* friends..."

"You're not even listening to me," Taylor said. "Hell, I thought you were getting on with it."

"God damn it, man, I've fucked it up for good now," I said.

"I don't like your tone, Thompson," Taylor said. I raised an eyebrow at him and he continued, "It seems to me that you are failing, my friend, failing to recognize, as you've done so many times this semester, that you are in fucking England, man." He produced two more cigarettes and we took turns lighting them as he went on. "When are you going to be back here? When are you going to be in another situation like this, man? You have just bedded a bona fide hottie, one of the hottest hotties here, and you are simply refusing to enjoy it!" He took a drag from his Camel, shrugged his shoulders, and said, "Why?"

I had never been comfortable using my size to intimidate others, but at that moment I looked at Taylor as hard as I could look at him.

"What?" he said. If he felt at all bullied he certainly didn't show it. "You didn't think about that before you brought her up here?" he said as he nodded toward my bed chamber.

"I didn't bring her up here," I said.

"What do you mean?" he said.

"She was here waiting for me, man," I said. "It was an ambush!"

"Sweet," he said, "ambush pussy."

"I'm not kidding, man!" I said.

"Listen all of y'all this is sabotage," he sang.

"Dude, she just wasn't backing down!" I said.

"That's fucking ninja and you don't even know it man," Taylor said.

"It's not fucking ninja!" I said. "What the fuck does that even mean?"

"Maybe you're right," he said. "A ninja could've gotten away from her."

"You're still high," I said.

"I'm going to try staying awake from now on," Taylor said as he hopped off of the window sill and started doing some sort of strange solo-waltz around the room. He stopped by my sleeping chamber and pulled the curtain open. He peeked in at Sara's sleeping form and then winked at me and said, "It's working for you."

"Fuck it, knock yourself out, dude," I said to him. "I wish *I* could get some sleep."

"You wish," Taylor said and he stopped dancing. "You wish that artsy little head case loved you as much as you love her."

"Be careful, man," I said as my eyes narrowed at him.

"What, are you going to kick my ass now?" Taylor said. "Dude, I'm trying to help you."

"I don't need any help," I said.

"I think you do, my friend," he said. "You've been pining over that bitch since you got here. It's run its course, man. You've got a brick shithouse lying in your bed right now, and it's time to move on." Taylor walked back toward his window sill and softened his tone as he said, "Haven't you gotten sick of it yet?"

"No," I said.

"Well I have," Taylor said. "She's playing games with you, man."

"You don't know what she's been through, man," I said. "She's not playing games."

"She may not know it," he said, "and you obviously can't see it, but you're wasting precious time, man. Days like these don't last forever. Whether you know it or not you made a breakthrough tonight."

"What the fuck are you talking about?" I said.

Then he smiled and said, "First day of the rest of your life, brother."

5:38 AM Friday (Hour 65:42)

I was sitting on the stone steps in front of the manor by the circle drive, smoking a cigarette, drinking a cup of coffee from the faculty break room, and waiting for the refectory to open. I couldn't remember how long I had been awake, but at that point my body was operating in some sort of weird limbo in which I no longer felt tired at all. In fact, I felt like I could barely remember what it was like to sleep, and it seemed like a lie to tell myself that I would eventually sleep again. I certainly didn't feel like I was in any danger from not sleeping. The only danger I felt was of losing Kat forever.

Apparently, participating in the poetry reading had not been the best idea. For that matter, getting drunk on evil scotch before I went had not been a very good idea either, and my decision making had gotten markedly worse after that. As the sun rose over my shoulder, I knew that I should be thinking about damage control, but I just didn't know where to begin. I was afraid that it was all futile at that point. The game was going be over as soon a she found out about Sara, and I knew that moment was coming.

Yet, despite all the bullshit that I had created for myself, my thoughts were still periodically drifting to that spherical model of time that I had seen in the woods when I was stoned. For the first time in my life, I wished that I had studied more science and math.

As the November morning chilled by bones, I thought about geometry, lines and segments, and how far away I'd have to be to see the true nature of existence. I was fascinated by the idea that walking a short distance on the surface of the earth might commonly be perceived as a line from A to B, while it was actually a segment of an infinite loop that traced one series of points around the circumference of the sphere. Somewhere in the woods it had occurred to me that time might share the same properties as distance. I wondered if this might make a relatively short measurement of time appear to be a finite line with a beginning and an end when, in actuality, it was an unperceivable segment of a similarly infinite loop. Then I realized that one person's lifespan was, indeed, a relatively short measurement of time.

At first, it had seemed like Taylor had made a good point when he talked about wasting time. Now I wasn't so sure. In 1995, we were fairly certain that the earth was a sphere, and that pretty much proved the model of three-dimensional distance on which my thoughts were based. As I finished my coffee, I wondered if the same could be true for time. If any distance that appeared as a straight line was actually a segment in a series of points that made up a loop around the planet, then could any measure of time actually be, rather than a line with a beginning and an end, a segment in a series of points on some cosmic-sized loop around a yet-unrecognized spherical realm of existence? I wondered if living was the same as walking. If we could travel forward through time, eons and eons past the moment of our death, would we eventually end up back where we started? Would we have a chance to do it again, to do it differently?

Because there is more than one loop around the surface of the earth. In fact, there are an infinite amount of loops. Every loop represents a different path around the earth, and together they all make up the three-dimensional sphere. But check this out, the loops are made up of individual points on the surface of the sphere, and every one of those individual points is also part of a number of other loops that all intersect at that same spot. Facing in one direction you are on the way to Edinburgh, face the other way and you're headed to London. Pivot again you're pointed at Dublin. You didn't have to move; the same spot was on all three courses.

And if time worked the same way, then each individual moment was a component of multiply histories represented by their respective loops around the realm. I tried to understand it. If time had no beginning or end, then what did that mean? Did we live the same lives over and over again? Could that explain *déjà vu* or reincarnation? And what about the other loops? Were we living parallel lives simultaneously, traveling different paths around the sphere and feeling that strange familiarity every time the lines intersected? I thought about that night at the Gregory Arms all those weeks ago, meeting Kat, and how I felt like I had known her all along. Maybe on one of those other loops, one that happened to intersect with that moment in time, we really were soul mates. Maybe there was an alternate dimension where Kat and I had gotten it right.

6:27 AM Friday (Hour 66:31)

I had wanted to eat breakfast alone that morning. Not only did I want to avoid another grilling from the nurses about my insomnia, I didn't want to see Sara and I certainly wasn't ready to face Kat. I was systematically scanning the room the entire time that I was eating; I needed to get in and get out. The refectory had been empty when I got there, but the long cafeteria tables were beginning to fill up as I finished my meal. I lowered my eyes in order to mop up some yellow egg juice with my last bit of ham, and when I raised them I saw Elwood sitting down at the table across from me.

"Hey Sammy," he said cheerfully as he settled into place, "morning, buddy."

"Good Lord, Elwood?" I said, "what the hell are you doing up this early?"

"What, man?" he said. "Maybe I got things to do."

"Yeah, sorry," I said. "I didn't mean anything by it. I've just never seen you out of bed at this hour."

"No, I know," he said. Then he looked to both side as if he was checking for eavesdroppers and said, "Hey listen, don't tell nobody this, but I'm kinda tryin' to turn over a new leaf."

"Oh yeah?" I said.

"Yeah," he said as he started in on his eggs. "I been thinking about tryin' to cut down on the drinking lately, ya know?"

"Really?" I said. "I never thought I'd hear that coming from you."

"Yeah, I don't know," he said. "I just got to thinkin' about it, you know? We're not gonna be here dat much longer, and I've wasted a lot of time so far. I mean, there'll be plenty of time to tie one on whenever I get back to Chicago. I guess I figure maybe I'll try growing up for awhile. See what that's like."

"Interesting," I said. "Let me know what you think."

"Sammy, you're a nut," he laughed. "D'you get any sleep yet?"

"Not yet," I said.

"Jesus, man, how long you been up now?" he said.

I looked at my watch and said, "Almost sixty-seven hours."

"What are you doin'?" he said.

"I don't know," I said. "I was going to get some sleep last night, but something came up."

"You go out with Taylor and the Brits?" he asked.

"Yeah, for a little while," I said.

"Don't you have that play tonight?" he said.

"Yep," I said.

He shook his head as he took a drink of his juice. Then he cut another piece of egg and said, "Listen, Sammy, I ain't tryin' to tell you your business or nothing, but you ain't lookin' so good."

"Yeah?" I said.

"Yeah," he said. "I mean, it was funny at first and all, but we're startin' to worry about you."

"You and your pet mouse?" I asked.

"See, just like dat right there," he said as he pointed his fork at me. "You ain't got no reason to be gettin' sassy with me. I'm just tryin' to help, buddy."

"Everybody's trying to help these days," I said.

"You ain't even been getting' along with Taylor last couple days," he said, "and you guys are thick as thieves."

"Thick as thieves," I echoed as I gathered up my tray and got up to leave.

"Hey look," he said, "like I said, I ain't trying to tell you your business."

"I'm sorry, Dan," I said. "I guess I *am* wearing pretty thin."

"Hey, don't worry about it, buddy," he said. "Just get some sleep, would ya'."

"Yeah, maybe I should do that," I said. "I don't know though. I'm liable to sleep for two days, and Lopez will fucking kill me if I don't show up for the play."

"Don't worry about it," he said. "I'm sure Lydia will wake you up in time for the play."

"Yeah, I guess I will," I said as I turned to go. "Was anybody up in the room when you came down?"

"Just Taylor and your girlfriend," he said.

"Shit," I said. "Sara's still up there?"

"Sara?" Elwood said. "Who's Sara?"

8:04 AM Friday (Hour 68:08)

Elwood was right; what was I doing? I started up the service stairs two at the time, but my legs were heavy and I had to slow down before I reached the third floor. My mind was groggy and I couldn't get my thoughts straight. What the fuck was she doing in my room with Taylor? No more drugs, no more drinking! The nurses were right; I was starting to lose control. Shit was getting ugly, and I needed to clear my head. I needed to fall back, to regroup. I needed sleep, but now there was no time. The gods in heaven didn't know what Taylor might be saying to her at that very moment. Based on our previous conversation, I feared he might have taken it upon himself to *help* me end my relationship by telling her about Sara. Or much worse…

I slowed my pace before the open door to the Vortex came into sight. I didn't want to appear as anxious as I was, but I had broken a light sweat jogging up the steps and there was going to be no way to hide that. As I rounded the last corner I saw Taylor perched on his window sill and Kat sitting in the Big Chair below him. I think she was talking and he was listening, but they halted their conversation when they saw me approaching. Trying to hide my heavy breath, I walked into the room as nonchalantly as I could. Kat looked up at me, her ice blue eyes piercing me through her glasses. Taylor watched from the window sill, but he said nothing.

"Hey," I said to her.

"Hey," she said back. She looked at the floor after she spoke. My guts were churning. I couldn't tell if she knew yet. What had that bastard told her? I looked at Taylor, but he just turned and looked out the window.

"So what's going on?" I said.

"What you mean?" she said. "Nothing's going on."

"I know, I know," I said. "I just mean what's up, you know, hello."

"Oh," she said, "nothing really."

"I'm gonna go get a cup of tea," Taylor said as he leapt down from the window sill. "Anybody want anything?"

"No, I'm good," I said as I stepped to the side so he could pass me on his way out of the room. "Do you want anything?" I asked Kat.

"No, thank you," she said.

There was a release of tension as Taylor extracted himself, but the confrontation was still palpably awkward. I tried to smile at her as Taylor disappeared down the hall, but I don't think I pulled it off. Finally, she spoke.

"I was actually looking for you…" she said but I cut her off.

"Listen, Kat, about the poem thing," I said. "I shouldn't have done that. I mean, I shouldn't have read it like that. I was drunk and I didn't think about it embarrassing you."

"I don't know why it did," she said as she shook her head. "I was drunk too. I'm just not always comfortable with that kind of stuff being out there like that."

"No, I understand," I said. "I mean I obviously didn't, but I do now. I'm sorry. That was presumptuous of me. I wish I could undo it."

"It's not that big of a deal," she said. Then she paused for a moment. Then she said, "I'm sorry that I stormed out of there like that."

"Oh, no, you don't have to be sorry," I said, and I reached forward and placed my palm on her bended knee. "I probably would've done the same thing if I were you. How embarrassing, some drunken idiot blubbering on stage about you. I'm the one that's sorry. Really, I'm sorry."

She looked up at me and smiled. I tried to smile back at her, but I wasn't able.

"It was good," she said after a moment.

"What?" I said.

"The poem," she said. "I thought it was good."

"Really?" I said.

"Yeah," she said.

"Thank you, Kat," I said. My smile came back.

"I wish you wouldn't have read it in front of everyone," she said, "but I thought it was good."

"I'm sorry," I said.

"Apology accepted," she said, and she smiled as she stood up from the Big Chair. "I just wanted to let you know that I know I overreacted last night. With the play and all...I didn't want anything to be weird between us today," she said as she took hold of my hand with hers.

"Don't worry about it," I said.

"So are we cool?" she said. She was absently moving my hand around with hers.

"Nothing's weird," I said.

"Good," she said as she passed me and headed for the door. She was still holding onto my hand, or maybe I was holding on to her. Our arms pulled tight between us as she moved away from me, and then I let go of her. "I've got some things to do before the play," she said as she backed into the hallway. "I'll see you there, okay?"

"Yeah, I'll see you there," I said.

"Goodbye, Sam," she said and I didn't like the way that it sounded. I was going to say something else to her, but my mind wandered off for a second. By the time I had formulated a response, she was gone.

9:16 AM Friday (Hour 69:20)

After talking to Kat, I had crawled into bed for a few minutes and tried to get to sleep. I knew that those few hours before the play would be my only chance. I remember how wonderful my bare, aching feet had felt when I moved them back and forth between the sheets, but my mind had been reeling and I never really got close to falling asleep. I knew I was going to eventually quit trying and get back up, but I procrastinated. I dreaded the rest of the morning, wandering around in my insomniac limbo, thinking about Kat and worrying about Sara. The fear drove my heart rate, and the bed became uncomfortable when I started to sweat. It was quarter past nine when I gave up and moved to the Big Chair.

The sweat on my upper lip began to dissipate as I lit a cigarette and looked out the window. It was another dreary day out there. The sky was gray and heavy. I looked around the empty room. I noticed that the calendar was still on the August page and the sink was surprisingly clean considering that it had been used regularly as a urinal. I felt the lights flickering in the room, and then I looked up and realized that they hadn't even been on. Then I looked at Taylor's collage piece, *King on Queen*. I was lost for a second in the regalia of

Her Majesty's dress and the King's deep blue eyes. I was quite surprised when I saw the lips on the post card move.

"Looks like it's gonna rain today, Tiny," Elvis said as I stared dumbfounded at the picture on the wall. "I don't know about you," he went on, "but I'm 'bout sick of all the rain, man."

One part of my mind knew that the postcard wasn't really talking to me, and if I concentrated I could tell that nobody else was there. But when he spoke I actually heard him, his velvet southern drawl echoing in my head.

"Hey I'm talkin' to you, man" he said after I had been silent for a moment, but I ignored him again. I needed some air. I had to get up and move, find some people; I didn't want to try to endure this kind of weirdness by myself. I could still hear the voice as I retreated down the hall. "Where you goin', Tiny. Don't leave me hangin', man."

Around the corner, down two steps, around another corner, and up three more I heard the familiar sound of Jerry's guitar and followed it to his room where I found him and his roommate Ben sitting Indian style on the floor beneath a red lava lamp swaying to the melody of whatever Jerry had been playing.

"Sammy, what up bro?" Ben said as I ducked into their room. I was fairly certain that Elvis had not followed me.

"I am," I said as I sat down against the wall beside them.

"How long now?" Jerry said. His fingers never stopped moving on the strings.

"Too long," I said. "I tried lying down just now but I couldn't get to sleep."

"Sure you ain't crankin', man?" Jerry said.

"I ain't crankin', man," I said. "The fucking hash monster got me last night, but I haven't had any speed."

201

"Did you get fucked up, man?" Ben said as he offered his hand for another slap-up session.

"Yeah," I said as I smacked his hand, "fucked up."

Jerry laughed. "Did you *get* fucked up or did you *fuck up*?" he said.

I snorted and shook my head at the same time. "Both," I said.

"You gotta watch that shit, man," he said as he chuckled.

"Yeah," I said, "…after last night."

"Hey you got any of that amyl left?" Ben asked, and I realized that those two cats might not be the guys to be hanging around if I was going to try to sober up. I reached into my pocket and found the little brown bottle that Taylor had given me. I tossed it to Ben and said, "Here, just hold onto it."

"You sure?" Ben said as he unscrewed the lid.

"Yeah," I said, "I've had enough."

"Cool," Ben said. He put the bottle to his nose and inhaled as I stood up to leave the room.

"Taker easy, man" Jerry said.

"I'm working on it," I said.

"Take her however you can get her, man!" Ben said. As I walked away I heard him giggling at his own joke all the way down the hall.

10:27 AM Friday (Hour 70:31)

I was sitting alone at one of the wrought iron tables in the conservatory when the rain started. Lightly, the drops began to hit the glass panels that made up the greenhouse ceiling of the room. I looked up and watched one as it hit and slowly began to trickle down in a crooked, lightning-bolt path from pane to pane as it was bombarded by a hundred others. I was mesmerized as the frequency and caliber of the drops increased, and soon the rain was beating down against the glass roof, washing in waves over the gutters, and onto the green grass below.

"You look like you've never seen rain before," I heard Lopez say before I ever saw her at the table with me. I jumped a bit as she materialized, and she looked at me as if I was being silly.

"God damn it, girl," I said, "don't sneak up on me like that."

"Who's sneaking?" she said as she kicked her feet up on one of the empty chairs. I wondered for a second if she was really there or if this was another hallucination.

"You get any fucking sleep yet?" she said.

"No," I said. It was not a hallucination.

"You're such a retard," she said. She sounded a bit exasperated.

"I know," I said as I nodded my head.

"I have too much to worry about today, Sammy," she said.

"You do," I agreed.

"Half of the lights we rented weren't delivered," she said.

"Got to have lights," I said.

"They wouldn't let us build the set in the great hall until today," she said.

"That's gonna be tight," I said.

"And now I have to worry about one of the supporting characters forgetting where he is, passing out on stage, or maybe even not showing up at all!"

"Lydia, it's cool," I said.

"Really?" she said and looked at me with her eyebrows high.

"It's been a struggle, indeed," I said, "but I assure you I will prevail."

She scoffed and said, "What movie is that from?"

"I don't know," I said. "I don't think any."

"Dude, you just talk like that now," she laughed.

"What are you talking about?" I said.

"Nothing, Sam," she chuckled. "Listen, I need the cast in the great hall at three, okay. We've got a few things to go over before curtain."

"Gotcha," I said, "three o'clock."

"Be there," she said as she stood up from the table.

"I will," I said and smiled at her.

"Don't be late, either," she said and she shook her finger at me.

"I won't," I said.

She smiled and shook her head before she walked off, and I thought about how Elwood was a lucky man. I noticed that the rain had slowed to a steady shower as she walked out the door and back into the manor, and I realized that it wasn't doing me any good to hide. I had dodged a bullet with Kat that morning, and I wasn't going to get that lucky again. I needed to talk to Sara. I needed to make sure we were all on the same page before I saw Kat again, and I only had until three o'clock to get that done.

12:20 PM Friday (Hour 72:24)

It had only been twenty hours or so when I started to notice the muscle twitches and body aches from the fatigue of being awake too long. For the first couple of days they would strike periodically, but if I would stretch out or focus on something else for a minute they would go away. As I walked around the estate looking for Sara that morning, I realized that they were no longer going to go away. The muscles in my back were so tight that I was actually starting to get a headache, but I trudged on.

As stealthily as my fatigued body would allow, I stalked the old mansion. I checked the library, the student lounge, and the writing lab. I walked through the state dining room, the great hall, and the long gallery. I climbed the service stairs and tiptoed down the forbidden fourth floor hall, checked with the cherubs at the old cedar staircase, and walked down the steps to the ornately restored second floor hall. The castle creaked and swelled as the rain came down steadily outside, and I was just about to give up when I saw her walking out of the refectory room with a Styrofoam cup of tea.

I froze a bit when I saw her. I had been looking for her for over an hour, but I hadn't really decided what I was going to say if I found her. Her first glance was at the floor as well, but she recovered faster than me and looked up at me with a tentative smile. "Hi, Sam," she said, and I let out the breath I had been holding. We had each stopped walking and there was a bit of space between us. There was steam rolling off of her tea.

"Hi, Sara" I said.

She didn't say anything. She just smiled at me, a mischievous, knowing version of her normal, perky smile.

"I'm on my way to meet someone," she finally said as she pointed down the hall in the direction that she had been walking. "Do you want to walk with me?" she said.

"Yeah, okay," I said, and I fell into stride next to her as she began down the hall.

"So," she said as we walked, "how are you feeling today?"

"Bout the same as yesterday," I said.

"You haven't slept yet?" she asked.

"Nope," I said.

"I figured when I woke up and you weren't there," she said. Her smile changed a bit, as if she were sad for me.

"Yeah," I said. I really didn't know what else to say.

"Listen," she said. "I'm not going say anything."

"What?" I said.

"To Kat," she said. "I'm not going to tell her."

"You're not?" I said.

"No," she said. "I don't know what there is between you two, but I know it would hurt her if she found out." She paused for a moment. Then she sighed and said, "and she would never forgive me."

"Then why'd you do it?" I said. For some reason hearing her talk about Kat's feelings was making me angry.

"Why'd *you* do it?" she said and smiled her mischievous, perky smile.

I didn't want to tell her. I didn't want to admit it to myself. I didn't even want to think about it so I just said, "I don't know."

"Yeah, you do," she said. I looked at her to see if she was right, and she was smiling right through me. "Look, Sam we can be adults about it, right? I wanted you. You wanted me too. At least last night you did. Maybe, you regret it now, but it was fun last night wasn't it?"

I smiled and shook my head. I don't know if she took that as an answer to her question.

"Look, Kat's my friend," she said, "and I know we probably shouldn't have done what we did, but we did it. We can't go back and change it now."

"What if we could?" I said as I stopped walking.

Sara stopped walking when I did. She turned to face me and said, "I had a great time last night, and if I have any guilt about what we did it's my own business. It's over. We did it. At this point, it would only be doing more damage to tell anyone else about it."

"You mean Kat," I said.

"Yeah, Sam," she said, "I mean Kat."

"I'm sorry," I said as I shook my head. My eyes were focused on a porous stone block in the wall behind her.

"Try not to be," she said as her smile returned, "Because I'm not going to regret it."

"Okay," I said and I looked back at her.

"Smile, Sammy," she said. "It's not that bad."

"No?" I said.

"No," she said. Then she laughed and said, "Actually, it was pretty good."

"Yeah?" I said. I tried to smile, but I don't think I did. I just stood there, waiting to see what would happen next.

"Yeah," she said. She leaned up and kissed me on the cheek, and then she turned and walked away. Turning back over her shoulder, she winked and said, "Let me know if you want to do it again sometime."

My mind was moving too slowly to answer her. I just stood there watching her ass move beneath her smart khaki pants as she bounced down the hall.

1:29 PM Friday (Hour 73:33)

Room 333 was oddly empty when I returned from my meeting with Sara. I strolled through the open door and sat down in the Big Chair as the rain hammered steadily against the window. I wondered for a moment where everybody was. In the months since I had been there, I could hardly remember the room ever being empty. All of the sudden, the place felt dreary and desolate, post-apocalyptic. I hadn't turned the lights on, and the white walls looked gray in the overcast light. The long desk was littered with books, first drafts, un-used post cards, and empty cigarette boxes. The foam rubber Rudolph mask was on the floor in the corner. Sitting on the throne, I wore the crown heavy on my brow.

For a moment, I flirted with the idea that everything might work out. I believed Sara, and I knew that if she wasn't going to tell Kat about our little soirée then there was no way she should have found out. I knew Taylor knew, but I had been loyal and discreet all the times that the situation had been reversed; surely he would do the same. Daydreaming, I wondered if it could really have been that simple.

But nothing is ever that simple. After all, I had been brought up Catholic, and I knew that sooner or later it would gnaw away at my resolve. Guilt was the basis of everything that we were taught at St. John the Baptist Elementary School. Sin was unavoidable, and it was only through repentance that we could benefit from Jesus' loving sacrifice. That's what the church had taught for two thousand years. Perfection was a trait possessed only by God himself. The rest of us were eventually going to fuck up, but the church had provided the holy sacrament of Penance for when we did. All we had to do was own our evil deeds, accept personal responsibility for our trespasses, and admit our guilt. The Son of Man had already died for our sins; all we had to do was confess them.

Years later, I would tell her. Out of the blue, all of the raindrops building until the dam just unexpectedly gave way one day. Perhaps over breakfast, would you like another cup of coffee? I cheated on you with your roommate at Harlaxton. We might have kids by then. She may even forgive me; she's the one who always said she didn't want to be my *girlfriend*. I hadn't thought of that yet; it wasn't cheating because she wasn't a girlfriend. But that only made me remember what she had said about names and categories. *It stopped being what it was when you put a name on it*, and the opposite was true as well. Because I had been willing to name it, I thought I had loved her more than she had loved me. Yet, just like her Donnie, I had been the one to betray her.

And now I was left to ponder Sara's philosophy. What possible good could come out of confessing to Kat? Did she not deserve the bliss of ignorance? If she never knew, then she would never know the pain. She would never wonder why, never live in fear that I might betray her again. If I could take it to my grave, keep it bottled up inside, then I could spare her the anguish of knowing what I had done. As long as I could swallow my guilt, we could still make it work…until my remorse overwhelmed me and the compulsive need for absolution made me spill the beans.

I wasn't any better. No better than Sara, telling herself what she needed to hear in order to get what she wanted when she wanted it. No better than Taylor, tearing through ass while his girlfriend waited back in Lexington. I had wanted mine to be perfect, and I was the one who had ruined it. And that reminded me of what Lopez had said about the play, about settling and perfection. *It's all going to be fine. Not perfect… just fine.* Oh shit, the play! What time was it?

2:59 PM Friday (Hour 75:03)

I winked at Lopez as I strolled into the great hall. She just shook her head and went on with what she was saying. The players were huddled around her by the giant stone fireplace, and I realized that, even though I had made it by three, the rest of the cast had been early enough that she had started her meeting without me. Quietly, I joined the rear of the huddle and began to look for Kat. She was in front, sitting on the lower mantle to the right of where Lopez was speaking.

Concentrating on what our director was saying, Kat seemed to be completely unaware of my entrance.

The gist of it was the lighting changes. There was going to be no tract lighting and they had only delivered one spot light. Lopez wanted to inform everyone that we would only be using the spot during monologues, and the rest of the play would have to be done under the dimmed house lights. I didn't understand how it made that much difference to us, but there are a lot of things I never understood about folks who take acting so seriously.

Lopez wrapped the meeting, and, as the huddle broke, I noticed Old Harold and a couple of my male classmates were finishing the set behind us. Lopez and Dr. White had agreed on a minimalistic production, but, despite its simplicity, the set conveyed the medieval majesty that one might expect to find at a Shakespeare play. It was just props really. The great hall of Harlaxton Manor with its grand stone and intricate woodwork was a perfect backdrop. The stagehands had only to place the appropriate furnishings in between scenes. Lopez had scoured the manor for interesting accent pieces, and she had received permission to use quite a few things. Among them I noticed a small collection of silver chalices, a sweet brass candelabrum, and somehow they had gotten one of the Viking long house tables up from the bistro. In the half light of the ancient room the stage looked rather impressive.

As instructed, the rest of the cast and I had come to the three o'clock meeting already in costume. The theme of minimalism was to be carried a step further with them. Lopez had instructed us to dress in black from head to toe, and she had planned on using some of our modest budget to rent an array of hats and headpieces from the lone costume shop in Grantham. Every character was to be adorned, and therefore identified by their distinctive headgear. I wanted the plumed burgundy cavalier, but that ended up going to Petruchio. As it turned out, Hortensio only rated an understated beefeater.

We tried on our hats and milled around the set while Lopez went off to talk to the lighting and music people. The atmosphere was intoxicating, and, for the first time, I began to look forward to the show as I familiarized myself with my marks. However, the lack of sleep was still affecting me, and my falcon was not as sharp as Petruchio's when I finally got to talk to Kat.

"I'm glad you made it," she said as our paths crossed.

"Me too," I said as I smiled at her.

She looked up at my face and then shook her head slightly. "You still haven't been to bed have you?" she said.

I dropped my eyes from her concerned gaze as I said, "No."

"Goodness, you look horrible," she said. "What did you do last night?"

I didn't answer her. Not only for obvious reasons, but I was a bit taken aback by her assessment of my appearance. I knew that I wasn't feeling up to par, but it had not occurred to me that my fatigue might be physically conspicuous.

"Sammy," she said as she put her palm on my chest, "I don't know whether to be impressed or to have you institutionalized for your own good."

"I think you need power of attorney to do that," I said.

She laughed unenthusiastically and said, "I was up all night too."

"You were?" I said. "What for?"

"Just nervous I guess…about the play and all," she said, "Sara was out all night too. She didn't get back to the room until like six in the morning!"

I could feel the sweat glands begin to warm up as I said, "Wow, really."

"Yeah," she said. "There must have been something in the air last night."

"I guess so," I said.

She smiled sheepishly and said, "Well, we each had a little too much of the *vino*."

"That'll happen," I said.

"Is Lydia mad at you?" she said.

"I don't think so," I said. "She came and had a talk with me earlier. I think we came to an understanding."

For some reason Kat was biting back laughter. When I raised an eyebrow at her she lost it and began chuckling heartily. In my dopey state, I had not realized that Lopez was standing next to me until I heard her speak. "Our understanding is: fuck my play up and you're a dead man Sammy!" she said.

"Wyatt," I said as I turned to face her, "I am an oak."

"Yeah," she said. "Just make sure you remember the lines from *this* show!"

"I'm golden," I said as I cocked my head back like I had everything under control.

Lopez laughed and said, "Sammy, you are quite literally a huge fucking dork." Then she turned to Kat and said, "And you look lovely as ever, my dear."

"Thank you," Kat said as she curtsied.

"No, thank you," Lopez said. "You're going to be great!"

"Awe, thanks," Kat said as Lopez turned to leave.

Lopez looked back over her shoulder, winked at us, and said "Break a Leg!"

There was a strange hot feeling beneath the skin on my forehead and just in front of my ears. I wondered for a moment if I had a fever. My eyelids felt swollen, but I had begun to grow accustomed to the headache. The excruciating part was the new level of discomfort in my lower back. Like a dagger had been shoved in between two vertebrae, the pain was sharp and had become constant. There was no longer any way to get comfortable. Sitting was the worst, but standing was not helping anymore either. Shifting my weight back and forth from one foot to the other, I decided that I had time to take a walk and try to loosen up. I sneaked out the rear door of the great hall, and strolled around the ground floor of the manor. I ended up in the entrance hall, lying flat on my back with my knees up, soles of my feet flat on the stone floor. I found that if I periodically pushed down with my legs and slightly lifted my body that I could relieve the pain in my back for a few moments.

As I lay there, I stared at the carved stone crown of the room, and my mind began to wander. I had felt better after Kat came to the room that morning. I had apologized for embarrassing her in the Bistro and she had said that we were *cool*. However, I was a nervous wreck when I talked to her at Lopez's pre-play meeting. She may not have known that Sara was with me, but she did know that her roommate had been out all night. Proverbially or not, Kat would be curious. I wondered how long that would last. Even if Sara and I could keep our secret, how long would it be before I could talk to Kat without feeling like that?

And then I realized that the pain had gone away. By God, something about the cold stone floor was doing the trick! Ah, sweet relief, as if I had awaken from a doomsday night terror and suddenly realized that I was again living in the time before the apocalypse. An unusual feeling of joy washed over me, and I begin to see a warm, white light as my eyelids closed. Delicious, euphoric sleep was seconds away, but then I remembered the play. I heard a sound like a balloon popping near the left side of my skull as I jolted awake. It took a few seconds for me to register that there was no balloon there, for I most certainly heard one pop; it was the mirage that had startled me awake.

5:21 PM Friday (Hour 77:25)

Groggy and afraid of falling asleep, I had returned to the great hall. I wandered on rubbery legs into the cacophony of activity in the old majestic room. The stage had been set at the front of the room, and Old Harold and a few others had begun to set up the rows of upholstered folding chairs that would serve as seating for the audience. They had opened a section of the wall between the great hall and the state dining room to allow the actors and stagehands access to the set, and that is where most of the players were milling about.

Before Lopez's production that semester, I had only been in three plays, all in high school. The backstage mood before all of them had been playfulness and frivolity. Sure, everyone was nervous, but the fear was exhilarating. That was part of what made it fun. Perhaps it was just the weirdness induced by my lack of sleep, but the mood in the wings that day seemed quite different. There was a solemnity and a gravitas that drove any trace of fun right out of the room. Maybe it was the material, some sort of reverence to Shakespeare that I had never seen shown to Meredith Willson or John Hughes, or maybe it was Lopez's depressing interpretation of what we had originally thought was a comedy. Tight lips and grim faces, as if we were condemned and awaiting our executions. Whatever it was, I didn't like it.

From across the room, I watched Kat for a moment. Sitting cross-legged alone in the corner, she appeared more relaxed than the others, but the tension was still evident in her posture. I wanted to go talk to her; I always wanted to talk to her, but I decided against it. Hers was the most important part in the play, and I didn't want to risk interrupting her pre-show ritual. Instead, I tried to concentrate on my part, tried to get into character, and when that didn't work I just focused on remembering my lines. All things considered, I decided that was enough to expect of myself. After all, I had never considered myself an actor.

6:30 PM Friday (Hour 78:34)

The curtain came up on our little version of Padua. Well, there actually was no curtain. I don't know how we would've rigged one in our makeshift playhouse, but the house lights dimmed and the small crowd became silent as the first actors entered.

"*I'll pheeze you, in faith,*" said the drunken tinker.

"*A pair of stocks, you rogue!*" said the alehouse hostess.

And we were off. No turning back now, no more time to be apprehensive. My first entrance was shortly after the *Induction*, and once I took the stage the exhilaration that had been missing before the show suddenly appeared. Finding my way though the choreographed chaos of entrances, exits, and scene changes, I became invigorated with adrenaline and all of the symptoms of sleep deprivation were driven from my conscious mind. Then something extraordinary began to happen.

Up until that point I had only read the lines of the play. Even at practice I was just saying my words at the proper time, after the other reader had finished his or hers. I had thought that I understood the plot and the characters, the sub-plots and the themes, but I had never really heard what the other characters were saying. As I played my part, I found myself watching the play, and, as I was watching it from within it, I began to feel empathy for the characters as if I was experiencing it right along with them.

"*I come to wive it wealthily in Padua,*" said Petruchio, "*If wealthily, then happily in Padua.*"

I had read the words before, but I had never really understood them. He was supposed to be my friend. I had brought him from Verona to introduce him to Katherina, and now, for the first time, I realized that he was not interested in her at all. He didn't care if she was a shrew, and he certainly didn't feel for her the way I felt for Bianca. The sod just wanted her money!

"*Why came I hither but to that intent?*" he said. "*Think you a little din can daunt mine ears?*"

All of the talking that Lopez had done, trying to convey her perception while I insolently daydreamed and waited for my turn to speak, was finally sinking in. I began to ponder as my friend from Verona spoke.

"*Have I not in pitchèd battle heard loud 'larums, neighing steeds, and trumpets clang?*" he said, "*and do you tell me of a woman's tongue, that gives not half so great a blow to hear as will a chestnut in a farmer's fire?*"

His bravado was well received by the others, but I looked at him a little differently than my character should have. I realized for the first time that I was beginning to mix the character I was supposed to be playing with my own. As I watched Kat play the lead role, I began to see the similarities between her and her character. I found the maid's rebellious spirit reminded me of Kat's own singularity and charismatic confidence, and I began to revere her in a way that Hortensio probably wouldn't have.

"*No shame but mine,*" she said. "*I must, forsooth, be forced to give my hand, opposed against my heart unto a mad-brain rudesby, full of spleen who wooed in haste and means to wed at leisure.*"

Why, Kate why? She was smarter than her father, than her sister, than the rest of us buffoonish suitors. Why did she fall prey to his scheming and ruses? Lopez had said she was choosing the lesser of two evils; I wish I could have remembered what she was talking about. All I could see was the evil; what choice had she really had?

"*Thus have I politically begun my reign,*" Petruchio began and I listened to him as if it was real. "*This is the way to kill a wife with kindness. And thus I'll curb her mad and headstrong humor.*"

And as I heard him speak, my reactions became genuine for I had become Hortensio, hearing his words for the first time. I was appalled as I began to conceive the fate that awaited this poor maiden. Emotionally, I began to hope for an alternative, some way to change the course of events that I knew was to follow. Runaway, Kate runaway! Climb out the window and stow away to the new world where at least hacking an existence out of the raw wilderness will not stifle your independence. There's no hope for you in Padua, no future but servitude one way or the other. Get out while you still can!

7:43 PM Friday (Hour 79:47)

"Come on, Sammy," Lopez said as the house lights came up for intermission, "I need a smoke."

It took my submerged brain a moment to register that the play had stopped, I was no longer Hortensio, and this strange little woman pulling at my shirt sleeve was my good friend from back in the real world. I followed her as she moved surprisingly fast down the steps, through the entry hall, and out the front door of the manor. Once outside, she bounced in the chilly air as I lit two Camel Lights and gave one to her.

"So…?" I said as she enthusiastically put the cigarette to her lips.

"I don't wanna say anything yet," she said, but her smile betrayed that she was happy with the play so far.

"Okay," I said, and I smiled at her.

"How are you feeling?" she said as she looked me over.

"I'm good," I said.

"You still haven't slept," she said. She was still bouncing.

"Don't worry about me," I said.

"I'm not," she said. "You're doing fine."

"I told you, I'm golden," I said.

"Right," she said. "Just promise me that you get some sleep before tomorrow's show, okay?"

"Alright," I said. "I promise."

"Did you look at the audience?" she said and I shook my head. "I think the whole room is full!"

"Probably nobody'll be here tomorrow then," I laughed.

Lopez stopped bouncing and took a long drag from the cigarette. She tilted her head to one side as she exhaled the smoke, and I saw her big hazel eyes shining through the cloud.

"You've done a great job, Lydia," I said softly as she stared off at the horizon.

She looked up at me and smiled. She put one arm around me and half-hugged me and I put my arm around her and hugged her back.

"Come on," she said. "Let's get back in there before they start without us."

7:50 PM Friday (Hour 79:54)

Back on stage, I tried not to draw attention to myself as I shifted my weight back and forth. The back pain was returning, and it had been joined by a crick in my neck that was making head-turns to the left more difficult than they should have been. My only solace was watching Kat perform.

"*Forward, I pray, since we have come so far, and be it moon, or sun, or what you please,*" she said. Her voice was strong and quivering at the same time. She was beautiful and enticing, but there was a heart wrenching sadness in her delivery. "*And if you please to call it a rush candle, henceforth I vow it shall be so for me.*"

My heart sank as I realized what she was saying. She was giving in, tired of fighting, resigning to accept the fate that everyone else had arranged for her. She was settling, and, as I watched her confess such, I couldn't help but think about Kat instead of Katherina. She was worthy of so much more than me. How could I ask her to settle after what I had done? If only we had been able to afford full costumes for the show, I would draw my sword in Act V and slay Baptista and that wretched Petruchio. I would emancipate that sweet, short-haired, ornery shrew, send her off with her independence, and fend off any who may try to follow her. I fantasized about *Hortensio the Hero* as the actual play continued around me.

"*Katharina, I charge thee,*" Petruchio said, "*tell these headstrong women what duty they do owe their lords and husbands.*" I wanted her to hand him a cup of hemlock instead.

"*Come, come, you're mocking,*" said the widow, "*we will have no telling.*" I looked at Kat and saw her bow her head.

"*Come on, I say,*" the rat said to her, "*and first begin with her.*"

"*She shall not,*" said the widow.

"*I say she shall,*" he retorted, "*and first begin with her.*"

Head still bowed, Kat walked to the front of the stage. The lights went down and the lone spot shown on her as she began to speak her final lines, "*Fie, fie! unknit that threatening unkind brow, and dart not scornful glances from those eyes…*" In the dark, I could not see if the audience had obeyed, but I knew the scorn that was still on my face.

"*To wound thy lord…*" she continued, "*It blots thy beauty as frosts do bite the meads...*" The sarcasm now obvious, the tragedy became apparent, and as she spoke it all sank in. "*Thy husband is thy lord,*" she said, "*thy life, thy keeper…*"

I watched her as she spoke and I saw the woman I loved. Finally, I understood why I loved her, and I understood how hard I had worked to crush that in her. I listened woefully as she continued, "*…no other tribute at thy hands but love, fair looks and true obedience.*" It was too late for Katherina, but I had failed where Petruchio had prevailed. Thank God it had not been too late for Kat.

"*I am ashamed that women are so simple to offer war where they should kneel for peace,*" she said as she knelt before him on stage and the house lights slowly came back up so the audience would be able to see the reactions of the other characters. We all stared on in disbelief as she continued, "*Or seek for rule, supremacy and sway, when they are bound to serve, love and obey.*"

Smugly, Petruchio smiled as my anger turned to despair. I saw mouths agape in the audience, and I reached for my sword that was not there. As if she were addressing them directly, Kat turned to face the audience as she continued, *"My mind hath been as big as one of yours, my heart as great, my reason haply more, to bandy word for word and frown for frown; but now I see our lances are but straws. Our strength as weak, our weakness past compare..."*

Lopez had them bring the house lights all of the way up, and in the eerie quiet of the brightly lit great hall Kat finished her monologue, *"Then vail your stomachs, for it is no boot, and place your hands below your husband's foot: In token of which duty, if he please, my hand is ready; may it do him ease."*

As we had practiced, there was a long pause after she finished speaking. Lopez had wanted to give the audience a chance for it to sink in. With the lights up I could see them, mostly classmates and faculty, and most of them were looking at Katherina the same way that I was looking at Kat. I felt a knot in my stomach, and I closed my eyes to fight back the tears.

A fella named Gabe, the actor who had been playing Petruchio, broke the tense silence. *"Why, there's a wench!"* he said, *"Come on, and kiss me, Kate."* She arose and did as she was told as the rest of the characters threw in their two cents. I watched Kat move in a posture that I never wanted to see her in again. Petruchio gloated. He told Lucentio that he had won their wager, and then he ordered Katherina off to bed with him.

As they exited the stage I realized that my final line was next, but whatever character I may have been playing was completely gone at that point. Lost in my own tumultuous emotions, I had tears on my cheeks and my voice was cracking a bit when I said, *"Now, go thy ways; thou hast tamed a curst shrew."*

8:41 PM Friday (Hour 80:45)

I had been lost in an underwater haze in the moments after the play ended. I was confused when Katherina and Petruchio returned; I didn't remember that from the script. I was afraid I had forgotten a non-existent Act VI until the house lights came up and I saw the small audience applauding. My panic subsided as I realized the actors had returned for the curtain call. Kat was smiling; the danger was over, but I was still standing there crying.

Amidst the commotion, I smiled and bowed along with the others as the tears rolled down my cheeks. Still in character, Kat coquettishly meandered upstage and the patrons began to stand as she did. She beamed and bowed, and the applause increased in volume as the audience got to see this version of Katherina one last time. The skin on my cheeks tingled as it dried, and I began to get a hold of myself. Awestruck, I watched as she took her final bow, and then she turned away from them and led the rest of us offstage.

A few knowing patrons had already slipped out of the back of the great hall and were waiting for us in the state dining room as we exited through the open wall that usually separated the two rooms. There were a handful of people waiting for Kat, and I saw Dr. White congratulate Lopez as Elwood inconspicuously smiled at her from across the room. I recognized the excitement in the air, and I realized that this was a bigger deal than any of the small plays I had been in before. There was a collective feeling of accomplishment among the players, like an army victoriously returning from battle, but I didn't feel like I was part of it. I didn't feel like one of the valiant. I wandered around the room watching it all as if I had been invisible until I heard Dr. Wallace's Edinburgh accent behind me.

"Mr. Thompson!" he said. I turned to face him and was a bit surprised by the proud smile on his face. "A most impressive performance, sir," he said, "most impressive, indeed."

"Thank you," I said as he reached out to shake my hand.

"My goodness boy, how did you make yourself cry like that?" he said as I tried to hide the befuddled look on my face. I didn't really give him an answer; I just shook my head.

"That bit at the end as she's talking about being the good wife and you're back there greeting like the rain," Dr. Wallace continued. "That was really quite good, Thompson."

"Thanks," I said again.

"I didn't expect your character's reaction at all," he said, "really drives it home!"

I nodded solemnly, as if I deeply understood exactly what he was talking about, but I didn't. I had no idea. The whole last act had been a tumultuous blur to me, and whatever emoting to which he may have been referring was not the result of my limited acting ability. It had been quite real.

I really didn't know what had brought it on; I think it was just some sort of process overload, all of the emotions, the stress and tension, collecting like moisture in a cloud until my whole brain was saturated to the point of explosion. Swollen in the back of my throat, the love for her, the disdain for myself, pulsed and swelled until I could no longer hold it down, and it burst as she said her final lines. An ecstatic, cathartic re-boot that cleared my head enough to allow me to function, the momentary break down left me vaguely wondering what had been so bad in the first place.

Black and white turned to grey as the imaginary world of the play had begun to blend with my reality. Kat *became* Katherina as Hortensio watched the play through Sam Thompson's eyes. I was content at first to just ride it out because I knew that when the play ended reality would still be there, black and white, right and wrong, measurable distances and facts not subject to interpretation. I was not prepared when the lights came up and the grey remained.

9:19 PM Friday (Hour 81:23)

"So where is everybody?" Taylor said as the two of us walked into the Bistro.

"Lopez said nine-thirty," I said as we sat down at one of the long wooden tables.

"So we're early," he laughed. "That's different."

"Yeah," I said. An informal opening night after-party had been Lopez's plan, but I had found that plans couldn't always be trusted.

"You want a beer?" Taylor said as he got up to go to the bar.

"No, man," I said. "I don't really feel like drinking tonight."

"Pussy," he said as he walked off.

As he disappeared around the corner, I saw Kat and Sara walk into the small bar. I smiled at Kat and they both smiled back as they walked up to my table. I held my hands out as if I wanted a hug and said, "You were magnificent tonight!"

Kat didn't hug me. She smiled as if she had known what I was going to say, and then she said, "Thank you. So were you!"

"You were all wonderful!" Sara chimed in. "I think that's the first time I've ever understood what was going on in a Shakespeare play."

"Yeah," I said as my goofy gaze stayed on Kat. "I think it came off pretty well."

"Yeah, it was fun," Kat said. "I can't wait to do it again tomorrow."

"I can't wait to see it again tomorrow," Taylor said as he walked up behind the girls with a cold bottled pilsner in his hand.

"Well, thank you sir," Kat said as she turned to welcome him.

"No, thank you," he said as he nodded at her. "It was a pleasure to watch you work, mademoiselle."

"Awe, thanks Taylor," she said.

"Would you ladies care to join us?" Taylor said as he motioned toward the empty chairs at our table.

"Alrighty," Kat said as she sat down across the table from me. Sara followed her lead.

"Can I get you anything?" Taylor said as he stood there like a waiter.

"No thanks," Kat smiled. "I think I overdid it a bit last night."

"Oh, come on," Sara said as she lightly slapped Kat's forearm. "Have one glass of wine with me."

For some reason Kat looked at me so I said, "I won't tell anybody."

"Okay," she said as she turned back to Sara, "one glass."

"I shall return," Taylor said as he set his own beer on the table and headed back to the bar.

"You're not drinking tonight?" Sara said as she pointed to the empty spot on the table in front of me.

"I don't think so," I said.

"Are you sick?" Kat said.

"No, I just don't feel like drinking," I said.

"How long have you been awake now?" Sara said as she took a quick swig from Taylor's unguarded beer bottle.

"Too long," I said. "I'm just about out of gas."

"Rubbish!" Taylor said as he walked up and set two glasses of red wine gently on the old scarred table. "You may be pushing the boundaries of human ability, but you are a mutant, my friend. You are nowhere near your limit."

"I'm going to have to disagree," I said as I smiled at his speech.

"What is the count, my brother?" he said as he sat down and regained possession of his beer.

I looked at my watch and said, "Eighty-one and a half hours."

"Oh my God!" Kat said.

"Seriously?" Sara said.

"Damn straight," Taylor said. "That's my boy."

"I'm sleeping tonight," I said.

"Good," said Kat.

"Like hell you are," said Taylor. "I'll bring *both* of these beautiful women up to the room with us if I have to."

I furrowed my brow as I heard his joke, and I tried to inconspicuously assess any response from either of the girls. Kat smiled tolerantly, but Sara shot me a mischievous glance that made my *spider-sense* tingle. My narrowed eyes made contact with Taylor's and I tried to silently tell him to knock it off, but in my fatigued state I was lacking the ability to execute such subtle diplomacy.

The girls thanked Taylor for the wine, and Sara bummed a cigarette from him. They were talking about something; Sara was giddy and laughing as Taylor spun one of his yarns. Kat was still excited about the play, and she enthusiastically told me about a cue she had missed in Act III and how she had improvised her way back on script. Recognizing the rhythm of her anecdote, I laughed at all the appropriate spots, but I wasn't really engaged in what she was saying. My mind was too tired; my ability to concentrate on anything, even her, had completely vanished.

Instead, as Kat talked to me, I watched the three of them, studied them. Sara was drinking her wine in gulps and sucking on Taylor's cigarette with what may very well have been analogous intent. She sat sideways, legs crossed in her chair, one smooth calf smashed against the other beneath the hem of her Capri pants. Taylor stood next to her chair casually holding his sweating beer bottle in his left hand. His hair was perfect. He rested his other hand on the back of her chair as he used his beer hand periodically to illustrate whatever it was he was talking about. Passionate and abuzz with energy, Kat leaned forward in her chair as she talked to me. The adrenaline rush of her performance was still fresh in her chemistry. Her eyes were wide and sparkling behind her glasses, and I remember thinking that was how I wanted to remember her. I wanted to paint her portrait. Years later, whenever I would reminisce about the semester I had spent in England and *that one girl* that meant so much to me, I would be thinking about this exact moment.

9:38 PM Friday (Hour 81:42)

The tiny bar in the basement of Harlaxton Manor erupted in applause as Lydia Lopez arrived fashionable late. Grinning from ear to ear, she took a large, exaggerated bow just inside the threshold and then took the arm of her escort, Elwood, who led her to our table as the applause died down.

"To all the cast and crew," she said in her director's voice, "I just want to say thank you. I really appreciate everyone's time and hard work. Everything was superb tonight. Everyone did a great job. Congratulations, and let's do it again tomorrow!" There was applause again as she sat down at the head of our table. She was positively beaming. "Okay fuckers, who's buying drinks?" she said.

"What'll it be, boss?" I said as I stood up from my chair.

"I think I'll try a cider," she said facetiously. We had all seen her *try* cider more than once before.

I smiled at her joke as I said, "Be right back."

But Elwood touched my shoulder gently and said, "I'll get it buddy."

"It's no trouble," I said, but I knew he wasn't going to let me so I sat back down.

"I got it," he said.

"Thank you, sweetie," Lopez said as he walked toward the bar.

"*Sweetie?*" Kat said as she raised an eyebrow at Lopez.

Lopez smiled at Kat's comment. She might have blushed a bit when she said, "He can be."

"He looks sweeter already," Taylor said as he gave me a wink.

"So is that like official now?" Kat asked as she nodded in the direction in which Elwood had walked off.

"Yeah," Lopez said. She was certainly blushing at that point. "I guess you could say that."

"So cool for you!" Kat said as she clasped Lopez's hands in a very girlish, celebratory kind of way.

As Elwood came strolling back to the table I shook my head at the caricature that he was. Acid-washed blue jeans taught over his skinny legs, he certainly didn't come off as the heir to an American liquor fortune.

I grinned at him as he sat down with us and then I said to Lopez, "So what d'ya think, boss? How'd we do?"

"Oh my God, it was perfect!" she said. She smiled at Kat and said, "You were perfect, my dear."

"Thank you, Lydia," Kat said.

"Gabe's Petruchio was perfect," Lopez continued. "You were even good, Sammy," she said as she smacked me on the arm.

"Yeah?" I said.

"Yeah," she smiled. "I didn't know you had it in you."

"Me neither," I said as I chuckled and looked at my shoe.

10:28 PM Friday (Hour 82:32)

"Did you ever notice how often the sphere occurs in nature?" I said. I hadn't had anything to drink, but I don't really think that I was doing any better than the rest of them.

"The *sphere*," Taylor said, "What like the shape?" He was on his third pilsner but he seemed fine.

"Yeah," I said, "the Earth, the moon, the sun and all the stars."

"And oranges," Elwood said. It never seemed to matter how much Elwood had to drink; he was always fine.

"Oh yeah, and blueberries," Lopez said. She was slurring a bit.

"Yeah," I said, "and various other fruits." I looked at Kat, but she didn't seem that interested.

"I love blueberries," Sara said. "I want some pancakes."

"What about subatomic particles," Lopez said. "Protons and neutrons, they're spheres aren't they?"

"I don't know, are they?" said Taylor.

"The models that they used in chemistry class always were," Lopez said.

"You see," I said, "we're even made up of spheres! Did you ever wonder where all the spheres come from?"

"Do you think they'll have pancakes in the refectory tomorrow?" Sara said.

"Good question," said Elwood.

"People make other shapes," I said, "right angles, squares and triangles and fucking pentagons, but God must have preferred spheres."

"You know," Lopez said, "there is a certain perfection to the sphere."

"Right," I said, "it's balanced and uniform and completely symmetrical."

"How about the pyramid?" Taylor said. "The pyramid makes perfect structural sense."

"Not without the force of gravity created by the sphere that it's sitting on," I said.

"What the hell are you talking about?" Sara said. She must have finally stopped thinking about pancakes.

"I had a vision last night," I said.

"You did?" Taylor scoffed.

"Yeah," I said, "in the woods as I was walking back from the carriage house. I saw myself floating in this sphere and for just a moment it all made sense."

"What made sense?" Lopez said.

"Everything," I said. "All of it. I saw everything from a different perspective, like a different dimension. The way time works, our lives, everything…"

"That sounds like a hallucination?" Taylor said.

They all laughed and I looked at him and said, "Yeah, maybe."

"I know how high you were," Taylor said.

"And you haven't slept in days!" Lopez added.

"Yeah," I said, "probably just drug-induced bullshit. The nurses warned me!"

"Maybe not," Kat said. I was surprised to hear her voice. She hadn't said anything in quite some time, and I had begun to think that she wasn't even listening to us. "I haven't been to church much lately, at least not since high school, but I've always believed in a higher power."

"You mean Jesus Christ?" Sara said.

"I mean *something* greater than us," Kat said, "something good and true and real."

"Something spherical?" Taylor said.

"Something that's too complicated for us to understand completely," she said.

"I'm not claiming to understand it completely," I said.

"I know," she said, and I noticed that her eyes were wide as we once again searched for the meaning together. "I've always thought of God as being the inherit goodness that binds the universe together. It's in all of us, right?"

"Like *the force* from Star Wars," Elwood said.

"Maybe, yeah kinda," Kat said. "Like an endlessly flowing river, and each drop of water is an individual human spirit. And when you take the drop away from the river, that's our life. And when we die the drop that was us goes back into the river."

"So we never really die?" Lopez said.

"Right," Kat said.

"But we cease to be ourselves?" Taylor said.

"Maybe," Kat said, "but we become one with the river."

"We become one with God," I said.

Kat nodded and smiled at me, and then she said, "And each individual drop of water is certainly a sphere."

"What the hell are you guys talking about?" Sara said.

"Blasphemy!" Taylor said as he raised his bottle toward us in an enthusiastic salute.

"He's a fucking Catholic," Lopez laughed, and I wondered if I was the only one at the table who knew that she was too.

"I need to go to the loo," Sara said. "Somebody go with me."

"I'll go with you," Lopez said as she struggled to get out of her seat.

"Why do you guys always have to go together?" Elwood said.

"It's just what we do, sweetie," Lopez said and she kissed him on the cheek as she slid past him.

"Are you coming?" Sara said as she looked down at Kat.

"Yeah, okay," Kat said, and she smiled at me as she got up to join them.

10:46 PM Friday (Hour 82:50)

For a moment I thought I saw numbers counting down in the upper right corner of my field of vision, as if superimposed on a television screen, but I couldn't make them out. I strained my eyes to try to look up at them, but every time that I did they moved off into the peripheral, just out focus. I knew I was running out of time, but I couldn't tell how much I had left.

Elwood and Taylor had started talking about the girls as soon as they had left to go to the bathroom together. Taylor had been asking about how long Elwood and Lopez had been together, and Elwood had been talking about how highly he had come to think of her in that short time.

"She's really smart," I remember Elwood had said. "I ain't never really been with any smart girls, ya know?"

"She's certainly one of a kind," Taylor had said, "I've always thought she was sexy."

"Thanks, buddy," Elwood said, "and you keep your God damned hands off of 'er!"

"Absolutely," Taylor assured him. "You guys are too good a match! One thing I'd never do is break up a good match." Then he pointed at me and said, "Besides, he's the one you've got to worry about."

"Sammy?" Elwood said as I groggily tried to catch up with their conversation.

"He's had a crack at those other two already," Taylor said.

"What are you talking about?" Elwood said as he rested his palm on my shoulder. "My man here ain't never been nut'n but in love with that little leading lady."

"Well he looked to be pretty fond of the other one last night?" Taylor said as he polished off his fifth beer.

"Hey man!" I said as I shot him a look.

"What?" he said, "It's just Dan, man." He looked a little off balance when he threw his arms up.

"No shit?" Elwood said, "You and Sara?"

"Yeah," I said as I nodded painfully, "but that isn't exactly public knowledge yet, okay."

"Yeah, okay," Elwood said. I could tell that he was a little stunned by the revelation. "So what about you and Kat?" he said sort of half under his breath.

"Yeah," Taylor chimed in. "I've been dying to know that myself. What *about* you and Kat?"

For some reason I was getting angry. Images flashed before my eyes as I visualized thrusting my open palm into the side of Taylor's face, driving his head into the stone wall behind him.

"I mean, damn! She was looking good on stage tonight my brother," he said. "You know, I don't think I ever really understood until tonight why you've been so fascinated with her. She was awesome!"

"Yeah," I said. "She was." I thought about knocking him out, visualized how his head would limply bounce back off of the wall. He was drunk enough that his reaction would have been slowed, and, even in my fatigued state, it would have been quick and easy.

"So how about it, Sammy?" Taylor said. "Are you still in love with her, man?"

I ground my teeth together as I thought one last time about hitting him, and then I decided to take it in a different direction. "No, man," I said as I smiled and shook my head. "I'm too young for love brother."

"No?" Taylor said as he grinned back at me.

"Nope," I told him again. "Like you said, dude, first day of the rest of my life."

"That a boy," Taylor said.

"So," Elwood interjected, "you and Sara, huh?"

"Yeah," I said. "I didn't see it coming either."

"Yeah, he got ambushed," Taylor laughed.

"Really," Elwood said, "so how was it?"

"It was pretty fucking hot," I said. I felt like I had lied even though I really hadn't.

"Better than Kat?" Taylor asked.

"Oh yeah," I said, "way better." That was certainly a lie. Well, the truth was that I didn't really know. Kat and I still had never actually consummated our relationship.

"Wow, really?" Taylor said. "I always suspected that Kat would be a fucking minx."

"I know what you mean," Elwood said, "but Sara does have a smokin' bod."

"Let me tell you," I added, "she knows how to use it too." I couldn't tell if they could tell, but I was laying it on a bit thick.

"Yeah," Taylor sighed, "but Kat's always seemed like one of those dam break chicks, you know. Like the naughty librarian, all that repressed energy built up and waiting to explode."

"Yeah," I said as I shook my weary head, "not really."

"So are you gonna start seeing Sara, buddy?" Elwood asked.

"I don't know," I said, "we'll see what happens."

"I'm going to make him bring them both up to the room tonight," Taylor laughed. "He's starting to think about sleeping, and they can take turns keeping him awake!"

"Right on," Elwood laughed.

"Right," I scoffed.

And then the three of us dropped the subject on cue as we saw the girls appear on the other side of the room. Always quick of wit, Taylor jumped *in medias res* to an observation that he had made about the end of the play, and the girls were quite at ease to find us discussing that when they rejoined us at the table.

10:56 PM Friday (Hour 83:00)

I had been enjoying the company, the socialization, hanging out with everyone, but the muscles in my back were beginning to ache the longer I sat with them in the Bistro. Also, I hadn't had anything to drink that night, and the inebriation gap between me and my friends was starting to get annoying. The conversation at the table had been degenerating to boring gossip and condescending ridicule of a few random individuals that were outside the group. I hadn't said anything in a long time. I was numb, detached; I was beginning to feel like a sociopath as I watched them. I listened as Taylor made a joke about a hippie chick across the room, something about how patchouli was no replacement for soap. I watched the rest of them laugh at her, even Kat, and I realized that I wasn't part of the group either. I remember wondering why they hadn't noticed it yet. Maybe I was a better actor than I thought.

But the show doesn't really go on. That's just a silly saying. All plays come to an end. Most of them only last a couple of hours; there's a limit to how long we can suspend disbelief. No one even acknowledged me as I got up to go to the restroom, and I wondered how long it would take them to notice if I just kept walking, out of the manor house, along the rail tracks, north maybe, up to the highlands. Maybe they would never notice, or maybe they would finally realize that I hadn't been one of them all along.

One last time, I looked back at that table, my best friends at that school. Lopez was slouched against Elwood half sitting on his lap. He was holding her drunken ass up, but his arm around her looked cozy and protective, like it belonged there. Sara was leaning on Taylor, her head on his shoulder, hanging on his every word, but he seemed more interested in Kat. Invisible to them from across the room, I watched her listen to him as she sipped her wine. Her blue eyes still sparkled behind her glasses, but this time they were sparkling at him. She giggled lightly, and I wondered if I was the only one that could see that divine aura glowing around her. Maybe it was just a figment of my imagination, a silly little daydream induced by my sleep deprivation. Or maybe it was as real as I had always felt it was, and her brilliance in the play had finally revealed it to the illustrious Taylor Beckett.

I almost went back to fight for her when I saw his hand on her knee beneath the table, but I was too tired. Besides, she hadn't really seemed to mind it there.

11:34 PM Friday (Hour 83:38)

A sense of relief washed over me as I trudged into the Vortex. The room was empty, quiet like a sanctuary. The moonlight shone through the old window panes and chased shadows across the floor. I kicked my One Stars off in the middle of the room and walked over to the window. The wind was still gusting and the trees outside the gates were swaying like dancers. It would be getting cold soon; autumn was almost over.

I lit a Camel as I eased back into the Big Chair. My trunk muscles relaxed as I leaned against the sturdy upholstered frame. I closed my eyes. Moving my right arm in a wide, rising arc, I brought the cigarette to my lips and inhaled. The smoke shot down into my lungs, delivered its addictive payload, and then meandered back up and out, hanging like a fog around my mouth and nostrils as it slowly dissipated. It had been a few hours since my last cigarette, and I was able to fully concentrate on this one. No interruptions, no conversation to keep pace with, I was a bit lightheaded, buzzing, almost high. God I loved to smoke. I just didn't want to think about what it was doing to my insides.

After all, I was only twenty. Consequences were hard to recognize at that age. My freewheeling lifestyle didn't seem irresponsible because I had no real responsibilities. There wasn't anybody counting on me, no mouths to feed but my own. Experimenting with drugs didn't seem dangerous because I had nothing to lose. It would never become a habit with me; I was way too smart for that. Staying awake for four days didn't seem like a big deal because there would be plenty of time to sleep later. Besides, sleep was a waste of precious time anyway.

I believed these things because I lacked the foresight to know any better. I hadn't experienced any consequences yet, and I didn't really believe that I was going to. I told myself that betrayal couldn't exist because I didn't owe anybody anything. I didn't have a girlfriend; I didn't want a girlfriend. At least, I tried to convince myself that I didn't. I had made no promises, taken no vows. I had been true to myself, right? And now I was free, as free as I should have been all along, free and completely alone.

I continued my mantra, the foolery, as I crushed out the cigarette and walked back to my sleeping chamber. The moonlight disappeared as I pulled the curtain behind me and I felt in the dark for that long lost stranger. Without taking my clothes off, I fell onto the bed and the springs creaked and bounced as they adjusted to my weight. The scene of the crime, the sheets still smelled of Sara Walters, and I began to deconstruct my motivations. Was it just too good to pass up or was it what I had really wanted all along? Had I just been tired of waiting or had I been lying to myself for months? How long would it keep me awake? How many nights? How many years?

I tried to put it out of my mind as I stretched my legs out on top of the covers. My body was relaxed, limp and comfortable, but my mind was working in circles, keeping me awake. I was regretting wasted time and then questioning my own regret. I was mourning lost love and then questioning my own sincerity. The blood red glowing numbers of my alarm clock ticked off one at the time as I lay there in the dark, and I began to concentrate on them to distract myself. The digital numbers were made up of dashes, and I watched

one of them disappear as the *eight* became a *nine*. Then
nothing for a moment; they were still. Then the one in the
center moved and the *nine* became a *zero*. Then, through the
ever open door to our room, I heard laughter down the hall,
and I knew they were coming.

Saturday

I felt like I was asleep, but I don't think I was. Perhaps I was in some sort of trance, hypnotized by the slow melodic movement of those red numbers on the clock. I could hear voices in the room outside my sleeping chamber. I recognized Taylor, but I didn't hear Elwood. There was at least one female with him, maybe two. They had been in there for a while, laughing and smoking. I could smell the fumes wafting in beneath the curtain in the doorway.

I opened my eyes and stared into the darkness. I was certain that I was awake. I heard the female voice again. She said something about riding the train to London. I couldn't make it all out, but I heard her well enough that I could tell it wasn't Kat. An unexpected calm came over me as the tension evaporated from within my spine. I had seen Taylor's work in the past. I had tolerated him and his victims as they thrashed about on the other side of the thin wall between our beds. Most girls were just girls and I realized that guys like Taylor would always be there to take advantage of that fact. I just didn't want to believe that Kat was like all the others. I wanted to believe that she was the exception, that she was immune. I wanted her on the pedestal.

Then the cigarette smell went away, then the laughter, and through the wall I heard the familiar dance begin. There was no more talking, but the breathing was slightly louder. I could hear the wet smacking sounds of their kissing and their awkward three-legged-race to his bed. As they bounced and scooted and took their positions, I questioned my decision about the voice that I had heard and I again wondered if he might have worked his magic on Katherine Graham. Before I could stop myself, my imagination placed her there underneath him, and I found myself silently flailing for the *off* switch.

I wanted to shut my brain down, to rid myself of the images that weren't really there, but I must have turned that figurative knob the wrong way. Although I was not able to block out what was happening in my roommate's bed, I was almost completely distracted from it by the giant, God-like hand I saw floating above me. Outlined in glowing red neon, the fingers moved slightly as the huge appendage hovered above me ominously. The fluorescent glow filled the room as I watched in curious amazement. The hand was as long as I was. The fingers were the size of my legs. It was large enough to pick me up and crush me, but I felt no fear. The red glow was warm and the rhythmic movement of the thing seemed oddly benevolent. The big red hand moved back and forth, swaying above me the way a mother's hand might sway over her infant in his crib. It was soothing and reassuring, and it had almost wooed me to sleep when the horse appeared.

The ice cold chill of panic shot down my spine as the red light that had formed the hand dissolved as white lightning bolts shot out of its palm. But the lightning bolts didn't flash and disappear like I expected them to. They hung over my prone body and glowed against the black backdrop of my room just as the red neons had done a second ago. With my eyes wide open, I began to catch my breath as the lightning bolts took shape. I saw the head of a furious horse and then the legs and the body and the wings. This electric Pegasus was further away from me than the hand had been, but I felt the fear welling in me as it flapped its lightning wings and headed straight for me. I was paralyzed, watching mouth agape as the monster swooped down to do me in. I tried to scream but nothing happened. I knew I should move, but for some reason I didn't want to.

And then I heard her voice. "Yes," she had said. It was the same word that I had heard on that park bench in Paris. It was the same voice.

I scrambled out of bed, falling into a crouching position low, close to the floor in the darkness of my room. I sat there still and listened. I could hear their breathing, the rustling of the sheets beneath them, but there were no more words.

Crouching in the cool, dark room, I felt beads of sweat forming on my forehead. My imagination was working again, showing me images that I didn't want to see. God damn it I was Hamlet again, struggling over whether or not to take action. I may have realized that it was too late for me to be her prince, but I would've settled for being her champion. I had wanted to protect her from any man who may try to taint the rare beauty of her life with his own. I had wanted to protect her from any man like me. Taylor was like me, young, free, full of life, and totally unworthy of her. I closed my eyes and saw him perched over top of her, his perfect hair brushing her cream colored forehead as he plundered Eden below.

I needed to hear her voice again to be absolutely certain. I had seen the way that he was looking at her in the Bistro, but that wasn't enough to be sure. Taylor was always at work over there. It could have been anyone, Audrey again or Alyssa or some new bird that I didn't even know about. Sara had been all over him in the Bistro as well, and after the previous night I certainly wouldn't put it past her to be up here again. The thorn in my brain was that word, *yes*. The way she had said it, that sigh, the strong exhalation, it was more than permission. It was a request, a demand even, just like it had been in Paris.

Speak! Say it again. Say anything...

Then my imagination answered. Inside my head I heard her say his name. *Yes, Taylor, yes!* I didn't like that at all. *Oh, Taylor, yes!* I had to make that stop. Quietly I crawled to the curtain that hung closed in the doorway of my sleeping chamber. I opened my mouth to quiet my breathing and slid my legs carefully along the carpet like a spy in an action movie. On my knees in the dark, I slowly opened the curtain, careful not to make a sound. When the curtain was open far enough, I pushed off my leg with one powerful, fluid movement and came to my feet in the dark common area of Room 333.

The curtain to Taylor's sleeping chamber was closed. I could hear the movement behind it, but I couldn't see them. My heart was beating fast. I could feel my pulse in my ears. The time had come to act, but I didn't know what I wanted to do. I wanted to draw back the curtain and see that it wasn't her, to confirm that she really was as special as I had always thought. Taylor wouldn't have minded and neither would his floozy. They would have written me off as a lost drunkard and went right back to what they were doing.

But what if it *was* Kat? What would happen then? There would be no good to come from me flying into a rage and violently beating Taylor. Kat would be screaming for me to stop, calling me an animal; the woman always sides with the loser. But how could I just quietly concede defeat? I would never be able to rid my mind of that image, his body poised above her, her delicate legs spread underneath him, pleasure-grimace on her face. I wouldn't be able to just go back into my chamber and go to sleep, laying there on the other side of the wall and listening to them as he finished with her.

So I retreated quietly out the door, made a left, and headed up to the fourth floor. It may have been more efficient to just peak around Taylor's curtain, but the risk was too great; I was too afraid of what I might see. Instead, I headed for Kat's room. I knew it might upset her, me banging on her door in the middle of the night, but if she answered then that would prove that it was someone else down in my room with Taylor.

12:13 AM Saturday (Hour 84:17)

I realized when Sara answered the door that I hadn't put enough thought into my plan.

"Sammy," she said as she stood there in her boxer shorts and her tiny tee shirt, "What are you doing up here?"

"Sara?" I said. She looked surprised that I was surprised to see her.

"Yeah…" she said, "this is my room. Were you expecting someone else?"

"I was…I..." I stammered.

"Were you ready to go again?" she smiled, and she coquettishly shifted her weight to one leg and pulled her tee shirt up just enough to expose her tight stomach.

My exhausted brain was distracted by her gesture. I lost my previous train of thought completely as I looked down at her taut abdomen, the curve of her hip jutting out above the waistline of her baggy boxers.

"Come inside," she said as she pulled me by my shirt collar, "before we wake someone up."

"Sara…" I said as I followed her inside. I was a bit startled when the door closed on its own behind me; it must have been spring-loaded or something. She put her arms around my waist and pressed her hips against mine. My body probably betrayed its natural instinct, but I stopped her when she tried to kiss me.

"Sara," I said again, and I could tell from her frown that she knew something was wrong.

"Oh," she said as she backed away from me with her head down. "You're looking for Kat."

I pressed my lips together tightly. Then I took a deep breath and said, "Do you know where she is?"

Sara began to shake her head slowly as she sat down on the corner of her bed. "I told myself I wasn't going to regret it," she said. "But you really love her don't you?"

"I don't know Sara," I said. "I don't know anything anymore."

"I'm so sorry, Sam," she said as she looked up into my eyes. "I was stupid and selfish." She paused and then she tried to smile as she said, "I just wanted that, you know? I saw how you always looked at her, and I just wanted that for myself."

"Sara," I said "It's all fucked up. It wasn't you."

"I just…" she said, "I don't know what I was thinking, you know?" Her eyes had welled up and she was fighting back tears as she said, "You said you never liked me."

I closed my eyes, shook my head, and exhaled before I sat down beside her. "Sara, I'm sorry," I said. "I should've never said that to you. That was wrong."

"I never even did anything to you," she said.

"I know," I said. "You didn't."

"Do you regret it?" she said.

"What?" I said.

"Last night," she said. "Do you regret being with me?"

Even in my fatigued state, I paused a moment before I said anything. I think for some reason I felt like I owed her an honest answer. I looked at her face, quivering as she held back the tears, and I remembered how content she had looked asleep in my bed the night before.

"No," I said. "I don't regret it."

"No?" she said.

I smiled and looked in her eyes and said, "No."

She smiled and then she looked at the floor and exhaled. "I'm glad," she said.

"I'll never forget it," I said, "I can tell you that."

"Good," she said and she smiled again. "I would hate to be forgettable."

"You're not," I said. My fingertips touched her cheek as I brushed a strand of hair away from her face. "You're a beautiful girl, Sara," I said, "I will always remember last night."

"Me too," she said as her eyes met mine, "It was special in a way, wasn't it?"

"Yeah," I said as I dropped my hand back to the bed. "It was."

"Thank you, Sam," she said. She smiled at me again and then looked back toward the floor.

There was a pause in our conversation and then I said, "She left the Bistro with Taylor didn't she?"

"Yeah," she nodded. "I'm sorry, Sam," she said.

"It's not your fault," I said as I stood up and walked over toward the window. I looked through the glass, past the green tinted slate shingles, and out over the moonlit grounds of the estate. "It's probably for the best," I said. Then I reached up and unlatched the window.

"What are you doing?" Sara said as I pushed the old steel framed window open and the cool air rushed in from outside.

"I'm gonna go for a walk on the roof," I said. "I've never been on the roof before."

"Sam!" she said.

But it was too late. I had already lifted my body over the wide stone sill and I was squatting on the steep roof looking back in at her. "Come on go with me," I said.

"Are you crazy?" she said. "I'm not going out there!"

248

"Suit yourself," I said. She said something back but I couldn't make it out. I was already climbing toward the ridge and the wind in my ears had blown her words away.

12:30 AM Saturday (Hour 84:34)

The church bell that I heard ringing down in the village was very faint from my perch on the roof of Harlaxton Manor. I remember being surprised to realize that they must have rang the bell twenty-four hours a day. The roof was maybe five stories up, and the wind was quite a bit stronger than I had expected it to be. With great difficulty, I lit a cigarette and sat there calmly smoking it, straddling the ridge with one foot on each side of the roof as the treetops swayed back and forth beneath me.

I thought about the last four days, and it was hard to remember my life before I stopped sleeping. I remembered Indiana, growing up in the suburbs, being a football star, and going to church on Sundays. I remembered being proud that I was going to be the first person in my family to ever graduate from college, proud that I was studying abroad, confident that I was going to be somebody. I remembered Sam Thompson, but I didn't know what had happened to him.

I knew that it was over. I knew that in a few minutes I would climb back down from the roof, walk quietly back to my room, and collapse into a deep sleep, but I wasn't quite ready yet. I wanted to savor it, to mourn it, those last few minutes of that ridiculously long day. It had been like living a short, separate life, perhaps parallel to the one that I should have been living. Everything that had happened in my life before those four days felt like a dream that I could barely remember, but I knew that when I woke up from my next sleep that it would be the other way around. Except, it hadn't been a dream, and when that long day was over the consequences would remain.

I knew how I felt about Kat, and I wondered how long it would take that to die. I didn't know how I felt about Sara, but I was too exhausted to think about it at that moment. I was going to miss my friendship with Taylor and living with him was going to be awkward, but we only had about a month to go. The thing that frightened me the most was that I did not know how much the experience had changed me. As I sat there smoking like a living gargoyle on the top of that old mansion, I realized that I wasn't sure who was going to wake up in my skin the next day, and I wasn't sure if I was going to like him.

I think I was trying to mark that moment in time, maybe to leave myself some sort of memento, a bread crumb on my path, when I took the burning cigarette out of my mouth and ground it dead into my left forearm.

1:09 AM Saturday (Hour 85:13)

I didn't expect to see Kat nervously waiting when I swung my lower body back in through the window and landed on the floor of their room. She jumped at my swashbuckling entrance and took a step back from me. I collected myself as I stood and then walked over and shut the window from whence I had come. "Where's Sara?" I said as I latched it closed and turned around to face her.

"She went to get someone to come get you down," Kat said. "She was starting to get worried."

"Oh," I said. "That's makes sense."

"We were both worried," she added.

"Yeah?" I said.

"Are you okay?" she said.

"Yeah," I said. "I'm a little sleepy."

Kat made what I thought was an odd face and then said, "Do you want to talk, Sam?"

"Why?" I said. Taylor's favorite word felt good rolling off of my tongue.

"I just thought you might want to talk," she said.

I did want to talk. I wanted to ask her if she had really been with him. I wanted to hear her say it. I wanted to ask her why, after all the moments we had shared, she had chosen him, but I didn't. Maybe I was afraid to hear the answers; maybe I knew that I owed her answers as well. Maybe I was just tired.

"What is there to talk about?" I said.

"Sam, seriously!" she said. "Not sleeping, climbing out on the roof, you're scaring the shit out of everyone."

"I don't know what else to say," I said. "I've already told you that I loved you."

Her eyes widened a bit.

"And you told me that I didn't know what I was talking about," I continued. "And I guess you were right about that. I didn't know what love was; I didn't know the first thing about it. I probably still don't. All I was ever certain about was how special you were. How one-in-a-fuckin-million you *are* Katherine Graham."

She looked up at me as I rambled. She didn't try to stop me.

"I know I've been a fool," I said. "I had my chance and I let it go."

Her eyes met mine and I could tell that she knew what I meant.

"What else is there to say after that?" I said.

"I don't know," she said.

"I don't know either," I said.

251

"We're just kids, Sam," she said. "There's a lot of road ahead of us still."

"Yeah, I know…" I said. My words trailed off as I visualized a blank canvas; the stark white emptiness was all I could see of my future. After a moment I said, "I wonder if I'll ever meet anyone else like you."

"I'm not all that you think I am," she said.

"Yes you are," I said. I reached for her hand and she let me take hold of it. I squeezed it softly as I looked into her eyes, and then she gently drew it back, forcing me to let go of her.

We stood that way for a moment and then she finally said, "I have something for you, Sam."

"Really?" I said as I raised an eyebrow.

"If I give it to you, you have to make me a promise," she said. "You have to promise to go downstairs and get some sleep."

"What is it?" I said.

"You have to promise first," she answered.

I smiled at her; I was still enamored by her strength. Her tiny elfin features glowed brilliantly in the aura that surrounded her.

"Ok," I said, "I promise."

She picked up her copy of the play, *The Shrew*, and flipped it open to the photograph that was holding her place. She turned the face of the photo so that I could see it as she handed it to me. It was a snapshot of her in her woolen coat, leaning against the railing of a ferry with the green suds of the English Channel behind her. She had one foot up on the rail and one foot on the deck of the ship. She looked absolutely radiant in the moonlight. It took me a moment to realize that I had taken that picture.

"Thank you," I said as I stood there staring at it. "You don't know what this means to me."

"Yes I do," she said. "I liked your poem, remember?"

"Yeah," I said as I looked into her sparkling eyes. "I'll make sure and get you a copy."

"You had better," she said. She smiled as she spoke, but she turned away when I looked up at her.

I dropped my gaze to the photo and thought about that night on the ferry. "You know I haven't taken enough pictures while I've been here," I said. "I think I'm going to regret that someday."

"Why?" she said. "You'll always have your memories."

"Memories fade," I said. "At least they do for me. Didn't you ever see a picture of something that you thought you remembered and then realized that you hadn't really remembered it the way that it exactly was?"

"Yeah," she said as her eyes rolled up and to her left. "The worst is when it's a picture of me, one of those photos that someone takes of you when you're not paying attention to them. On a fun night when you were just relaxing, doing what you normally would do, and if you'd have known that someone had taken a picture you would've expected it to look great, but then you see it the next day and find out you were wrong."

"Well now I'll always know my memory was right," I said as I held the photo up to let her know I was referring to it.

"I look like a goof it that picture," she said.

"You look like a goddess," I said.

"Thank you," she said and she looked away from me again.

"I'm going to miss you," I said. I saw some surprise on her face as she looked back at me.

"We've got a whole month left before we leave," she said. "I'm not going anywhere."

"Right," I said, "but I'm going to miss what it was."

"*What it was?*" she said.

"Whatever is was," I said.

She looked up at me. Then, pressing her tiny lips together, she shook her head and exhaled through her nose. I'm not sure what I expected her to say, but I was still surprised when she never said it. She just looked down, at her shoes maybe or the floor, but definitely away from me.

"Do you ever think about how you're going to remember this?" I finally said.

"Harlaxton?" she said.

"Yeah, years from now," I said, "Do you ever wonder if any of this...this place, all the other places you've seen...all the people you've met...will any of it mean anything to us ten years from now? Do you ever think about that kind of stuff?"

"Yeah," she said, "I guess so."

"Do you ever wonder if you'll remember it, you know, like it really was?"

"I don't know," she said. "I haven't taken very many pictures either."

"Well let me ask you this," I said, "how do you want to remember it?"

"I hope I remember it exactly how it was," she said.

1:50 AM Saturday (Hour 85:54)

I don't remember thinking about anything in particular when I finally crawled into bed that night. Not Kat, not Sara or Taylor, not the oozing burn on my arm. I don't remember at all what my final thoughts might have been at the end of that day. I just remember looking at my watch when I hit the stop button on the timer. It said *1:56 AM*. I'd been awake for 86 hours. I repeated the number to myself a few times in hopes that I would remember it when I awoke. It seemed like one of those details that might be important to me later.

[exeunt]

Acknowledgements

Earnest gratitude to all the mentors whose inspirations and shared wisdom have helped shape this work, especially Miss Rebecca Haynes, Col. Thomas R. Mason, Mr. John Lloyd, Margaret McMullen, Dr. Sam Longmire, Gabe Merrill, Jane Friedman, and my lovely editor, Kathleen Wallace.

Thanks be to those who subjected themselves to early drafts: Audra Douglas, Abbi Cook, and of course Kathleen Wallace

In the event that any of the characters from this book have borrowed or stolen certain characteristics or eccentricities of friends and acquaintances from long ago, I offer a collective thank you...*and apology.*

About the Author

Andrew Mason was born on March 2, 1975 in Paradise, Indiana. The oldest of three boys, he became a confirmed Catholic in 1989 and an Eagle Scout in 1992. After graduating from Castle High School in 1993, he attended the University of Evansville in southern Indiana. His first work of short fiction, *The Unfortunate Tale of Ralph the Monkey*, was published in the Evansville Review in 1997, and he earned a BA in English literature from UE in 1999. Mason lives with his wife and family in Smythe, Indiana. His first novel, *86 Hours in England*, was published in 2011.